THE PIRATE KING'S THIEF
REALM OF DRAGONS AND FAE

ALISHA KLAPHEKE

To my girl gang

SHROUDED MOUNTAINS
REALM OF LIGHTS
Vineyards
Hunting Lodge
Caer Du
Gwerhune
The Fae Forest
FJORDBOK
The Veil
Border River
Midhampton
Veilbury
SAXONION
Isernwyrd
Strykeford
White Sea
DEIGS
Masdam
Glass River
LAQQARA
Leptis
Luxurium
Skull Desert

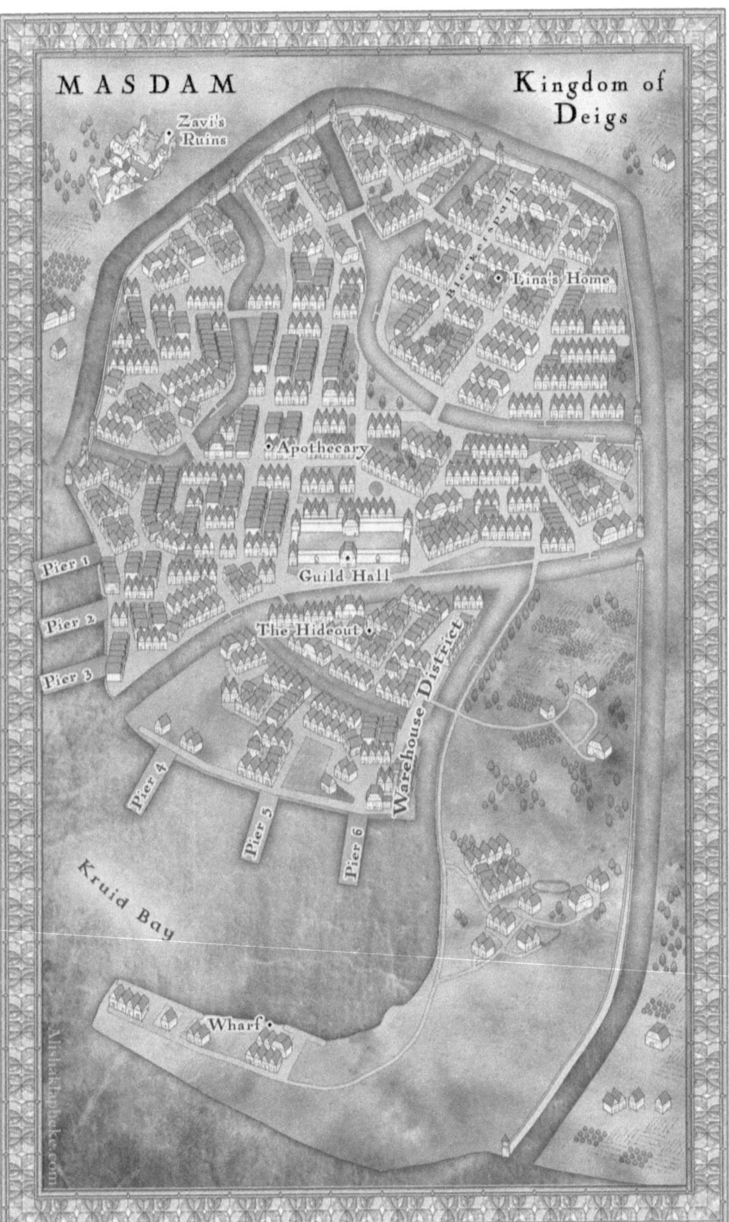

MASDAM
Kingdom of Deigs
Zavi's Ruins
Lina's Home
Apothecary
Guild Hall
The Hideout
Warehouse District
Pier 1
Pier 2
Pier 3
Pier 4
Pier 5
Pier 6
Kruid Bay
Wharf

LINA

Stealing was wrong. I knew that. But honestly, I couldn't summon up any guilt. Snatching coins and nicking daggers provided hope. Someday, we would have enough stashed money to disguise ourselves and escape the men who lorded over us.

My fellow thieves and I walked into The Last Dock, a tavern well out of my rich father's sphere of activity. A deliciously deep voice curled through the air. The song's lyrics told of friends lost and found, of lovers and long nights at sea. It was beautiful. I stood on tiptoe to see the bard, but the crowd was too thick and I was too short.

Phoenix nudged me forward. "Come on."

Finally, I saw the bard singing. He was a handsome, dark-blond man playing a battered lute with his tattooed fingers. Jaw shadowed in stubble, he wore a black scarf about his head, two large gold rings on his right hand, and a pair of tall leather boots. His homespun shirt wasn't tied properly, and his broad chest showed in a slice of tan skin above the dirty fabric. Launching into the bawdy chorus of the tune, he gave me a grin. I found myself smiling back, which surprised me because men were generally my enemy. His scarf shifted with his movement and the tip of one pointed ear showed. My stomach dropped. He was part Fae. My smile slid away, and I turned my attention toward the crowd. I had good reason to hate Fae, and I didn't care to think on my past at the moment. It was time for some fun.

A table of dice-throwing merchants glanced my way appreciatively, but I passed them and instead cozied up to a man drinking at the bar top.

The dirt of a long overland journey muddied the hem of the drinker's fine woolen cloak. More importantly, he possessed a very shiny dagger that hung from his belt. Gold, rubies, diamonds, and sapphires always caught my eye. Something about the colors of a flame drew me in. That's why my two friends—my fellow thieves—called me Moth. I licked my lips and initiated the scam.

I cast the man a come-hither look. "Lovely night for dancing."

He did a double-take, then dipped his head respectfully even though his hungry gaze snagged on my breasts. I wouldn't lose a wink of sleep robbing him blind. The traveler glanced behind me at Phoenix. My light-skinned blonde friend played the role of my chaperone. Phoenix was a Deigs merchant-woman who had lost her children when her husband divorced her. She loved stealing as much as I did.

Father believed I was at my aunt's townhome, tending to her multitude of cats. He thought I had finally given up my efforts to avoid gaining a husband. My wedding was all but planned. Well, he was wrong.

"Indeed. I love to dance," the wealthy traveler said as he set his goblet on the bar top and offered his arm.

Phoenix followed closely until the traveler and I reached the expanse of the tavern floor that had been cleared for dancing, then she melted into the crowd, her clever eyes always watching.

My second friend, Star, took up a spot by the back door of the tavern with her dark arms crossed, ready in case things went wrong and she had to use her military training to get us out.

I slid my hands over the traveler's shoulders and grinned wickedly. "My father would be horrified if he knew I was here."

His eyes widened, and he glanced at the front entrance.

"Oh, don't be worried. He never comes around this part of the city."

Letting out an arrogant huff of a laugh, the man snaked an arm around to the small of my back. He leaned close and set his lips against my ear. I shuddered. "And my wife would likewise be scandalized."

My stomach turned, but I forced a lilting sound of surprise and lightly smacked his shoulder, pulling away from him a bit. "Oh, I do love a bit of naughtiness."

He tugged me close again and I let him, using my body to distract him from the fact that I was relieving him of his coin purse and knife. As he danced with me, and I use that term loosely, I also decided that without his shiny dagger, his multitude of rings was just silly, so I snatched those as well. Once I finished my work for the good of my friends and myself, I led him back to his drink. He found the goblet he'd set down earlier and drank it in full. I glanced toward Phoenix and she winked, meaning she had already put the sleeping aid in.

"I'm headed to sleep, my sweet." The traveler slurred the last two words and leaned heavily on the bar top. "Won't you join me?"

I patted his hand. "I couldn't possibly, but thank you for the invitation."

"Now, see here, woman." The traveler gripped my hand and pressed my fingers into the rough grain of the bar top.

Pain shot up my arm.

And there it was. The reason I loved stealing. "If you don't remove your hand from mine in two seconds, my chaperone will make mincemeat of your liver."

He inhaled sharply and glanced over his shoulder to see Phoenix standing there with a smile made for dark alleys. The traveler released me and tried to walk away, stumbling into a group playing cards by the hearth. The card players shouted as he upended their table and, soon enough, punches were thrown.

With Phoenix at my side, I maneuvered through the crowd toward the front door, where Star now waited. I would have sworn that woman had magic for how quickly she could move. She opened the door and I took my cloak from Phoenix and began to follow the two of them.

A hand locked onto my upper arm and held me fast against something hard and warm. A prickly sensation ran up my shoulder. I turned to see the handsome half-Fae bard. His dark eyes glittered. The slightly slitted pupils contracted as he looked down at me and lifted an eyebrow. Heat shot through me and flushed my cheeks. Stupid attractive Fae.

"I'm afraid I can't let you leave with that man's treasures," he whispered.

Stones. He knew. "I'm sorry," I said in my best sweet lady voice. "I have no idea what you're talking about."

His Fae strength was evident in the hold he had on me. He chuckled darkly and ran his free hand down my stomach to my side where I'd stashed the dagger in a pocket I'd sewn into my dress for just this purpose. My skin seemed to spark in the wake of his touch.

"Why do you care?" I asked, giving up the ruse. Phoenix and Star remained still and watching, steps away, the moon painting them in blues and whites.

"Because the barkeep hired me to watch for criminals such as yourself."

I couldn't quite fight the grin that perked up one side of my mouth. Criminal. "Well, what are you going to do, then? Haul me back in to face the keep? Punish me yourself?" I glared, daring him.

"Moth! Give it back and let's go," Phoenix said sharply.

But I didn't want this arrogant half-Fae bard to win. This was my game and I'd never once been caught. "What if I give you the coin and I keep the dagger?" The dagger was just so very pretty.

His eyes sparkled, but he shook his head. "How did you get such light fingers? I'd have thought a woman of your status didn't need to steal."

My temper flared hot and fast like a lightning strike. "Don't pretend to know what my life is like."

I bumped my body against his. His grip loosened a fraction with his surprise and I spun and took off. A cart passed by, blocking his advance.

"Don't come back here, firefly," he called out. "Next time, I won't waste time with verbal sparring no matter how much pleasure I take in it."

His low voice echoed in my ears as Phoenix, Star, and I hurried to our hideout. Had that sensation I'd felt been mere attraction or was there some magic hanging from the bard? Father had a few magical objects at the house and they gave a gentle sort of shock, for lack of a better word, when I touched them. Perhaps the bard wore something with power, something from the Realm of Lights, the land of the Fae. But why would I care? Shaking my head, I pushed the image of the bard's off-kilter grin out of my mind. Damned Fae.

ZAVI

"No, I swear. I did nothing. I just had to speak to her. Forgive me, barkeep." Zavi slid his lute to his back and adjusted the shoulder strap as his boss continued grumbling about giving rich customers plenty of space. Employers always thought Zavi was about to run off with the dockmaster's daughter, but really, that had only happened once. All right, twice, but the second family were more merchants than dockmasters...

"...if you want to hold this job, keep your Fae fingers to yourself."

Anger snapped through Zavi like a whip.

The barkeep froze like a rabbit in the gaze of a wolf. Smart human.

Because of whatever injury or curse had been set on him five years ago—the bitter taste of dark magic never quite left his tongue—Zavi had no idea who he really was, but he knew he could kill in the blink of an eye. And not only because of the Fae strength that ran through his blood. No, he was trained to fight—to fight very dirty, in fact. Sometimes, when anger lit him up, that confidence showed in his gaze and made folks pause. Humans either froze like the tavern owner or stupidly attacked in blind fear.

Zavi took a slow breath and nodded. "Apologies. I enjoy playing here. If you will it, I'll stick around and mind my manners."

The barkeep blinked repeatedly, then stuttered a "yes" before hurrying back to his coin box.

Zavi shook his head and left the tavern as dawn's light cracked its way into the starlit clouds. He hadn't intended to scare the keep even though the prejudiced fool deserved a bit of frightening.

He tore the scarf from his head, and, rubbing his hands through his hair roughly, he cursed his life for the thousandth time because not only could he not remember his past beyond his time singing in various taverns up and down the coast of Deigs, but he also knew nothing of the murderous talents he somehow possessed. A familiar, ripping sort of agony tore across his side, and he pressed a hand over the scar there. It had to be related to his memory loss because it pained him every time he tried to remember his life before the most recent five years, which he'd had living as a bard.

The luminous eyes and coppery hair of that woman shimmered into his mind, easing his pain. So gorgeous. And full of fire. His breath caught as he recalled the scent of her—peonies. He'd seen a great deal of thieving during his days in Deigs, but never one like her. So quick, so clever. He clicked his tongue. Such a criminal, that one. A grin pulled at his mouth. If she came around again, he would find a way to strike up a conversation. Her hands had been as smooth as ivory. Those fingers had never seen hard labor. She was wealthy, a lord's daughter or perhaps the daughter of a successful merchant or other such businessman. He didn't care about the money, but he wanted to know her story and why she had been at the tavern, nicking from men like it was a dance she knew by heart.

Footsteps sounded from the alley behind him. Zavi whirled to see a pale-skinned man coming at him with a knife. "Just give me your coin, bard, and I'll leave most of you intact."

Zavi threw up an arm to halt the man's downward strike, then hit the man with the heel of his other hand. Blood burst from the mugger's nose. The arsehole bent over, but he kept hold of the weapon, which was actually quite impressive. Zavi grabbed the attacker's wrist, keeping the knife at a distance as he braced his free arm against the man's neck. Zavi rammed a knee into the attacker's stones and disarmed the fellow as he went down.

It was all over in a matter of heartbeats and Zavi hadn't even had to think. His body had simply responded. Flipping the knife and catching it, Zavi left the mugger in the street for the Watch to pick up, and then Zavi aimed for home.

Who had Zavi been and why had he lost his memory? The bitter taste of a magical artifact flooded his mouth. He was used to the sensation after five years of experiencing it. But the frustrating—and frightening—part about it was that he held nothing magical on him. He'd experimented with every-thing he normally wore on his person, and none of it held magic. Curses could only be passed through artifacts or straight from the Witch of Saxonion or the Druid who lived in the Fae lands. Perhaps one of them had wrought this special evil on him, then stashed him on a boat to Deigs, where he'd woken one day as lost as he was now.

He tucked his new knife into his belt and walked the last of the cobblestoned street until he reached the castle ruins where he'd taken up residence. A moss-covered stone gate and an old dog with a face that told a thousand tales greeted him.

"Everything good here, Wolfling?" He scratched the dog's brindled coat and smiled as the fantastically foul creature let out a woof.

The dog trotted alongside as Zavi bumped the door open with his foot and climbed the wide stone steps to the one livable chamber in the age-old fortress. Tossing the lute onto the bed and grabbing his collection of notes about his tattoos, Zavi found a comfortable spot in a hammock he'd strung up between two columns near the arched windows.

About the only thing he knew was that he'd been a pirate. He had the mark of one once arrested and charged for piracy —an inking of a wave with a sword through it. Plus, his love of rum and hammocks were pretty strong indicators.

The tattoos running along his hand and down his fingers most likely symbolized battles or challenges, as they were a collection of arrows, swords, and skulls surrounded in droplet shapes that probably pertained to bloodshed. He really hoped each droplet didn't stand for a life he'd taken. Or if it did, that those he'd killed had needed to be taken down for the safety of others or himself.

A dragon soared across his other hand, talons reaching down each finger. Perhaps he'd had a nickname that revolved around dragons. Or maybe he'd visited the Shrouded Mountains at some point to see the fire-breathing mountain dragons and simply appreciated their viciousness.

What had the copper-haired beauty thought of his tattoos? Her gaze had said she was intrigued, not put off like many. Not surprising that a woman who had no need to be a thief would be attracted to someone outside her usual circle. But that flash of rage in her eyes when he'd mentioned her life... Well, hopefully, she would return to the tavern soon.

Lying back in the hammock, he set his notes on his stomach and closed his eyes. He knew some things, such as world geography, a few points of culture and history from various kingdoms, and the basics of living. Each time he thought of a fact, a piece of knowledge about life, he wrote it in his notes and marked it with a star. Visions and what might or might not be memories—those flashes of moments that accompanied pain—went into the notes as well, but he marked them with a circle. It was very tough to know what was true and what wasn't. For the first three or so years, he hadn't had pain, but now the torture erupted in him fairly often.

As Wolfling curled up beneath him, he imagined a ship on a stormy sea, conjured up a fake memory of a pirate crew, and tried to see a version of himself among their ranks. He hoped it might jostle his mind free of the magic, if only for a moment.

He opened his eyes and his sight grew blurry, nausea following. Sometimes he had visions, but it was always tough to tell which ones might have actually occurred in his past. His imagination was powerful and whatever magic had been set on him made his thoughts tumble into hallucinations.

Blinking, he saw a vision of a bearded man with brown eyes. Zavi's chest constricted with some unnamable feeling. Fear? Kinship? Loyalty? Who was that? He shut his eyes and focused on the hazy features that felt as familiar as his own reflection, though the man didn't look much like him, aside from the eyebrows, perhaps. Worry for the man wrapped Zavi's heart and squeezed tightly, and a vague sensation of desperation haunted the edges of this memory. Because this was an actual recollection. It was too visceral, too gut-wrenchingly packed with emotional weight not to be a real memory. Was this a fellow crewman that he had sailed with? A captain? His captain? No, that didn't feel right. Someone closer, then. A friend. A twinge of rightness swam through Zavi's chest, but that wasn't exactly the answer. The foggy image of the man turned and laughed, the sound echoing. Then blood splattered the man's face and a scream split the memory into a thousand razor-sharp pieces.

Zavi gasped as realization swept through him with the warmth of love and the horrid chill of fear.

This was his brother. And something very bad had been done to him.

Pain like the cut of a rusty blade drove through Zavi's side. Every time he tried to remember anything, the agony in his side erupted. This time, it was worse.

As his brother's face faded, fire burned its way from his side up his ribcage to his heart, where the dark magic shook him like a beast with prey latched in its jaws. He cleared his mind and stopped trying to remember, if only to catch his breath. The image fully disappeared and the pain dissipated.

He had a brother. Curiosity about his life was one thing, but this? This was an entirely different thing. What had happened to his brother?

A name echoed through his mind and nausea swamped him again.

Emiel.

Emiel was his brother's name.

Zavi breathed slow and deep until the nausea faded and he could think again.

Only a general sense of danger and hurt lingered from the memory. Could Zavi help his brother if he broke the curse and remembered everything?

Fingering his ribs, he had a terrible idea.

What if the magical artifact that held the curse wasn't *on* his body but *in* it?

His temples pounded. What if...

He unsheathed his dagger and set the point against the scar he'd had for five years, the spot that had pained him for the last two years.

Star glanced at me as we climbed over the old-style high threshold of the doorway into our makeshift second home. "Firefly? Perhaps because of your hair?"

"Fireflies don't have red hair." Phoenix crossed the cracked flagstone of our cheap flat, plopped down in her favorite ancient high-backed chair, and began pulling out her hairpins.

I sat on a stool and shucked off my heeled boots. I'd have to put the atrocities back on before heading home, but at least my poor feet would have a short break.

Squatting, Star stirred the glowing coals in the hearth. "But they glow and red hair glows in candlelight."

I smiled at her back. "I believe that was a compliment. Thank you."

"Wasn't," Star said. "Just a fact. Another fact is that you couldn't tear your gaze from the bard's well-fitted trousers."

I threw a boot at her. Without a glance backward, she raised her forearm and deflected my flying footwear.

"I was not staring at him."

A snort came from the pantry, where Phoenix was rummaging, chucking empty crates and old fruit from the dim interior of the flat. "You were!"

"Enough of this." I went to the table and poured out the coins I'd nicked, the dagger, and the rings. "Let's see what we have." It was a lovely hoard.

Star and Phoenix joined me and we tallied our winnings and added them to the growing total figure inked into our book.

Phoenix chewed the inside of her cheek and scowled at the book. "What do you think? Maybe another two months and we might have enough?"

Enough to book passage to the southlands and to buy the silence of the captain and his crew so Father couldn't follow me. "I think so. Star?"

Star rubbed her chin, then nodded. "If we work as often as we've been doing lately."

"I have to get this new suitor off my back or he'll eat into our evenings," I said.

"Is Papa still buying the whole visiting auntie excuse?" Phoenix asked, her tone souring at the feigned endearment for my father.

"As long as I appear when summoned, he doesn't really care. But I'll be asked to sit quietly at far more gatherings if Lord Arseface doesn't leave off."

Glancing at me, Star asked, "What's your plan there?"

"I have to figure him out first, see what would make him dislike me. I'm supposed to have wine and play Knocks with him tomorrow afternoon."

Mouth tilting up slightly, Phoenix rapped her fingers on

the table and made the coins jingle. "Will you crush him or let him win?"

"Oh, I will crush him and see how he responds to that. When a man loses, I can see the inside of him as easily as a painted picture."

The ladies nodded, and we set to preparing our traditional post-thieving drink—jenever. Phoenix set out the tulip-shaped glasses, which I'd pilfered from my mother's secret stash in her sewing room, and Star poured a serving into each.

I raised my glass and the now crackling fire cast lovely colors over the surface. "To us! Freedom at any cost!"

They echoed our motto and we drank down the powerful spirit. The juniper and malt flavor woke up my tongue and I shivered as the drink burned down my throat and warmed my body. We settled into the straw chairs at the table and put our feet up, queens of our own dilapidated castle.

I looked into the fire, taking comfort from its heat and its beauty. The bard's face flashed through my mind and I recalled the frisson of power that had crawled over my shoulder at his touch. "Did anyone feel anything magic around that Fae bard?"

Star poured us another round. "We weren't close enough. What did he have?"

"I don't know. Maybe the necklace he wore? Or one of his rings?"

"With a half-Fae, you never know," Phoenix said. "They all seem to possess some sort of magical artifact."

Star frowned at Phoenix. "How many Fae have you actually spoken to?"

Tucking her hair behind her ear, Phoenix shrugged. "I don't know. At least two."

"Two is plenty to make such an observation," Star said sharply.

Phoenix exhaled. "Everyone knows they have magics we humans don't."

"True enough, but with those part Fae who don't live with their kind, I doubt they have much going for them. Else why would they be here rather than there? The Realm of Lights sounds so beautiful." Star blinked at the dancing fire.

"I wonder if they hate those with human blood and throw them out," I said.

Phoenix lowered her feet to the floor and leaned forward on her elbows. "Eh, I have a surprise for you two," she said, changing the subject.

Star and I exchanged looks. "Well," I said, "out with it. I have to leave soon or Mother and Father will have the Watch out looking for me. One twenty-year-old spinster missing!" I snorted a laugh and Star grinned.

Phoenix disappeared into the back room where we had a single bed for nights when one of us needed to stay. All of us had homes, but none were delightful, to say the least. Phoenix lived in a hovel below the chandler's place, just off High Street. She cooked and cleaned for him because he'd lost most of his sight and wasn't married. Star lived with a group of former warriors like herself. They crowded into a flat near the docks and she claimed the place was never quiet for even one moment of time. I, of course, lived in a fine house on Bleekerspath with my father and mother, Lord and Lady Casparji. It was one of those gilded cage situations that I felt bad complaining about when some in the city starved. Nonetheless, it was driving me to madness putting up with Father's insistence that I marry horrible men who would do with me exactly as they pleased.

I swallowed and looked to Phoenix, who had emerged from the back room with a cloth-covered basket. "What's this?"

Star stood up and eyed the basket. Even though Star hated everything about being a soldier, I could easily imagine her on the battlefield, assessing risks and standing ready to launch an attack. It was nearly time for the king of Deigs to reclaim her as his warrior. Her three years of earned time away from the military would be over in two months.

Phoenix slowly withdrew the cloth from the basket. "Now, don't move too quickly. She just hatched." Phoenix reached into the dark of the basket and retrieved a...

"Is that a ball of leather?" I squinted at the uneven texture that my mind couldn't understand.

Star's hands went to her mouth. "Stones, Phoenix. Where did you find her?"

The ball of leather unrolled to become two green wings, a serpentine body with four legs, and a head that boasted eyes far larger than they should have been for a creature that size.

"A pocket dragon?!" Never once had I seen one. I'd heard about them from foresters and charcoal men who wandered the wilds, but the tales of us Deigs folk having them as pets were ridiculous stories that rich men's tour companies had invented.

Holding the tiny dragon out to Star, Phoenix practically lit up. Her gentle handling of the dragon reminded me that she was a mother and would always be a mother despite the fact that her children had been locked away from her.

"Be careful with her snout. They are very tender for the

first six weeks, as the bones beneath haven't yet fused." She gingerly placed the sleepy-eyed creature in Star's outstretched hands.

Star brought the animal close to her and whispered to it in the tongue of Fjordbok, where she had lived for a while as a youth.

"What did you say?" I reached out a finger and stroked the dragon's pliable spines. She blinked up at me and I knew we'd be keeping this baby beast for the duration of its existence.

Smiling, Star said, "I gave her a blessing of luck and power." She scratched the dragon's smooth-scaled neck and the creature cooed, flapping her wings lightly. Regular Fjordbok folk didn't have magic, but Star's blessing was a kindness nonetheless.

"I thought perhaps she could help us nick smaller items," Phoenix said. "Once she is mature, that is."

"How long does it take?" Star handed the dragon back to Phoenix.

"About a week."

I stared as the dragon curled up in the bottom of the basket and went back to sleep. "Wow, that fast? How long do they live?"

"Nearly as long as us." Phoenix deposited the dragon in the back room, then came out with one of the crates we used to store our earnings.

The city bells rang midnight.

"Time to go."

After tugging my boots back on, I went to the hook at the front of the house and donned the thick black cloak I kept solely for returning to my house at the end of each night of stealing. The cloak's hood more than covered my red hair and draped low over my face.

"Meet you in front of the cordwainer's shop tomorrow?" I asked.

Star finished her drink and set her glass by the crate. "Yep. As planned. Don't forget the wig."

"Ah. Yes," I said. "No problem. Good night, ladies."

Phoenix waved absently as she tucked the lovely dagger in beside the sack of coins and the large gold necklace I'd stolen last week. "See you then!"

Keeping my eyes open for movement in the shadows, I hurried through the streets as quickly as my fancy boots allowed, and soon I was slipping back into my gilded cage. I had enough time to sleep and to sharpen my wits for tomorrow's courtship games. I could handle two more months. After that, I'd be on my way to freedom. I wondered what song that horrible Fae bard would sing about me after I was gone. Hopefully, the final verse of my song would feature a long journey away from the chains of my father's household.

A memory of my friend, Sophia, washed through my mind's eye. She had been twelve when the pirates killed her and not a day passed when I didn't miss her. Every time her family had visited mine, we'd holed up in my bedroom and told stories. Hers featured the golden sands of her home kingdom, Laqqara, as well as a multitude of barn cats that they had on their saffron plantation. Her stories had always made me laugh until I cried. I remembered her little smirk and how much I'd loved slipping away from our parents and into the market with her. The three years of age between us hadn't meant anything. We had been friends from day one, from the first time her parents had sailed here to negotiate with Father.

Since her death, I'd written her family time and time again. They had never answered. Not once. But surely, if Star, Phoenix, and I showed up there, they would speak to us. They would help us get started in Laqqara. Sophia's parents were kind where mine were calculating.

And now, they would be instrumental in my and my friends' plan to start a new life. Star could be Aramia again if she wanted to or take a third name and begin fresh. Phoenix could be Greta, mother to Bram and Sanne, once more.

Somehow, we would get Phoenix's children, then we would flee her ex-husband as well as escape my parents' control. Star would break away from Deigs and escape the military's demands. They'd be after her to return to service in two months if we didn't leave. But if we managed it, Star would have a lifetime to heal from the visible and invisible wounds that war had given her.

Yes, it would work. It simply had to work. We were out of choices and nearly out of time.

❧ 4 ❧
ZAVI

The dagger's tip pierced Zavi's skin, and he locked his jaw as pain bloomed at the spot. He made a small clean slice over the spot that pained him, tossed the dagger to the windowsill, and felt about the area to see if any foreign objects hid inside his flesh.

"Ach!" A string of obscenities flowed from him at the same pace as the blood from the self-inflicted wound.

Nothing but flesh, at least as far as he could tell. He needed a mirror. Leaving the hammock, he rummaged around the chamber for his shaving mirror. His beard didn't grow out like a full human's would have because of his Fae blood, but sometimes he felt the need for a completely smooth chin. He supposed that was his Fae heritage popping up. The second drawer of his nightstand proved to hold the mirror. After grabbing a cloth from the bathing room to clear away some of the blood, he held up the mirror to view his side. It was difficult to see, but—was that something green?

Digging his fingers in and hissing at the pain, he felt

something diamond-shaped. The blood slicked his fingers, so he took up the cloth and used it to grip one pointy end of the object.

He pulled.

Hot agony roared across his ribs and into his heart. He fell back onto the bed, shouting curses. The object remained firmly embedded in his side.

Wolfling yowled and jumped onto the duvet beside him.

"I'm alive, thanks for asking. But I don't know for how long." With a shuddering breath, he sat up and pressed the cloth to the wound. "Know where I could find an apothecary in this side of the city?"

The dog grunted and licked his hand.

Zavi raised an eyebrow. "Well, I would prefer not to walk that far, but if you say it's the only location."

He cleaned himself up and chuckled darkly at himself for imagining conversations with an elderly canine, but his pride wasn't injured by his madness. When you had no memories to speak of, you didn't have a reputation or status to protect either.

Once he had the wound bound, he set off toward Pink Street to get someone to sew up his folly.

THE APOTHECARY'S SHOP LOOKED LIKE IT HAD BEEN crafted from three different buildings. The steeply pitched tiled roof was common enough in the city, but the shutters were painted a wild yellow. The morning sun reflected from the nearby canal onto the shutters and Zavi winced against the brightness. A door that looked plucked from antiquity stood halfway open and creaked noisily as he let himself in. A large woman with a young girl in tow stood at the countertop speaking to the apothecary. The apothecary rubbed her forehead of wrinkles as if in thought or dealing with frustration.

"No, no," the apothecary said, pulling her silver hair into a knot on the top of her head, "don't even think of giving this to her without a meal. She'll toss it all up again."

The woman nodded and pushed a handful of gladecoins across the wooden countertop. "All right, apothecary. Thank you."

With a foul glance in Zavi's direction, the mother-daughter duo left and Zavi approached the counter. The apothecary had her back turned and she was organizing glass bottles—of only the Old Ones knew what—on a long shelf.

"I need stitching up, please," he said. "I have money."

"Wait on the bench."

"I'm bleeding quite a bit. Can we hurry this along?"

She scowled over her shoulder. "Your bad decisions can't mandate my schedule."

"How do you know this wound was a result of my decision?" he asked. She was right, but he couldn't help inquiring.

"You have the accent of a southlands pirate, that's how."

It was as if she'd turned on a light inside Zavi's mind. A southlands pirate. He stepped closer, his stomach bumping the countertop. "I don't have the look of a Laqqaran."

"No." Her tone held confusion. She'd think he was mad. He basically was. She went back to her bottles, muttering something about pirates.

"I'm not a pirate now. Just a simple bard with a hoard of problems."

Slamming a round-bodied red bottle onto the shelf with enough force to crack the thing, she exhaled. Whirling, she stared him down. "Fine. But you'll pay handsomely. I'm no healer. You should be at his place, not mine."

"I've heard enough about the healer to know you are worth the extra coin."

A laugh came from the apothecary and she rounded the counter and waved him to the bench. She examined the wound, muttered something incoherent, then disappeared into the back of the shop. Reemerging with a small basket, she tilted her head at him.

"Are you part Fae?" No measure of hate colored her words. She was simply curious.

He moved his tousled hair to the side to show one of his pointed ears. "Yes, but apparently I didn't inherit much of the healing power my full-blooded kin possess." It was odd that he knew so much about the world and yet so little about his own life.

Nodding, the apothecary washed the wound with a damp cloth, then smeared a vanilla-scented ointment around the area. He did his best to hold still. Perhaps this woman knew about magic and curses...

"Do you see anything odd inside the wound?" he asked.

She paused in her ministrations and squinted at him. "I didn't but I'll look if you can stand it. This has to be painful and yet you've not wriggled once. You have a high tolerance for pain."

"A good thing for both a pirate and a bard who writes songs about idiot drunkards."

With a snicker, she turned him so that the window's light illuminated the wound. As she searched the wound with gentle fingers, hot agony rode up his side and into his chest. He tried to keep breathing as sweat poured down his face.

"I do see something," she said, quietly. "There is some sort of arrowhead, perhaps, in here. We will have to get that out."

He gritted his teeth and exhaled, trying hard not to shout from the pain. "Please do."

"This will cost you twenty-five."

"Make it thirty," he said through his clenched jaw, "and tell me what you know about the object once it's out."

Frowning, she examined his face then went back to the wound. "Deal."

"Deal."

After an incredibly painful few minutes with tweezers, the apothecary had the object free. Magic washed over him like a rogue wave and he promptly blacked out.

❧ *5* ❧

LINA

I sipped on a warm spiced wine and cider mixture and watched the sun slide from its peak to shine into the receiving chamber, where we hosted casual guests like the incoming Lord Arseface. Four tall chairs with velvet cushions sat in a semi-circle by the hearth. I chose the one nearest the fire and leaned back. Fatigue dragged at me, but not because of my late night. No, that infused me with excitement. This tiredness resulted from knowing I was about to endure my would-be husband for at least two hours. I eyed the Knocks board that Mother had tucked up beside the hearth. I'd been playing the strategy game since I could move the tall pewter pieces, and I was very, very good. I couldn't concoct fantastic explosions from chemicals—that was Phoenix's talent. Nor could I fight with a sword like Star. But since Star had trained Phoenix and me, I wasn't horrible with a dagger or with fighting dirty, and I was aces at playing Knocks.

As the fire crackled, my mind conjured the face of the

bard with his roguish grin and that flash of Fae fang. I swallowed and shook the image from my head.

Mother floated in, already muttering judgments against me even though she knew well that her nitpicking did little to alter my behavior. It was long past time I leave this place and claim a home of my own, but of course, as per Deigs law, I wasn't permitted to do that unless I did so with a husband on my arm. I finished the goblet of wine and poured another.

Mother grabbed a lock of my hair that had fallen from its pins and rammed it back in place. "Don't drink too much. It'll loosen that dangerous tongue of yours."

"My tongue doesn't matter today. You know he'll blather on every single second about his blessed boat. And when he's not yapping, Father will be."

Mother glared and began smoothing my hem. "Sit up straight."

I did as she instructed, but my teeth ground together and she noticed, her gaze missing nothing.

"I had an interesting talk with a sacred lady of the moon yesterday," she said.

My heart shivered and I gripped my goblet so as not to drop it. The sacred ladies at the House of the Moon lived a cloistered existence on the outskirts of the city. They said prayers for those who paid and claimed to help the poor, but I'd never seen evidence of that. All I knew was that I would go fully insane if I was imprisoned behind the same walls for the rest of my life. I wanted to see distant lands, to dance at parties, to eat all the foods the wide world had to offer. I wanted to live.

I set my jaw and tried to remain calm. "I would die before you shoved me into a moon house."

Straightening fast, Mother stared at me. "If you fail to win Lord Drukker's hand, you won't have a moment to yourself. Sara will sleep at your feet and will accompany you to the moon house when they invite you. There is no escape from real life, Lina."

The wine turned in my stomach and I fought to keep it down. I wanted to lash out and yell, but that would only induce more of her threats. And these weren't empty threats. Mother was fully capable of ruining my life, and the entire time she would believe she was doing the right thing.

Father strode in talking with Lord Drukker.

Lord Drukker had dark blue eyes and blond hair. He was well dressed and handsome, but that beauty was only a surface thing. He was incredibly ugly on the inside, always dropping little comments that Mother called compliments but I deemed insults. Phrases like "You'll make such a wonderful wife once you shed all that silliness" and "If you took half the time you waste on the market to learn how to host, you'd be the best one in the entire city." I'd had and loathed suitors before Drukker—a womanizer with an obvious foot fetish, a guild leader who only spoke to command me and thought women were far, far beneath him, and an overly religious prick who wanted me praying every hour of the day while he slept his way through the city—but my hatred for this suitor was a special blend I saved just for him.

Father finished his sentence as they came toward Mother and me. "...and if the king demands a tax on that, I will simply move the operations to the lowlands."

Drukker chuckled. "Wise. I'll come to you when I know more."

I took a deep, slow breath.

Nodding to Drukker, Father held out a hand toward Mother and me. "Lord Drukker, our ladies await our company. Is there anything finer?"

My jaw ached from grinding my teeth, but I stood and dipped a quick curtsey as the men joined us at the hearth. Keeping my face devoid of the anxiety raking its talons over my heart, I glanced at Drukker, but he didn't meet my gaze. Sara slipped in and served the cider wine all around. I gave her a smile. She returned it quickly, her gaze flashing toward Mother in fear.

Drukker placed his goblet on the arm of his chair. "Lady Lina, how has your morning been?" At last, his foul eyes latched onto me.

I'd researched dragons in our family library, but talking about wild animals wasn't going to lessen the time of this little visit. I wanted this visit over and done with as quickly as possible.

"I did some reading."

"Oh?" He glanced at Father as if it were amazing that women read. "And what subjects tend to catch the attention of a woman these days?" He gave Mother a condescending smirk.

Heat poured through my veins. Although I had one thousand problems with Mother, I would defend her to this pig.

"Mother enjoys keeping up with the latest tax laws. I heard you two discussing. You should ask her advice if you want to know about the new four-sixty-two adjustment. I'm not overly fond of such topics and instead dig into history, such as the rebellion of 982."

Drukker's jaw fell open, but he quickly slammed it shut.

Father's features went stormy and he closed his eyes briefly, holding himself back from crossing the short distance between us to strike me. I didn't look to see Mother, but her glare burned my cheek like a candle's flame held too close to the skin.

Smoothing his pale blond beard, Drukker clicked his tongue. "I'm not familiar with the rebellion. Tell me about it." His forced smile wasn't fooling anyone and his fisted hands on the arms of his chair said if I were already his wife, I'd have been suffering some consequence for my tone.

Mother abruptly stood and nearly toppled my wine. "The food has arrived. Sara!"

Sara popped her head into the room, a question on her face.

"The food is ready, isn't it?" Mother said, the question more of a demand.

With a quick nod, Sara left again but soon returned with a tray of afternoon treats. Stroopwafels whose caramel scent almost made the company tolerable sat in a stack beside a plate of appelflap. A bowl of custard tempted me to dive in and forget all my worries, but I held back.

Sara made each of us a plate of goodies and handed them out. Before Mother could snatch my plate away—she insisted I was getting too fat—I started on the appelflap, enjoying the buttery puff pastry and the tart fruit inside.

The morning wore on through a small lunch. Mostly, the men blathered on about their boats, shipping delays in the trade industry, and who might land a deal with Rietveld, the most powerful merchant in the kingdom. The man was little better than the pirates he dealt with. Of course, Rietveld deemed the pirates merchant sailors, but no one was fooled.

The sooner this visit was over, the sooner I could prepare for tonight. I ate and let the rest of them chatter on, biding my time in my cage.

Father drew out the Knocks board, dice, and cards, and he challenged Drukker to a game. They were tied for the first half, then Drukker let Father win. If he'd have won, Father would have seen it as poor manners. Just another example of how stupid Deigs culture was.

"I'd like to play next." I might as well have a little fun. "Master Drukker?" I gave him a sickly sweet smile.

Drukker inclined his head and Father left his seat so I could sit at the board.

Mother's fingers snagged my elbow before I could settle into the chair. "Don't forget the rules, darling."

"How many times have I played this old game, Mother?" I laughed lightly and brushed her hold from my arm. I joined Drukker and eyed the board, not wanting to look at Drukker more than I had to.

Mother and Father went to the bookcase in the far corner. They were giving us space to talk. Mother called in Sara to play the small harp she'd brought with her from home.

Music filled the room and Drukker dealt us four cards each. I had a jester, the two of pines, a moon, and the five of ships. My fifth roll of the dice sent me into the labyrinth. I glanced at Drukker. The gleam of happiness shone in his eyes.

"Oh, no, you'll have to ask a favor," he said, his voice quiet and laced with meaning. He thought we'd be married soon and I'd have to ask him for favors to do anything at all.

"I don't think so. Not yet, anyway." I smiled and played my jester in the circle at the center of the board.

Drukker frowned. "You can't do that."

"The jester invents stories, yes? He can portal from one end of the board to the other. Why wouldn't he be able to help my piece leave the labyrinth?"

"It's just..." Drukker glared. "You know that's not how it's meant to be played."

"There is no rule against it." I lifted my piece out of the labyrinth and set it on the first square of the board.

Sara's harp music grew louder, the song building toward an end.

"But you're back at the beginning with no progress at all. You're not very good at this game, are you, dear Lady Lina?"

"I'd rather return to the start than be indebted to another player." *To you.*

"Foolish move." He rolled, moved his piece, and played the ten of coins. "I'm nearly to the finish line now." He moved the dice in front of me.

"I wave my roll." I scooted the dice back, then played my moon card. "I get one answer."

Sara began a new tune on her beautiful stringed instrument, a low melody that brought to mind dark nights in darker forests.

He eyed the board and then studied my face. He was obviously rather confused as to why I wasn't worried about losing.

"Fine," he said. "Ask it."

"Do you have any torches in your hand?"

Blinking, he looked at his cards, then back at me. "No."

"Good. I will use this," I said, playing my pines, "and this." I turned my ships card over beside the pines. "I claim the double."

"But you didn't even advance. You can't just create a fleet and win."

"Can't I?"

His nostrils flared, and his color was high in his cheeks. "I will see to it that your contrary ways end once you are mine."

Father strode over, leaving Mother reading a poetry book in the window seat. Despite myself, I began trembling. Father would punish me for this.

"What is the problem? I hope you are having a fine time," Father said tightly.

He regarded the board while Drukker's features fell into an emotionless stare that was directed at me.

Father set his hand on the table. "A fleet to win during phase one? That is genius, Master Drukker."

Drukker stammered. "Yes, but..."

"It was my move, Father. I'm so glad it pleases you." I grinned at them both.

Standing abruptly and disrupting the dice, Drukker claimed it was time for him to leave.

Sara took her harp and bowed before leaving. Father and Mother wished Drukker well, then left us, their low conversation echoing down the corridor outside the hall.

Drukker snatched my hand and kissed it gently.

I fought a shudder.

"My lady, you will benefit from a strong husband." His lips touched my hand once more, then he whispered, "And you *will* bend to me. Of that, I have no doubt."

A shiver rattled down my spine and I wrapped my arms around myself. Oh, how I longed to retort with something like *I'll see you dead first, darling,* but I had to hold my tongue. Getting into a sparring match with Drukker here wouldn't end well.

Drukker's steely eyes said he couldn't wait to have control

over me. I pulled away from his grip and watched him leave, feeling like I'd escaped the executioner of my soul for the last time.

When Drukker was truly gone, Father stepped toward me, grabbed my chin, and forced me to look up at him. His intense hold shot pain through my jaw. With his dark gold eyebrows furrowed, he stared at me until a vein in the side of his forehead throbbed.

"You will marry Lord Drukker within the month or you will go to the House of the Moon. You will spin wool, clean privies, and stare at the same four walls for the rest of your miserable life, you ungrateful little monster."

My chest sank and I fought to keep breathing steadily. I would shrivel and die there, my mind shrinking to pea-size and my spirit going dark inside me like a forgotten candle. It wasn't the threat of hard work or a humble existence. It was the lack of freedom, of adventure, of saying what I wanted to say and finding all the beauty and joy in the world. I would be well and truly trapped. The pain from Father's hold on my chin didn't faze me because my mind was fully tangled in one question: Which was worse—a life with Drukker or a life at the House of the Moon?

Mother stood to the side, agreeing to Father's treatment of me simply by standing there and not uttering a word against it.

I tried to step back, to shake my chin out of his grip, but he held firm until tears sprang to my eyes. "Bruises don't look good on a lady, Father."

He bared his teeth and released me. Turning on his heel, he said, "You will attend the boating party tomorrow and there you will accept Drukker's proposal." He stopped and looked at me over his shoulder. "Unless you have another noble suitor I don't know about? It doesn't have to be Drukker if you do."

My heart lifted at the scrap of consideration he offered and I hated myself for feeling anything but loathing for the man who had sired me.

"You know I don't, Father."

Mother joined him at the archway leading out of the chamber. "Well, then, it's settled. I'll have Sara ready a dress for the event."

As soon as they were off to other parts of the house, I hurried to the kitchen. Sara stirred a large pot over the fire.

"Please tell my mother that I'm off to market to buy a new set of earrings to match my dress." There were three places I was permitted to visit on my own. The market, my aunt's home, and the tutor's room above the guild house. "After that, I'm visiting my tutor. I will dine at the guild house with her."

Sara paused in stirring to bow her head briefly. "Yes, my lady."

"Think she'll believe it?" I cracked a smile despite my aching jaw.

She grinned then covered her mouth with her free hand. I gave her a quick thanks before popping upstairs to grab the black cloak I had hidden under my mattress and rushing out of the house.

I practically ran for the hideout. I had to change into my disguise before meeting Star and Phoenix at the cordwainer's shop. As I walk-jogged my way along the canals, dread took up residence in my chest and chilled my heart. I was shivering by the time I arrived at the hideout and it wasn't only because of the cold rain that had started to fall.

We didn't have the money yet to sail away and I was out of time. My mind raced through other plans, new ways to gather funds. I didn't like any of the ideas. I wasn't going to whore myself for the money. I had my limits. And I couldn't ask for money from my decrepit old aunt. She would definitely tell Mother and Father.

Maybe if I stole enough tonight, and then accepted Drukker's engagement ring, I'd have enough? It would have to be one hell of a ring.

Hmm. What if I sent a message to Drukker that hinted at my openness to accepting his proposal but also mentioned the size of the gift indicating his level of commitment to me? Would he take the bait and make certain he presented a costly ring? Perhaps he'd ditch the one he had and purchase a new and larger emerald or ruby.

After digging through the closet near the hideout's bedchamber, I donned a black wig and a homespun dress dyed a garish red. The neckline was outrageous, the cut between my breasts nearly plunging to my navel with lace that did very little to cover my cleavage. A pair of rough ladies' boots served well enough for footwear. I also took the jeweled dagger I'd nicked yesterday and set it into the thigh sheath Phoenix had made for me.

The event Phoenix, Star, and I were attending this evening was a dance of sorts where many different types of folk would gather to celebrate Port Day. The day commemorated the completion of the first port built in our city of Masdam. Truly, it had been the first port in the Kingdom of Deigs, for Masdam was the first city. Father never wanted anything to do with the celebration because he didn't like mixing with folk of lower status, so I wouldn't see him or Drukker, who was also a complete snob.

I threw on the black cloak and covered myself as best as possible, waiting to enter the street during a pause in the traffic of horse carts, noblemen on steeds decked out in tassels, and fine carriages. Stepping out from under the hide-out's front overhang, I walked into the misty rain. The cobblestones clicked under my shoes.

The pickings at this get-together would be rich indeed. Plus, Star, Phoenix, and I would be able to dance and drink in disguise, enjoying ourselves without worrying about what society wanted from us. The only issue was that we were dressing as whores and that sometimes brought up some problems. Nothing a dagger and a well-placed knee hopefully couldn't handle. It was worth the trouble because no one would balk at whores dancing with anyone and everyone or drinking the night away.

A flutter of warm excitement did a lot to chase my dread away as I rounded a corner and saw Phoenix and Star, also disguised, waiting for me in front of the cordwainer's awning, beside his collection of heeled and flat shoes.

I linked my arms in theirs as they welcomed me. They needed to know my time was short, but I couldn't get my lips to form the warning. If we did amazingly well tonight, we could leave right away. If we found the right captain to bribe. If, if, if.

"Time for some fun, girls," I said, pushing my worry to the side.

We laughed all the way to the warehouse where the uncommon party was already in full swing.

6

ZAVI

Zavi woke up on the floor of the apothecary, blinking away daydreams of a copper-haired beauty with quick fingers and ferocious eyes that, quite frankly, scared him. His vision cleared to reveal an old woman staring down at him.

The apothecary pushed a gray lock of hair behind her ear. "I tried to drag you to the back room, but you're too big of a man. Fae. Whatever you are. If you're awake enough now to listen, this is what I found and what I think it is."

He felt his wound and realized she had stitched him up. What a blessing this fine woman was! She held out an emerald-colored stone cut into a diamond shape. It was no bigger than a gladecoin. He sat up and the room spun.

The apothecary put a hand on his shoulder to steady him. "You're cursed, friend. I hate to be the one to tell you. But perhaps you already knew?"

"Yes. I can't remember anything past the last five years. Well, I know basic things like how to speak, obviously, my name, and how to fight and sail." He didn't want to think of his brother Emiel's face now because the pain would return. Plus, it might be wise to keep that information to himself. So, like he had many times lately, he pushed the memory away and swallowed the frustration and agony of being completely unable to help Emiel.

"But you don't know your past?" the apothecary asked, bringing Zavi back to the moment.

"No. I get flashes of memory, but not enough to piece together properly. I feel..."

"Hollow?"

Zavi nodded as another wave of nausea swept over him.

"Unfortunately, you must have a very rich and powerful enemy."

Somehow that didn't surprise him. "Why is that?"

"Because you've been cursed with a memory stone."

That made sense. He'd known it had been something to do with memories. Holding a hand to his stomach, he tried to focus on the apothecary's face, but the room kept spinning.

"I might vomit."

"I'll probably have to put it back inside you. I'd hoped that wasn't the case, but..." The apothecary went to the back and returned with a bucket and more clean cloths. She set the bucket beside the bench. "It's a rune-etched magical artifact made of sea emeralds. It's placed inside the victim, but one piece is kept and hidden." She held the diamond-shaped stone that she'd removed from his side up to the light. A silver set of initials sat on the bottom left edge. K.V. "Until the piece is reunited with the artifact and the magic is unbound, you'll continue to be blocked from your memories. I suppose your Fae blood fights the magic and that's why you have some of your memories still. Full humans forget absolutely everything except tasks which have muscle memory built in."

"Those initials. Could they be a maker's mark?"

She squinted at the object. "I've seen initials carved on artifacts, but they usually point to the owner or dealer rather than the maker."

"How do you know so much about artifacts?" It wasn't the question he really wanted to ask, but his mind was still processing this revelation.

"I don't know everything." She crossed her arms over her apron and pursed her lips, eyeing his stitched-up side. "I used to buy and sell them, but I gave it up. Too much criminal activity. I'm too old for that shite. I'm not sure you registered what I said earlier. We have to put the piece back where it was."

"In my side?"

"Yes. I'd thought you could simply carry it around, but you look far worse with it outside your body. You'll have to find the missing piece first, then remove the memory stone, then replace the piece so the stone is whole."

"This is...a lot. Thank you very much."

"I can tell you're a good one. I'm not charging for the second bit of cutting and sewing."

"No, I insist." He fought the dizziness to pull a small bag of coins from his trouser pocket. Pressing it into her hand, he gave her his best attempt at a grateful smile. "Please."

She tilted her head in sympathy and accepted the bag.

"How do you know I'm a good one? I'm pretty sure I'm not."

"Good ones never say that. Plus, you talked while you were on the way to passing out."

"Stones, what did I say?"

A laugh bubbled from her as she cleaned the curse piece with alcohol. She handed him a cup of something that smelled bitter. "Drink this and you won't feel the work quite as keenly."

He did as ordered, noticing she hadn't answered him. The room faded to gray and it only seemed like seconds had passed when she helped him sit up again.

"Finished?" he asked.

"I am. The drink I gave you makes you a bit foggy. It should fade in a minute or two."

His middle was bound with clean linen that she'd knotted neatly at his stomach. She helped him lower his shirt into place.

"Any ideas on Masdam folk who might have the ability to secure a memory stone?" he asked.

Shaking her head, she gathered all of her items and placed them in the bucket that he thankfully hadn't been forced to use. "If I did, I wouldn't tell you. I don't want trouble. Just know that the stones are rare and incredibly costly. Your enemy is a rich man. Or a rich Fae." She glanced at his ears, then quickly away.

The room's details bloomed into focus. Light streamed through the windows and illuminated the glass bottles on the back shelves as well as the deeply worn wooden floorboards. He stood and thanked the apothecary again.

"I wish you luck! It might be a good thing that you forgot who you were. I noticed that pirate tattoo..."

"Do you do inkings? I'd love to have it covered or altered."

"I don't, but you could try the blacksmith's second son. I heard he does them for a decent price. Oh, I should tell you one more thing. If you don't find the missing piece of the stone soon, the memory loss will be permanent and it might also render you senseless."

The artifact would ruin his mind? Zavi swallowed and nodded. "Thank you so very much. For everything. I should have asked for your expertise long ago."

She waved as he opened the door. Three customers bumped past him and into the shop.

The street was busier now, carts and horses everywhere. A town crier's bell grieved across the plein—an open space where merchants hawked their wares and children ran to and fro kicking rag balls.

"Storms approach from the sea! They land in a matter of days, maybe hours!" the crier warned.

Zavi hurried along the cobblestones toward his ruined fortress and his bed. Fatigue made it impossible to consider investigating who might have the missing piece of the memory stone.

The initials on the stone blinked through his mind. K.V.

Tonight, he would begin his search. The Port Day celebration was this evening and he'd been hired to sing and play for one segment of the dancing. Even if his mysterious nemesis wasn't in attendance—he might be too fine for such a raucous event where folk of all classes gathered—surely there would be gossip. He'd find out who the richest were here in Masdam. He already had a small list in his head. He'd find his way into their circles and root out his target. If he ended up without leads, he'd spread his search to the rest of the kingdom and beyond. Hopefully, his mind would remain functioning long enough to enact this plan. If not, well...

A one-legged, blind beggar sat on the corner of Blue

Street and Night Avenue. The man's wrinkled hand extended beyond his ragged tunic as he asked passersby for coin. Zavi pulled his emergency coins from the secret pocket sewn to the inside of his belt and handed them over.

"May the Old Ones bless you," he said to the beggar.

"May they bless us both."

"Aye to that, good man. Aye to that." Zavi left, praying to the gods that he would be spared a future as a fog-minded beggar.

7

LINA

The Port Day celebration organizers had transformed the warehouse into a party that looked like something from the Fae realm. I could despise Fae and still appreciate the paintings of their court and King Lysanael's vineyard. Rose-colored candles burned from stands along the edges of the room and flickered with golden light from chandeliers hung from the ceiling's rough-hewn beams. Long lengths of rose-and-turquoise-dyed linen fluttered from the beams as well, the fabric undulating in the breeze that passed through the small, high windows of the building.

Sophia would have loved this. My heart ached with the familiar pain of loss. If she hadn't been killed, she could have been here, enjoying our little band's hijinks.

"We're in the clouds!" Smiling, Phoenix spun around one of the fabric panels. A tiny dark shape crawled out of her cloak and flew to her shoulder.

"You brought the dragon?" I reached for the wee thing

and she jumped onto my outstretched hand. Her body was warmer than I'd thought it would be. "You're supposed to fly, not jump, little sweetling." The pocket dragon rubbed her muzzle against my palm, then hiccuped. A spark hit my thumb. "Whoa! Maybe don't light me on fire." With a forked purple tongue, she licked the spot she'd accidentally burned and I laughed.

Star took a turn holding her as we gave our cloaks to the doorman then made our way around the edges of the crowd. "I can already see that her scales are more defined."

"Yes," Phoenix said as we each took an offered mug of what smelled like apple ale from a passing server. "She is growing very quickly."

"But she's not any larger," I said. The ale was cold and tart. Delicious.

"It varies, but they generally don't get much larger. They just grow sleek and their scales and snout harden."

The music started up and that same sultry, deep voice from the tavern poured through the gathering. My heart beat triple time. It was the half-Fae bard. I couldn't help it. I enjoyed the Fae's singing. It meant nothing. He was Fae and was therefore not a person to trust. My own experience had taught me that fact. Plus, he was a male and all the males in my life—Father, Drukker...the list went on and on—were selfish and commanding. No, I wasn't going to let the bard's voice tempt me to let a male enter my life. I didn't want a lover or a husband. I certainly didn't want a Fae partner. I only wanted freedom.

"Oh." Phoenix stood in front of me and it was obvious she had been talking to me and I hadn't caught more than that one word. "It's that bard again, hmm?" She wiggled her eyebrows and grinned slyly. "Maybe when he is finished, you can ask him for a dance?"

I glared and began to answer, but Star nudged me while Phoenix slid the dragon into her dress pocket.

"She isn't interested, Phoenix," Star said. "You know that."

"Do I?" Phoenix tapped her feet to the bard's song. "I'm headed to the feasting table to do some shopping." She winked and melted into the brightly dressed crowd.

Why was she goading me? Normally, she wouldn't.

Shaking her head, Star faced me. "What is going on with her?"

"I don't know. I guess she thinks the Fae is handsome."

"If you are interested," Star said. "I can do the harder work tonight and you can relax and have fun."

"No. I want nothing to do with him. Let's get to work."

"Moth," Star said quietly, "I would never push you, but that incident in your childhood... It was years ago. You can't blame every Fae for what one—"

Sweat bloomed on my forehead even though I felt cold. I set a finger on Star's lips. "I appreciate the fact that you don't push me. Let's keep it that way."

She cocked her head and grimaced but then shrugged.

Phoenix returned with a tiny goblet of something that smelled like pine. She downed it. "All right. Let's wiggle into the fray and have some fun."

Nodding, I led Phoenix onto the dance floor while Star hung back. The bard's voice faded and his song concluded. Everyone began lining up for a reel. Finally, my head felt clear. I couldn't have stood for another minute of the bard's distractingly beautiful voice.

Phoenix stood across from a doughy man with a shirt

hemmed in fine embroidery. He wore a pair of black boots that also spoke of money. I watched as their turn came and Phoenix walked a slow circle around him, her right hand moving quickly in and out of his trouser pocket while her left touched his arm to distract him.

My partner wore a mummer's mask and a plain linen shirt, but the rings on his fingers and the gold of his trouser belt buckle said he had plenty to go around too. I danced a ring around him as the reel called for and relieved him of a tiny coin purse he'd had tied to his belt. It slid easily into the pocket sewn into my dress.

The reel had us all changing partners several times until we met the one with whom we would dance the final bit. This one wore a mask similar to my first partner...

My heart froze in my chest.

I knew that blond hair and the set of that jaw and the curl of that particular beard.

Drukker.

Before I could dart away, he had his hands at my waist and was spinning me around.

"You're a lovely girl." His voice was as smooth as a snake's hiss, though his breath stank of strong drink. "I believe we have met. Perhaps at the harvest festival?"

Sweat prickled across the edge of my wig. "I don't think so," I said in a southlands type of accent that was probably terribly inaccurate. "I need to meet someone. I'm sorry."

I tried to break from him, but he held me firm. His dark blue eyes widened in his mask.

"Lina?" His voice mixed confusion and rage.

Twisting quickly to the side, I broke his hold. I pushed through the other lines of dancers, and sweat stuck my clothing to my skin. Drukker caught up and snatched my dress, fisting a handful of the material and yanking me backward. I nearly fell into a woman, who swore like a sailor. Drukker whirled me around, held my wrists, and put his face in mine. He'd torn his mask away at some point.

"What in all the hells do you think you're doing here? You demean us both."

"And yet, here *you* are just the same as I am. How is it different?" I knew the answer, of course, but I wanted to hear him own up to his double standard. I don't know why I tried. Pointless, really.

The confusion furrowing his brow slid away, and he glared. He released me, drew back a hand, and struck me across the cheek. Shouting a string of curses, I stumbled into a man and woman, who caught me. The metallic tang of blood filled my mouth and I fisted a hand, ready to clock Lord Arseface.

An elbow came out of nowhere and struck Drukker's temple, driving him to the floor. I gasped, then fought a laugh —not the proper response, but damn if it wasn't glorious seeing Drukker knocked out like that. The awful toad of a man was out cold, mouth hanging open and eyes shut.

The person who'd hit him turned to look at me as he shook out his arm.

I blew out a breath. "Damn it." It was the bard, grinning wickedly with his Fae fangs and all.

My heart beat three times in painfully quick succession. His collarbone peeked from inside his disheveled shirt and I wondered what the smooth skin there would taste like.

Stop it, I shouted silently at myself. *Rein in the lusty party mood, you fool. He is a Fae.*

"Thank you," I said tightly.

Two men nearly as broad-shouldered and tall as the bard picked up Drukker and dragged him away. They wouldn't let him back in, thankfully. The organizers never allowed reentry after a skirmish. What would happen with Drukker now? Would he tell my parents? If he did, would my mention of him also being in attendance work in my favor even a little bit? Or would this just go to the hells and tangle my life further?

The bard bowed and swept a hand out dramatically. "At your service." His dark half-Fae eyes with their barely slitted pupils watched me through his thick black lashes. "I like your disguise," he said. "Repay me with a dance?"

So he did know it was me.

Something about the way the bard's dark blond hair fell over his forehead when he bowed warmed my cheeks in spite of myself. Gods, I hated Fae. And pirates. But could I still despise this former pirate after doing such a lovely job dousing Drukker's lights? I squinted at the bard. Maybe. Maybe not. He wasn't the Fae pirate from my past, from that terrible night. I didn't remember much about my kidnapper's face, but I'd never forget the grass-green shade of his irises around those fully slitted Fae pupils. A shiver washed through me and this one was far from pleasant. At least the bard had given up pirating. Sure, pirates stole like my friends and I did, but they committed far worse crimes—and those against innocents.

Phoenix pushed through the crowd. "Are you all right? What happened? Wait. Is that Drukker they're tossing into the street?" Being taller than me, she could peer over the crowd.

"Yes." I took the bard's hand to start the dance. A shot of heat ran through my fingers and up my arm.

He glanced at me. "Hmm. Interesting." His gaze traveled over my face and stayed there despite the fact that my décolletage was presented boldly in this naughty dress.

"What did Drukker want?" Phoenix asked.

"He didn't realize it was me at first, but when he saw through the disguise... Well, he wasn't happy to see me here. He wanted to dance in anonymity through this gutter, as he would call it." Such hypocrisy.

Star appeared at my side. I hadn't seen her moving through the crowd, but she was talented in that way. "Anything I need to do? It's already been a fruitful evening." Wiggling her eyebrows, she patted her side, where stolen items surely hid.

The musical cue for the reel to begin sounded across the dance floor and the bard's feet moved gracefully. I waved to Phoenix, who frowned, and Star, who slid her hand into a man's pocket while laughing. I let the bard lead me in an intertwining circle with the other dancers. He was ridiculously graceful.

"All Fae are physically gifted, yes?" I asked.

His eyes smoldered and a grin plucked at the side of his mouth.

I glared. "You know I was talking about dancing."

"Of course."

I studied him, willing myself to give him a portion of trust. It felt like trying to nick a rusted dagger from its sheath.

"What is your name?" I asked.

He probably wouldn't give me his true name because Fae could control anyone with their true name, and he wouldn't know for certain whether I did or did not have even the tiniest bit of Fae blood. When the new queen had taken her throne in the Fae's Realm of Lights, every human and Fae had been tattooed with a rune devised by the incredibly powerful Druid to counteract the magic. But old habits died hard for Fae, or at least, it seemed that way from stories about their culture.

"Zavi."

He rubbed the side of my hand with his thumb as we rotated around another couple. Sparks danced down my body. Was it because he was Fae or was it just attraction?

The crowd was growing more raucous and the reel fell into a chaotic dance. Zavi grinned, took my waist in his hands, and pulled me against him. Before I could stab him or some such action, he was spinning me around and I found I didn't hate the feel of his body brushing across mine. The power just in his grip, in those fingers, threw my imagination into a whirlwind. Never had a man looked at me like this, like he was simply enjoying my company. Yes, there was a bit of lust in his gaze, but joy flickered there too, and a complete disregard of who he knew I was—a lord's daughter. Kissing him wouldn't be like having to kiss Drukker or any of the other uptight lords my family had presented to me for marriage. No, this roguish pirate turned bard would have experience, tricks—knowledge of how to please a woman. My throat tightened, and I held to his well-muscled shoulders as he lifted me high in an exaggerated move of the reel we were supposedly dancing.

I was breathless, shocked... No male had ever affected me like this.

He took my hand and pulled me out of the dancing and toward a woman pouring ale at a long table. Grabbing each of us a mug, he nodded toward two seats. I took one, for the first time at a loss on what to say. I didn't know myself at the moment.

"Why are you frowning? Didn't you enjoy that?" He downed his ale in one go.

I drank mine just as quickly, ready to stop worrying about him because it didn't matter how my body had responded to him. I wasn't interested. "I was thirsty."

He looked down at me, his pointed ears showing a bit through his tousled hair. I shook my head. Gods, he was lovely. His smooth skin, that shadow of a beard on his sharp jawline, those cheekbones...

"Glad I could help," he said. "I have an idea."

"About what?"

"See that man there?" He pointed out Master Rietveld.

"The richest man in the city aside from the king when he visits."

"That's the one. Wouldn't he be fun to steal from?"

I laughed and reached for the pitcher of ale the woman had left for us. Pouring myself another mug of the tart drink, I glanced at Zavi. He was studying me with those clever eyes of his.

"You believe stealing from a man surrounded by enormous bodyguards would be a nice way to pass the time? That maybe slipping past a bevy of trained dogs and into his house, or ship, would be a pleasant diversion?" I put on my rich lady voice and laughed again.

"You could do it. You and your friends. I've never seen someone as capable as you. Why do you steal?"

"I'm here with you because you knocked Drukker into next week. I'll give you one more moment of my time in gratitude, then I'm gone."

"Fine. But please, I'm curious. Why do you steal?"

I leaned close and his scent danced over my nose—the salt of driftwood and the aroma of bergamot.

"Do I smell terrible?" He lifted his shirt and sniffed.

I had to smile, but I wasn't about to tell him what I thought about his scent. "I live in a cage," I whispered before taking another sip of ale. "I want out. To escape." It was more than that. My father was abusive and he was about to hand me over to a man just like him.

"Where to?" Zavi asked.

"Not why? Do you understand why?"

"Women have no freedoms here. I easily fathom you imagining a better life in a place where you choose how your day goes."

I blinked. He actually did comprehend my reasoning.

He chuckled and shut my open mouth with a finger to my chin. "Don't look so shocked. Not all of us males are like the Deigs richies you are forced to meet. I wonder... Why don't you steal from your own house? Wouldn't that be easier?"

"Father somehow set a magical trace on the valuable objects in our home. They can be beyond the walls for a short span of time, but not long. And I have to help my friend get her children back from her ex-husband, and Star can't go to war again..."

The drinks had gone to my head. I was an idiot. I shouldn't have been telling him all of this. He was a Fae and a male. A terrible combination.

"I must go. I'm sorry," I said, starting to leave.

"If you succeeded in a big job, you could have the funds for a long, long journey away from here in a day's time rather than scraping your way and hoping Drukker's advances don't slam you into his version of a cage before you have the chance to escape."

I couldn't think about this. Stealing from Rietveld was a mad dream. Forget a violent marriage or the House of the Moon, I'd end up in prison. "Thanks again for the rescue."

Leaving before he could call me back with another interesting comment, I searched the dance floor for Star and Phoenix. Once they were at my side, we exited the warehouse and I only looked back once, wondering if Zavi was watching.

I had to focus because the only important question right now was—had my friends and I stolen enough to secure an off-the-books sail to Laqqara tomorrow?

❧ 8 ❧

ZAVI

Behind a tower of used wooden crates, Zavi watched the richest man in Masdam—Rietveld—hand a well-known crime lord a sack of coins. Zavi had been trailing Rietveld since the end of the Port Day celebration.

That crime lord whom Rietveld spoke to was thought to be dead—he had once been the talk of the tavern—but there he was alive and well, albeit missing a leg. Interesting. A wooden peg had replaced the limb, and it didn't seem to be slowing him down at all as he left the dock and slipped into the shadows of the back streets.

The crime lord's name was Kal Vancing. K.V. A match to the initials scratched onto the memory stone.

Rietveld grinned, showing a straight line of very white teeth, and a buzzing sounded in Zavi's ears, making him shudder. From the way Rietveld had treated the servers at the celebration, Zavi knew he was a monstrous person, but why would Zavi have such a strong reaction to him? Kal was just as bad a person. Zavi focused on Kal, and the irritating sound in his ears faded. He looked back at Rietveld, and the buzz started up again.

The apothecary's voice echoed in Zavi's head. Maybe Rietveld really was the one who had cursed Zavi. The curse seemed to be reacting to him, making that odd sound in his ears. Rietveld could have purchased the memory stone from Kal. Excitement burned through Zavi's blood. Masdam was the only city in the whole kingdom of Deigs, so it wasn't crazy to think the rich man who'd cursed him would be here, where Zavi had woken up five years ago.

He might be wrong. But he might be right.

Zavi's brother's face surfaced in his mind. He pushed it away. He had to remain alert; this was no time to fall unconscious to the ground.

Rietveld tossed a leather satchel to his assistant, a skinny human male with close-cropped hair.

Ears buzzing quietly like he had a minuscule bee trapped in his head, Zavi followed Rietveld down a series of winding alleyways.

Zavi had seen Rietveld many times—at the tavern where he worked now, near the piers from time to time, and around the guild house during festival days. He wondered if the buzzing had always been an effect of the memory stone and the noise of the surrounding city had simply covered the sound.

The path narrowed and a tunnel yawned, open and dark. Rietveld and his man walked inside and Zavi followed, hoping there would be a way out and some noise to cover his footsteps.

Flickering torches appeared in the tunnel, lighting the

heads—one bald and the other nearly shaved—of Zavi's two subjects of study.

His goal for now was simply reconnaissance. Where did Rietveld keep his money and most valuable items? A safe? Behind guarded doors? In his brightly painted townhouse on Pelican Canal or in some off-site location?

Once Zavi knew the probable location of the memory stone, he would tell the gorgeous Moth, Lina—he'd heard that bastard at the celebration call her Lina—and lure her into helping him. It would help her too.

Lina was a marvel. So wild and clever. That tongue of hers...

He could easily imagine several ways that sharp tongue could be his undoing. Swallowing, he recalled the flicker of rebellion in her quick gaze and the way her pink lips shifted to the right when he pleased her and she wished he hadn't. He could kiss his way from that mouth all the way down her curvaceous body until she was calling his name and demanding more. She could order him around anytime.

Was she so against his very presence because he was half-Fae or was it simply because he was a male and she had been treated poorly by the males of this kingdom for so long? Or was it both that were strikes against him? Probably both.

"Eh! Who are you?" Rietveld's assistant started toward Zavi.

His heart flipped once and he retreated quickly, using his Fae speed to slip out of the tunnel and into the street. The assistant ran from the underground corridor as Zavi lodged himself behind a boarded-up and locked-down leather merchant's cart. The wise choice would be to head back home, but now that Zavi had a trail to follow, he couldn't let himself consider waiting another day to discover more. With the assistant still running in the direction he likely thought Zavi had gone, Zavi returned to the tunnel and followed it to a set of double doors etched with Rietveld's family sigil of sail and cliff. He pulled a black mask from his belt and tied it on. It covered his hair and the set of his brow. If seen, at least Zavi might not be recognized later. The double doors opened with a gentle push. The stupid assistant had left it ajar.

Perfect.

The doors led into another corridor, this one lined with stone walls and glass-cupped torches. A scent like hot metal and fruit floated on the air. He swung open a door on the left. A chamber filled with scrolls and books sat in the dark, only a slender beam of daylight streaming through a high window. Moving to the next door in the corridor, Zavi kept his footsteps silent and held his breath. No sounds of other humans trickled to his ears. This door opened to a room lit like the last one, but there were no books here. Just a large desk, a high-backed wooden chair, an empty fire grate, and a series of paintings along the wood-paneled walls.

No, it can't be this easy.

He huffed a laugh as he moved the first of the paintings to reveal a safe.

Come on, Rietveld. At least be a worthy enemy.

Zavi took his eating knife and a long metal stick from his belt and began to work the lock. The safe gave way to reveal... A stack of parchment. Deeds, guild agreements, horse purchases. Nothing related to what Zavi was after. He sighed, replaced the items, and stepped toward the second painting. A squeak stopped him.

"You had better have a grand story," an unfamiliar male

voice said, "or your life is at its end."

Zavi's heart should have sped up, but because of whatever training he'd had, he found himself breathing deeply and slowly as he rotated to see who had spoken. "Hello, there. That's a lovely sword. Care to duel?"

"Not really. I doubt you could even give me a good fight."

"I don't know." Zavi unsheathed his sword. "I might surprise you." He grinned, showing his fangs.

The man's throat bobbed, but he held his ground. "With those eyes, you can't have much Fae blood."

Zavi shrugged. "I guess you're about to find out."

Before the man could offer some retort, Zavi rushed him. The man parried Zavi's first blow, so Zavi shifted his weight and slashed toward his shoulder. He didn't want to kill the man. He'd ended one life with his mysterious skills only by accident during the first days after he'd become aware of himself. Those had been dark days. Murder wasn't something that filled him with any sense of victory. It was a tragedy and he had no desire for more blood on his hands. Plus, he really didn't want to hide a body and a crime. It was far more trouble.

The man swept his blade left, then right. Zavi ducked to avoid injury, then knocked the follow-up attack back with his sword. They parried and danced, striking at one another. This man was rather fast for a human.

"I'm impressed," Zavi said.

Glaring, the man muttered, "Don't patronize me."

"I would never."

The man panted, his face gone a dark red with effort. "You're just playing with me, aren't you?"

"I thought it best to give you a good match," Zavi said. "You'll be even better for it."

"Cocky arse."

"I've been called worse." With a lunge and a spin, Zavi had the man by the throat, sword tip at the fellow's ribs. "Drop your blade."

The man did so, his weapon banging dully on the red carpet. "If you kill me, you will be ending your own life."

"I doubt you could pick me out in a crowd."

"Perhaps not."

A grin tugged at Zavi's lips. "Wise fellow. Have a lovely nap." He rapped the man on the head, then lowered his body to the ground beside his sword.

Footsteps sounded far down the corridor outside the half-open door. If he returned later, there would be guards here or the items in those poorly veiled safes would be moved to different locations. He had to check those safes now or never. He sheathed his sword.

Hurrying to the next painting, he made quick work of the lock. Gold bars. He could steal one for Lina, but then she'd have no motivation to help him. Plus, it wasn't easy to hold a gold bar in one's pocket, not a bar the size of these. But perhaps if anyone saw him, they'd only believe him to be extravagantly endowed. Chuckling, he locked the safe up again. The footsteps grew louder. The third safe held nothing at all. Hmm. He wiggled the metal pin into the fourth's lock, but this one was older and had suffered from Deigs' sea air, and rust colored its edges.

Well, damn. He wasn't going to get into this one.

Whoever was coming down the corridor was slowing their pace. Had they noticed the door was open?

Zavi crept to the door and peered out. A large man had his back to Zavi and was lighting a pipe. Zavi slid out of the room and down the corridor the way he'd entered. Once he was free of the building, he slipped his mask from his head and took a deep breath. Stars glittered overhead as he hurried over the cobblestones. His decision not to steal a bit of gold weighed his steps. He might have held back on shedding blood, but he could have saved Lina and he had chosen not to. No matter how he rationalized his behavior and compared it to beasts like Rietveld and the renowned crime lords, no matter how much he wanted to be the hero, only one thing was true. If he'd stolen gold for Lina, she could have escaped within a day, but he'd walked away. He was the villain of the story.

LINA

Back at the hideout, we appraised our take for the night. I played the scene of the bard's elbow hitting Drukker's face over and over in my mind, and I could not stop grinning. The bard's laughter echoed through my head. It was such a great sound, so full and free. And the way he had danced... So graceful and bursting with joy. His grip around my waist had been so warm. In another life that didn't include my memories, I might have wanted his hands all over me.

I pushed the last of my grabs, a ruby and gold ring, toward the small dragon hoard we'd assembled on the table. Star found the last of our jenever and poured a round. I drank mine down quickly.

Eyeing our take, Phoenix pursed her lips, then clicked her nails on the table.

"Not enough, is it?" I said, my voice shaky.

"Not to bribe a ship captain and his men," Phoenix said, "but maybe there's an avenue we haven't explored yet."

"I'm supposed to marry Drukker in a month."

Star froze, her tulip-shaped glass halfway to her lips. She touched my hand. "What?"

I nodded. "Yes, and I'm attending the boating party on his horrible arm tomorrow." Leaning on the rough grain of the table, I put my aching head in my hands.

Sophia would have had ideas on how to deal with all of this. She'd been the leader in our mischief. I swallowed around the lump in my throat and curled my fingers, remembering how we'd made pinkie promises to tell one another everything to do with crushes on boys. What would she have thought of Zavi?

"Will he mention tonight to your parents?" Star asked.

Rubbing my temples, I daydreamed of the southlands. Laqqaran women of twenty didn't have to deal with controlling fathers. I could not wait for the day I was one of those free people.

An imagined moment flitted through my thoughts. Zavi lying beside me on a brightly striped blanket by the Glass River at Laqqara's border. His hand slipped up my side, the heat of his fingers warming me though a thin tunic. His breath on my neck...

I shook off the stupid daydream. "Not sure," I said, finally answering Star. "He could get away with a lie something along the lines of a servant or client mentioned seeing me."

"He'll need to explain his banged-up face." Phoenix eased backward and crossed her arms. "Your parents aren't stupid. They'll know that those two facts are most likely related."

"They won't care," I mumbled. "They'll see what they want to see. As usual. I'm guessing that Drukker will hold it over my head at the party tomorrow."

Phoenix took a healthy swallow of her drink. "So what if he tells your parents?"

"They will put me in a locked room until my wedding day. Have no doubt of that."

Star slammed a fist onto the table, jangling the coins, daggers, and rings. "Do you have a plan?"

"If he proposes tomorrow with a big ring, I can accept and add it to our loot?"

My friends' guffaws tugged a smile across my lips.

Once we stopped chuckling, Phoenix said, "Sadly, I don't think one ring will do it for all of us to gain passage." She exchanged a heavy look with Star.

I stood up. "No, no, no. You aren't going to sacrifice your escape by paying for mine."

"But we aren't in a situation like yours," Star said. "We can wait."

"No. We are getting your children out, Phoenix. And Star, you don't belong in this cage of a kingdom any more than me. I'm not going to the southlands alone. I love you both. I refuse to go without you."

Exhaling, Star shook her head. "Fine."

I grabbed my cloak. "Fine is right. I'll think of something and we will get away. But first, I need sleep and time to ponder."

Across the table, Phoenix grasped my hand and squeezed. I forced the tears searing my eyes to go right back where they'd come from and I left before the tears could defeat me.

The street lamps' flickering light made the rain on the cobblestones sparkle as I hurried home. I had to do a bigger job to pay for our escape, and perhaps tomorrow would provide such an opportunity. The entire upper class and the nobility would attend the boat party. Surely, I could find information to steal a larger stash of coin. The location of a vault. A numbered combination for a locked room of gold. A miracle in the form of silver. Anything was possible.

Or at least, that was what I tried to convince myself of as I slipped back into the house.

As I walked beside Mother down the bay's edge toward Master Rietveld's ship, a bellowing singer on board both relieved me and turned my world to pain. He was terrible. Though I couldn't see the fellow, his less than dulcet tones let me know the Fae bard hadn't elbowed his way into this event. I hated that I was disappointed. I took two scraps of linen from the bag at my belt—cloth that I used to dab my nose as needed on chilly mornings—rolled them up, and stuck them in my ears. It was that bad.

"What are you doing?" Mother tugged my hand away from my ear.

"Saving my precious hearing. The real question is why aren't you doing the same thing?"

She ripped the cloth from my hand and tossed it into the sparkling water of the bay. Her glare told me that I was about to follow the bits of cloth into the dark blue.

"Come. Your father is playing one and thirty with Master Rietveld."

She shoved my back, forcing me to lead her up the walkway and onto Rietveld's ship. Polished railings and masts that scraped the wispy clouds framed a party of nobles in silk, highly regarded merchants laughing, judges eyeing the crowd, and guild leaders ordering wine passed around by impeccably dressed servants.

Thankfully, Drukker had yet to make an appearance. Gods, would he ask me to marry him in front of everyone? My stomach rolled.

Across the decking under a pale blue shade tarp, Rietveld tapped a thick finger on the gaming table. The dealer passed Rietveld another card. Father turned to lift a hand to us in greeting.

The men at the gaming table stood as we approached.

"Master Rietveld, you know my esteemed wife."

"Of course, Lady Casparji."

"And I'm happy to introduce my daughter, Lina."

I gave a quick curtsey as Rietveld inclined his head.

"Drukker has his eye on this peach, does he?" Rietveld asked.

Gosh, I loved being referred to as fruit. I gritted my teeth.

"He does," I answered, forcing a smile.

Everyone's eyes widened at me, but I dipped my head submissively and soon they went on to talk trade and cards once more. Mother dragged me away from the table, then pushed a glass of wine into my hand.

"Sip it like a lady."

"I know how to drink wine, Mother. I'm twenty years old, if you've forgotten."

"You know nothing of how to behave, as you have shown clearly just now."

I shook my head. "How can you stand it?"

"Stand what?"

"How they treat us? Like we are nothing but chattel to be

bred. Why do you just go along with it? They educate us, then they don't let us use what we know."

"It is the way of things. Besides, I wouldn't want to be in charge of running a business or making all of the decisions. It sounds exhausting."

"Don't you grow bored?"

"Your father discusses issues that concern the world outside our home."

"I think that's actually called *lecturing*."

She gave me a flat look. "That's enough of your tongue. Here comes your husband."

I coughed on a mouthful of wine, covered my lips with my hand, and managed to swallow the sweet liquid before Drukker slid up. He looked like a poodle that had crept into the stables and tangled with a draft horse. He wore a tunic, its hem embroidered with ships and waves. His hair, curled and styled, was tied at the base of his neck—all the better for viewing that lovely black eye.

The Fae bard's rich laugh echoed through my memory. I still would never trust a Fae, but the bard was different from what I had expected. Bold, but so completely unlike any other male. He had been flirtatious, but not pushy, seemingly wanting to please me. Last night had been truly interesting. I wondered where the bard was spending his day...

Drukker bowed low to Mother, then cut his eyes to me. His gaze exuded naked fury. "Good day, ladies."

Mother made a sound of surprise. "My, my. I didn't notice your injury until you came close. What happened, dear Master Drukker?"

I tried so hard not to smile. It was impossible. I covered my mouth with my glass, downing the rest of my drink.

"I fought off a brigand on my way home last night."

I ran a finger along the edge of my wine glass. "So I assume this brigand looks far worse than you today?"

"He will get justice. Make no mistake about that."

"I have no doubt," Mother said.

Drukker was all crow and no peck. He had no idea who Zavi was. Drukker had been out cold and hadn't even seen the hit coming.

"What would you like to do?" I spun to view the ship and the entertainment provided for this year's event. I had to start playing nice if I was going to get that ring. That hopefully very large, very expensive ring.

Mother gave me an approving smile as Drukker cleared his throat. We were all such fabulous actors.

Drukker nodded toward a slender table of men and women setting whalebone pieces into tiny cribbage board holes. A deck of cards sat in the center of their play and each held a few cards in their hands. "How about a game of cribbage?"

A server who looked strangely familiar walked by. Something about the set of his shoulders and the glimpse of his profile... The crowd swallowed him up, so I couldn't get a better look.

Beside the cribbage players, a large woman sat at a circular table around which a half-open curtain had been tied up to serve like a small tent.

"Oh, I prefer to speak to the oracle." I started toward the woman in the shadows.

"Foolish nonsense," Drukker muttered, catching up to me and taking my arm roughly.

"Is there a type of nonsense that isn't foolish?"

"What?"

"Nothing. What do you have against the oracle? It's only a bit of fun like all of these other games."

"Oracles always pretend to know everything."

"Um, yes, that is the point, after all. It would hardly be entertaining if you asked them a question and they just replied with a shrug."

"That's not what I mean and you know it."

I did know it. He hated watching a woman play at being more knowledgeable than a man. Typical Lord Arseface behavior.

"Well, Master Rietveld must be all right with her since she is right here on his fine ship." I turned to give Rietveld a smile, not that the man was looking my way, but it was enjoyable to watch confusion twist Drukker's face as he tried to figure out how well I knew the powerful merchant.

"Does your father often play cards with Master Rietveld?"

He didn't, but Drukker didn't need to know that. "Rietveld knows you are interested in marrying me. He said as much today."

"He mentioned me?"

"Greetings," the oracle said as we ducked into her makeshift tent. The fabric blocking the sunlight made her face glow a pinkish shade. She wore a pirate's scarf about her head and had her eyes painted heavily with kohl. She looked amazing.

"Hello." I took a seat on the stool opposite the oracle. Drukker stood stiffly beside me, not making eye contact with the woman.

The oracle took my hand. Her fingers were smooth and

warm and she wore a ring on every finger. It was nice to see some rings that I had no desire to steal.

"Choose a necklace or choose to fly," the oracle said in a dreamy tone.

Drukker snorted and crossed his arms.

"Can you tell me a bit about each choice first?" I asked.

"Splendor can be yours, but happiness comes only with courage."

"Cockamamy..." Drukker muttered.

But he didn't understand poetry or art or the will of one's spirit. The oracle was using intuition, a very female power.

"I can't help but try to be courageous," I said.

The oracle smiled, but her gaze flashed toward Drukker briefly. "You shall see a lion and a pool of oil in your dreams, but the jewels will be yours if you stay the path."

"What jewels?" Drukker let his arms fall and tilted his head as if truly interested.

"Not the kind that sparkle in the sun, but the type that hold you up."

The type that hold you up. Something valuable. "Friends."

A grin stretched the oracle's red-painted lips. "Courageous and wise. You will do well if you avoid the oil and the knife, if you see your way to laugh and dance with the lion."

The lion... I wasn't sure what that meant. The oil and knife seemed to be some sort of trouble, and, well, I had plenty of that. She wasn't wrong there.

I stood, took a gladecoin from my bag, and set it on the table. The coin was gone before Drukker could open his mouth to argue.

"Such a scam," he said as we left the tent.

"I would lose more than one gladecoin at the gaming

tables, so which is wiser? Visiting the oracle or losing some of my allowance in front of a group?"

"I don't like all that ridiculous talk. She was spewing random words. None of it made any sense."

"It made sense to me. Your mind takes the nonsense and places it in the puzzle of your life. I learn things from the oracle every time, or, at the very least, I'm comforted and strengthened in my resolve."

"Your resolve?"

We stood at the base of the steps that led up to the captain's wheel. Drukker's gaze attempted to pin me down, but I started toward the long table of food set near the blue and yellow flags flapping along the railing. Drukker snatched my arm.

Someday, I would go one entire day without a person grabbing me. Someday.

"May I ask you a question?"

There was only one instance in which a man like Drukker would lower himself to request something from a woman. This was it.

He was going to propose.

With a glance at Father, who had finished his game and was standing beside Rietveld and two other businessmen, Drukker went to one knee. He never let go of my arm.

"Lady Lina, will you marry me?"

I didn't have to fake happiness as he pulled the biggest ruby I'd ever seen out of his pocket to slip onto my finger. Now that was a ring made for bribing.

"Yes, Master Drukker. Of course!" I really threw myself into the act.

The idiot seemed to truly believe I'd had a change of heart

because his disgusting smile appeared genuine as he swept me into his arms. He kissed me, his lips too wet, his movements sloppy. The kiss only lasted one second but that was one second too long.

For the rest of the party, I accepted congratulatory toasts and well-wishes from strangers and from men I'd seen in our home with Father on business.

As I broke from the festivities to catch my breath, I overheard Rietveld talking to a man I didn't know. I stared over the railing at the sparkling water, then held out my hand as if I were completely enamored with my engagement ring and simply needed a womanly moment to enjoy it all to myself.

Rietveld spoke quietly and quickly to the man beside him. "...put it in the Brightstreet vault."

"But this artifact isn't something you want your crew to find," the stranger said.

The wind washed Rietveld's reply into whispers that I couldn't hear clearly. "...don't permit anyone to put anything else in there. Not when my plan is near to fruition. You know what risks I take with this."

"Fine," the stranger said. "So you'll have it on the ship. When do you sail?"

"In three days. Do not make me wait. This comes first. I don't want to waste this opportunity," Rietveld said, his tone sour. "They have given up searching for him and will replace him soon."

Two vaults? It was no surprise really. Rietveld was the richest man around, possibly richer than the queen herself. But what were these items they were discussing? The stranger's item had to be dangerous or illegal if the stranger didn't think it should be placed in a vault on a ship. Rietveld's artifact had to be truly rare. He wasn't going to let it out of his sight. And what was this opportunity he spoke of and the one the mysterious "they" were seeking?

I grinned at the ruby ring weighing down my fourth finger. Rietveld's secrets and vaults meant nothing to me now. With this ring plus the loot we'd stashed at the hideout, we could bribe a lesser ship's captain to get us across the sea as far as the southern border of Saxonion, and then it would just be a day's hike into Laqqara. First, we had to get Phoenix's children from her terrible ex-husband, but then we would be on our way. Our plan was truly going to happen!

"I'm surprised you are so happy, daughter." Father's voice made me jump.

"It's a lovely ring."

"You have always liked shiny objects." He almost sounded like a kind and loving father, and my heart broke for the thousandth time because I knew the truth.

I steeled myself before looking him in the face. "May I set the wedding date?"

"That is up to Drukker and me. You know that."

"Father, please?" I blinked innocently, wondering if he could be swayed to think of me as a doting daughter even for a second. "I have given my *yes* to Drukker. I have obeyed."

"You have." He took my hand and patted it like I was a child and not a woman. "I suppose I could have a word with Drukker. What date do you have in mind?"

"The full moon."

"I had hoped you would marry sooner than that. Before I have to deal with the cinnamon imports coming, but I suppose the full moon would be quite romantic. Your mother and I were married beneath a full moon too, so this might please her as well."

"Thank you!" I threw my arms around him as tears resulting from a very special type of rage seared my eyes. If only this could be real—my father showing me true affection instead of manipulating me to fit into his life plan. If only I could love him as I pretended to. I did love him, despite my best efforts not to, but not like this. Not with this type of joy. No, the love I couldn't shake for Mother and Father was some instinctual pull that I tried over and over to cut from my shattered heart.

Swallowing, I settled back on my heels and gave him a feigned look of contentment. "I won't let you down."

Nope, I will fully live up to your very low expectations, the expectations hiding beneath this false show of care and joy. He saw me as a failure and a freak. And I would be exactly that the minute I set foot on a ship bound for a country full of free women.

Leaving him with an excuse to speak to a friend, I weaved through the crowd. I slid an emerald off the slim finger of a man who refused his wife's request to leave early, snagged a gold chain from the neck of a drunken half-Fae merchant visiting from the Shrouded Mountains, and neatly stole a fine silver cloak clasp from Father's accountant. All in all, it was a very productive day and I was more than ready to sneak off to the hideout to leave Phoenix and Star a message about leaving tonight.

❈ 10 ❈

ZAVI

The boating party was still going strong when Lady Lina Casparji walked off the ship behind a cluster of ladies who didn't seem to notice she was there. Looking left and right, whipping that glorious copper hair like a flag, she split from the group and headed away from the piers and down an alley.

Zavi trailed her. Surely, she had heard what he had on that ship. Though he now wore his usual clothing, earlier he'd disguised himself as a server and stood near her as she'd gone to the railing to admire her ring. Rietveld and the man Zavi now knew was simply called Thad all but discussed having a memory stone right there. And what had Rietveld meant about timing? Well, Zavi had to get onto Rietveld's favored ship, a larger but less fancy craft floating at the edge of the bay. Rietveld had the missing piece of the memory stone that was in Zavi's side. And Lina was the one to help steal it.

He was a villain for dragging her into this, but he couldn't help himself. She would get it done and he was out of options.

His brother, Emiel, could be dying somewhere or might already be dead, his blood on Rietveld's hands. Zavi had to undo this curse and take action, and he couldn't sneak onto a ship and steal without another person to back him up. Especially if Rietveld knew him—and Zavi had no idea if the powerful merchant did or not. At the end of this heist, Zavi would make certain Lina and her friends had all they could possibly need to escape Deigs. Her friends had to be in on the plan to leave. They were too close to break away from one another willingly. He would make it up to Lina and she would never have to see his face again.

"What are you plotting back there?" Lina said, her voice stopping him cold.

"You know," he said. "To steal from the richest man in the kingdom."

"That plan is outrageous."

He spread his hands wide. "Well, there isn't really a plan at all, so it's early to name it."

Lina finally halted her steps and turned to look at him with those fierce eyes of hers. "A bit of advice. Don't sneak up on someone who has been trained to fight by a former Deigs soldier."

"You're worth the risk."

Her lips twitched like she was almost ready to smile. "So this job. Would it be in a house or on a ship?"

"Ship." He came close and her peony scent wrapped him in daydreams about how soft her hand had been in his during the dancing at the Port Day celebration and how that soft hand would feel sliding down his chest and beneath the waistband of his trousers.

She studied his face. "What are you thinking about?"

"Throwing you up against that wall right there and seeing if you want what I do."

"I thought you wanted fine goods or coin, not carnal pleasure." But her cheeks blushed, telling him that the thought—and the feeling of connection between them—hadn't been his alone.

A part of him wanted to tell her everything, but what if exposing what he knew somehow endangered his brother? He didn't know enough, so he would keep that part of his tale to himself until he knew for certain what was the best choice.

"Can't a fellow have it all?" he said.

Her eyebrow lifted and she didn't respond, but she fidgeted with her dress as if her hands needed to stay busy. He grinned. Those eyes of hers saw far more than she let on.

"I know you don't approve of me, or like me, but maybe you want me."

She chuckled. "I like that you don't care that I don't approve of you."

"You have your opinions. I'm fine with that. But I wouldn't mind serving you up some delight in this shadowed alley." This was a wild idea, but he couldn't help himself.

"Delight? As in..."

"A kiss."

Tilting her head, she studied him, her gaze sliding up and down his body. "What would you want in return for this kiss? Would you be expecting more than that?"

She was actually considering this? His heart drummed fast and his blood ran hot. "Touching you in any way is the best of rewards. I need nothing from you aside from permission. And no, a simple kiss would be perfect."

"I thought you wanted to discuss a heist."

"Yes, well, I was going to try to talk you into sneaking onto the prettiest boat in the bay, but that can wait. We both appear to be sidetracked."

"I can't kiss you. I hate Fae."

"Why?"

"One tried to kidnap me when I was young. He was complicit in the murder of my dearest friend."

Ah. That explained a great deal of her behavior. "I'm sorry that happened to you."

And he honestly was. What a horror to live through as a child.

He remained still, not getting closer or making any sudden moves. This was like some grand dream, her talking to him like this. He didn't want to spook her and ruin everything.

Waving a hand, she dismissed the subject, but a darkness clung to her gaze as if a part of her remained in the past. He longed to know who had threatened her in that way. Shedding blood would be a joy in her name.

Yes, he was well and truly hooked by this siren of a woman. Her song wasn't music, but the boldness in her wild actions, her rebellion against a society that tried to chain her down.

"But I find myself trying to trust you," she said, watching him, weighing whatever she saw in his eyes.

"Because I smashed your fiancé's face?"

A grin spread her lovely lips. "Exactly that."

A laugh bubbled from his chest and he slowly closed the short distance between them. His body was an inch from hers and the heat coming from her made his head swim. To merely feel her against him, her clever gaze boring into his eyes... She would be his undoing. He'd never wanted a female like this.

She eyed the end of the alleyway, then set her focus on him. The look she gave him sent a bolt of heat right to his cock.

"All right. One kiss," she said.

"You have kissed someone before, right?" he asked, keeping his gaze on hers.

"Not properly. Not with anyone I chose to kiss."

"That is a tragedy."

"Indeed." She stepped backward until she leaned on the wall of the building shadowing them. Her lips parted.

A low growl vibrated from him, his body reacting before his mind could catch up. Gods bless this day.

He gently pressed himself to her, searching her gaze for any signs of discomfort. "With one word, I will step away. This is your game, my lady. You are queen here."

Her lips lifted.

"Oh, you like that, do you? I can give you more of that treatment, my liege," he whispered.

She didn't speak, so he leaned in and set his lips against her velvet neck. She breathed in, and a little shiver of delight appeared to run through her. He kissed the spot where her pulse jumped and touched her skin with the tip of his tongue. A gasp left her, her chest moving against his.

"More?" he whispered against her tantalizing skin.

"Yes. Much more."

"You demand it?" he asked.

"I do." Amusement laced her words and his heart lifted at the tone.

He smoothed his palms up her neck, enjoying her quick

breaths, and he cupped her face. Her eyes were wide and luminous. With his mouth, he drew a line along her jaw, then he found her lips. She tasted sweet like summer wine. Another growl rumbled from him; he couldn't stop himself from the primal utterance. Her fingers curled into his sleeves and she tugged him closer.

Kissing her fully but slowly, he explored her mouth with his tongue and kept her pinned to the wall with his hips. She kissed him back, her movements tentative and a little clumsy. He didn't mind at all. Everyone had their time in life to learn.

Her hands drifted to his shoulders. Her fingers dug into him sharply and he delighted in the pinch of her nails. Her hair was silk tangled around his hands, and when she rolled her hips against him and moaned, his hands shook with the need to rip her dress and ravish her until she was shouting his name.

"I should go." Her voice was more breath than word.

He eased back a step. "As you command."

She almost seemed to glow with her own light. "Maybe just a minute more."

He'd never heard a more perfect phrase.

11

LINA

I was dizzy in the best way and I had no idea what I was doing.

Phoenix had told me about this type of kissing once during a late night at the hideout when we had imbibed far more jenever than was wise. Star had confirmed it. I loved that I was having my turn at it. To the hells with Drukker. He didn't own me and never would. I would take pleasure from this near stranger because I wanted to. Zavi was handsome and he had treated me unlike any man, or male, I'd ever encountered. I loved his voice, enjoyed his humor, and delighted in his conversation. Did I trust him? No. But it was only kissing. No harm in that.

Zavi's scent of salt and bergamot enveloped me, and his hands smoothed over my sides in a way that reminded me of my earlier daydream of him by the Glass River. Every sweep of his fingers sent wonderful shivers down my body. The turn and shift of his arm muscles under his tunic made it difficult to breathe and the feel of his hips against me... That was absolute bliss.

He set his forehead against mine, and with his scent so close... It felt intimate. Truly intimate. As if we weren't near strangers, but two people who cared for one another. Panic stabbed me. I had let a male get too close.

I set my hands on his chest and pulled my head back.

He cleared his throat and nodded, understanding in his gaze. "I will leave right now if you tell me to."

"You will?"

"Of course. You are in charge."

Relaxing my arms so that I wasn't pushing him away, I bit my lip. I was in new territory in so many ways.

"No. Don't leave," I said, surprising myself. "I want knowledge they have kept from me." And I simply wanted him. But I couldn't say that out loud. I couldn't be that vulnerable with a male.

"Then may I kiss you once more?" The slant to his eyes and mouth almost said he was feeling shy, but with those fangs peeking out from under his lip, he was too dangerous-looking to be considered shy.

"Please."

He set one hand against my cheek gently while his other hand gripped my lower back, easing my body so that it was flush against his. Heat rolled through me. His thumb dragged across my lower lip and my stomach tightened, hot need pooling low inside me. His mouth pressed into mine and I parted my lips. His tongue twisted over mine and he held me to him like I was the greatest treasure. Moving his kiss to the underside of my jaw, he whispered against my neck. His warm breath along my skin made me feel like I was falling, weight-less, lighter than air.

"Firefly, I would happily take ages upon ages to discover what makes you gasp the loudest."

Gods, I was undone. Though I was nervous about doing this wrong, I tried to let go of my apprehension. I nipped his ear and he let out a quiet snarl. He extended his tongue and dedicated himself to my collarbone. I was absolutely melting in the weight of his embrace and I could feel exactly how much he was enjoying himself as well. I ran my hands through his hair, dislodging the black scarf he had tied around his head. It fell to the cobblestones.

If this kept up any longer, I was either going to throw him down next to his scarf or explode with frustrated desire.

I broke away, panting so hard that it was impossible to attempt to be coy. "That was amazing. I am angry I haven't done more of that in my life."

He smiled and brushed my hair behind my ears. "Are you satisfied?"

"Definitely not," I said.

Raising his eyebrows, he laughed. "But you need to go."

"I do. I plan to leave tonight, so I doubt we will see one another again."

"Tonight?" He stepped back, adjusted his trousers, then bent to pick up his scarf.

"I think this," I said, raising my engagement ring, "will provide me a means to escape at last."

His shoulders fell, but he nodded. "I'm glad. I wish you well."

"Thank you. I hope you manage to steal a king's sum from that horrible criminal."

He set a hand on his chest and bowed slightly. "Happy travels. I hope the stars see you to your true home."

"That's a lovely sentiment. You really are a bard now, aren't you?" I couldn't fight a broad smile that stretched my swollen lips.

He held out his hands, palms up. "I try."

I could have stared at him all night long. "I wish you well too." Part of me wished I could just fall into his arms again. "May the Old Ones bless you."

He lifted my hand and kissed my palm, tickling the sensitive skin. "Farewell, firefly."

I swallowed and turned to leave for the hideout. That was that. It had been enjoyable. Fun. I had trusted someone with Fae blood for the first time in years. Everything was going well. Zavi was a stranger. No one to me. I would be gone from this place by dawn and I was thrilled...

So why did I feel bad walking away?

12

ZAVI

Well, that was not what Zavi had expected at all. And he couldn't stop shaking his head. What a wonder she was. So bold. She definitely didn't belong in this kingdom. Sadly, he had made no progress in persuading her to help him with the heist, but he couldn't rummage up any negative feelings. The sun sank lower in the orange sky as he continued to trail Lina, keeping a block away and ducking into alcoves and shop doorways when she turned. Was she watching for him or for Drukker? Maybe for her parents. Perhaps all of them.

The warehouse district wasn't the best spot for an evening stroll on your own, especially for a young woman, but Lina didn't seem bothered by the growing shadows or the clusters of workmen gathering in clouds of pipe smoke to watch her walk by. She wasn't ignorant. She'd shown that at the tavern and at the Port Day celebration. Stealth, distraction, and quick thinking were some of her strengths. Maybe she knew how to wield a dagger hidden in the folds of her skirts. He hadn't felt any blades hidden in those lacy folds. Swallowing, he adjusted his trousers and smiled. He should have given her one of his daggers. She had mentioned something about being trained by a soldier.

A dark blue and rusted structure lorded over the cobblestones where Lina slipped between buildings and disappeared. Hurrying to catch the door or spot where she'd hidden, he kept one eye on the way they'd come. He also didn't want her family or fiancé surprising them. But he'd been too slow. A slender set of worn wooden doors might have led to her escape, but it could have been that dark space between the blue warehouse and the pale yellow one a few feet behind. He didn't want her to know he'd followed her, so he shouldered into the archway of what smelled like a former chandler's shop and concealed himself in the shadow of its half-open hingeless door. The sour odor of tallow and sweet beeswax clouded his ability to scent humans that might come upon him, but it would mask his scent from any half-Fae like him hanging around. No full Fae would be in this part of the world.

And there he waited to see what the lovely firefly would do. If she tried to bribe any of the pirate lords' lackeys, he would most likely recognize them and be able to steer her away from a scam. Crossing his arms, he watched the fading sun paint the tall broken windows of the pale-yellow warehouse in stripes of melon and persimmon. Was this Lina's castle, a hideaway like his own tumble of ruins? Was he the villain watching someone he wanted to use for his own plans or was he truly being protective of her in a kind way because of the high regard he held for her?

He closed his eyes for a moment and took a breath. Could it be both?

No, he was lying to himself. This whole thing was a fiction he'd crafted to soothe his conscience. He needed her. She had an in with Rietveld and had stealth to spare. He bowed his head, letting the weight of what he was about to do crush him. He deserved every ounce of the burden.

13

LINA

I dipped the quill into the ink and finished the note for Star and Phoenix. I just hoped they would see it quickly.

I have climbed the mountain. Gathering the lambs now. Meet me near the stars.

~Moth

Swiping the quill's soft goose feather across my chin, I eyed the makeshift dragon lair in the storage alcove. A squawk sounded and a mewling followed.

Should I bring the dragon with me in case she could come in handy?

The mewling grew more insistent, so I walked over and lifted the lid of the basket. A pair of golden eyes blinked up at me.

I reached in and scooped the tiny dragon into my arms. She was warm like a coal from a forgotten hearth. Her lime-green wings fanned out in a stretch and her tongue flicked like a snake's as she scented me.

"Yes, you have met me. Now, if I bring you along, can you tempt some sweet children to follow me but keep your cute noises to yourself? We will need to be very stealthy, little emerald."

The dragon flew up and snuffled into my ear. I pushed her snout away with a fingertip.

"That tickles."

Her scales were soft and finely detailed with scalloped edges and barely visible veins of gold. I petted her head, and she shut her wide eyes and made a purring sound.

"All right. You're a little too big for the pockets on tonight's outfit, but you could fit in there." I pointed to the bag on the table.

The dragon, Emerald for now, leapt from the crook of my arm to fly. She landed less than gracefully on the table, knocking the ink over. Black spread over the wood and I rushed to grab the bag and my note.

"Shoo for a moment, you little monster." I waved her to the chair and she obeyed, her sharp teeth clamped around the handle of the satchel. She tugged it from under my arm as I set the note above the fireplace. Using one of the old rags we had stashed in a bucket by the door, I cleaned up the ink. I really hoped bringing the dragon wasn't a mistake.

❦

PHOENIX'S FORMER HUSBAND HAD NOT BEEN A MAN WHO loved luxury. Unlike some of the other rich fellows of his ilk, he spurned the typical tiled and brightly painted townhome in favor of the sober-looking structure looming over me. A towering building made of plastered stone, his home stood along the finest of the new streets beyond the northside canals. Unadorned wide windows eyed me as I crept between tree shadows in the small courtyard out in front of the home. The last of the day's sun poured heat across shrubbery that had been cropped to within an inch of its life. A serpentine path wound through the shockingly tidy garden, and I hurried along, the dragon in my bag bumping lightly on my back. The eastern side of the house had a side door, Phoenix had told me. Servants used it at dawn and throughout the day, but they left the premises via the front door as their master bid them. Phoenix said he insisted on checking everyone's personal items to be sure no one was stealing the silver. I had to chuckle. His former wife was one of the best thieves in the entire kingdom.

I wished I could have met Phoenix earlier than I had. A memory of her sitting in the filth of the alley, wearing a ripped and dirty dress, blinked through my head. Her weeping had been so guttural that I had slipped away from my parents as soon as I'd had the chance and gone back to her to see how I could help. That had been two years ago.

Two hedge bushes framed her ex-husband's side door and the handle shifted easily under my grip. Still unlocked. That meant the staff hadn't yet left for the day. This wasn't going to be easy. I'd definitely have to do something about the governess, if indeed the children still had one. They were older now, but not out in society yet, so it was likely the governess remained.

But I'd worry about her once I made it past the kitchen and the downstairs staff.

I eased the door open and entered a quiet pantry stocked with bottles of dark wine, jugs of mead labeled with a bee and crown maker's mark, and sacks of grain.

Emerald snorted and I twisted to see she had come up out of the bag and was looking about, her wings slightly spread as if she was about to fly into those grain sacks and have a treat.

"Oh, no, you don't. Now is not yet your moment." I pushed her back gently and a spark hit my palm. "Ow!" I covered my mouth too late and held my breath.

There were footsteps beyond, but not immediately outside the pantry.

I blew out a sigh and urged Emerald back into the bag. "Stay. If you spark me again, I'll toss you out the door and you'll have no fun with the children at all."

A sad growl came from the bag and vibrated along my back. Shaking my head, I slid out of the pantry and into the kitchen proper. Extending the length of my home's main hall, the place held long tables where bowls of covered dough had been left to rise. A fire snapped at the far end of the room and a stout fellow stirred a pot on an iron stove. He seemed wholly focused on his deliciously scented curried beef stew. I was glad for his intense focus because my stomach took that moment to compete with Emerald's growl. Wincing, I stepped back to hide in the shadow of the shelving that held countless stacks of vanilla-colored crockery plates, soup tureens, and blue platters.

Peering around the edge, I saw the cook glance my way. I froze. His eyes narrowed and he tilted his head.

Please be quiet, Emerald.

"Annie?" The cook's voice was deep and rough as if he barely used it or perhaps smoked too much.

I kept one hand on the strap of the bag, ensuring it would stay put.

The cook went back to his stew and began whistling. I was safe for now. When the cook finally turned his back to me to grab a cluster of dried rosemary hanging from the ceiling, I made my move. I shot across the expanse of the kitchen, glad I had changed into a tunic and pair of trousers at the hideout. My skirts never would have permitted this kind of speed. I was out of the kitchen and up a winding set of stairs before I heard the clang of the stew pot's ladle start up again. Phoenix, Star, and I had studied the blueprints of the house, so I knew these stairs led to the former nursery now turned tutoring room. Maps of the world and the waterways that Deigs merchant sailors often sailed covered the plastered walls. Two doors were set into the opposite side of the room and I headed for the one on the right, which, unless something had changed, led to the children's bedchambers.

In a large chamber with high ceilings and dull curtains, the children each sat on their beds, reading by lantern light. Their backs were to me, thankfully, and I stepped quietly inside. The blue of twilight grazed the carved wood partition that separated their beds. I shut the door with careful but quick movements, then straightened.

"Your mother is alive," I said quietly.

They both jumped a bit and whirled to face me.

I held my arms wide like I was trying to keep them from running past me despite the fact that they both appeared frozen on their beige duvets. And that's when I noticed the bruises. Damn their father.

"Mother?" The girl—a slip of a thing named Sanne, who

was seven or eight—blinked, her eyes glistening with unshed tears.

The boy, Bram, stood first. Wearing a sleeping gown marked with his father's sigil—a white shield with a black eel and an axe—the boy had the rawboned look of a ten-year-old or somewhere close to that age. With my mind whirring and my nerves on edge, I couldn't remember exactly how old they were. I wished I'd thought to ask Phoenix for a piece of information that would prove to the children that I knew her.

"Who are you?" Bram crossed his arms and glared. "Our mother died." His voice broke on the word *mother*, but he held his head high. "I'm calling for the governess. She has a dog." He raised an eyebrow.

"I love dogs. Please do call her." I had to keep them calm. "But before you do…" I reached around and tapped the bottom of my bag, feeling Emerald's bony rump. "It's your cue, lovely."

The dragon crawled quickly out of the bag, scratching my neck ferociously in the process. She took to the air and flew in broad circles, her green scales catching the lanterns' flickers and the pale light from the window.

The children dissolved into a mess of "ooos" and "aaaawwwws" as they ran in circles underneath Emerald.

Her blonde ringlets bouncing, Sanne clapped her hands. "She's so small!"

I had to get them quiet. "Shhh, now. You'll scare her."

"Dragons are never afraid," Bram said, still glaring.

He reached for Emerald, who squawked and flew a tight circle around his head. She was playing with him and I wished I could relax and enjoy this sweet moment. But we would be discovered soon. I had to get them out of here now.

Sanne stretched her arms out in front of her. "Please perch on me!" She covered her mouth and lowered her voice to a whisper. "Please perch on me."

I slipped a bit of meat from the bag at my belt and raised it high. "It's time to go on a trip. I swear on the dragon that your mother lives and she wants to see you tonight. We leave now."

Bram looked at the floor, thinking. Then he raised his chin and rubbed his eyes. "But we aren't dressed."

Sanne looked toward the window. "It's almost night."

"That doesn't matter for this trip. Follow us." I opened the door a crack, listened, then emerged with Emerald now on my shoulder and the children on my heels.

"This is fun," Sanne whispered.

"I don't think Father would approve of a trip like this," Bram said.

I led them back down the corridor and the stairs and to the kitchen, where I stopped them with a hand held at my side. I set a finger to my lips and they nodded, excitement shining in their eyes. They may have been barred from seeing their mother, which was a tragedy, but these children had obviously not been ill-treated beyond a strict upbringing. They held very little suspicion of me in their eyes. Phoenix would want to change that, to bring them up to be wise about the dangers of the world. She wouldn't want them to grow up with a false sense of security. She'd want them to be strong and clever. I hoped I'd get the chance to help her raise them.

The cook was tidying up for the night, setting the stew pot away on a low shelf. He whistled as he worked and I waved the children to follow me across the expanse of the room.

Once we passed through the side door and into the first breeze of the coming evening, I finally exhaled.

Barking exploded from the front of the house.

14

LINA

Bram peeked around the corner of the house. "Trout!"

I grabbed the back of his sleeping gown and yanked him back. The dog was named for a fish? Bram stumbled over a row of ferns planted along the back of the house and toppled into Sanne, who fell back on her rump.

"Hey! Watch it!" She scrambled up and smacked Bram on the arm.

The barking came closer.

"We must go before...before Trout finds us. It's part of the trip. Sadly, no pups allowed. Only dragons."

"I don't like Trout anyway," Sanne said, a scowl in her voice.

I turned them toward an orchard that lined a stone wall at the back of the property. We jogged into strips of moonlight created by an orchard of orange trees. I took Emerald from my shoulder and lifted my arm to get her to fly.

"Follow her," I whispered to the children.

Trout must have been distracted, because the barking had

ceased. Could the governess have taken the dog inside? Could we be that lucky?

The kids took to climbing the stone wall. In this fine neighborhood, the wall wasn't made for protection but for looks, so it was easy for Bram to find footholds and spots to wedge a hand. Soon he was at the top and reaching down to help Sanne. I boosted the girl up and he took her hand.

Sanne grunted as she climbed with our help. I passed her, sat beside Bram with one leg over each side of the wall, and grabbed her arm to lift her to us.

"You can climb down on your own, yes? You're doing very well," I whispered to Bram.

He beamed from the praise as if it was the first time anyone had ever given him a good word. Before I could give him a few tips on landing, he was down and leaping into the tall grass outside the property line. Raising his arms to Emerald, he grinned and a gap showed where one of his incisors should have been. The dragon swirled through the air, then dropped onto Bram's head, making him laugh.

"Shh," I whispered as I climbed down side by side with Sanne.

Her little bare foot slipped and I snagged her elbow before she fell.

"Oh," she said, looking up at me with big eyes like her mother's, "that was a close one."

I gave her a smile. "It was. But you can do this. And I'm here. Bram will help you down once you are a little farther down."

Bram came close to the wall, Emerald now on his shoulder, licking her front talons. "Jump, Sanne. I will catch you."

She awkwardly detached from the stones and I held my

breath as she fell into Bram. They both tumbled to the ground, but their smiles said they were just fine.

The moment my boots hit the grass, barking erupted from the other side of the wall.

Sanne clutched onto Bram.

"I don't know who you are," a deep voice said, "or what you were after, but I have sent for the Watch and they will be here before you can make it to the canal."

"Father..." Bram's voice was a breath and his face paled.

"The Watch?" Sanne began to silently cry, silver tears running down her plump cheeks.

I crouched low. "Get on my back. We are going to run now."

"Away from Father?" Bram asked, but he didn't seem upset about it. More like this was an opportunity he hadn't imagined. "No more punishments..."

Sanne pressed her head against my back.

"Come on, then," I said, waving as I dashed into the dark.

Bram trailed me as shouting rose from the front of the property.

We ran and ran until I was certain no one was following us, then I took the children to the hideout.

❧

PHOENIX AND STAR WERE THERE, AND TO SAY THERE WERE tears would be an understatement.

"My babies!" Phoenix crushed the children in a hug and they held her, Bram kissing her cheek, his tears blending with hers and Sanne saying *mother* over and over.

Bram coughed and sniffed. "He told us you died."

Bastard. Over my dead, rotting corpse would their father ever see them again. What a monster.

"I thought you were in my dream," Sanne mumbled into Phoenix's tunic.

Both Phoenix and Star had dressed for the journey. It was a good thing too because with the Watch seeking us, we had to move fast and with extreme stealth.

Once everyone had a satchel packed, and I had our hoard stashed in Emerald's bag over my shoulder, we set off. We should have split up the goods, but there was no time.

The streets were not as empty as I would have liked. We couldn't wait for full night now that the Watch was on us in addition to my parents, who by now had to have realized I wasn't at the boating party anymore nor was I at home. Sanne slipped in a puddle and Phoenix caught her as we hurried down one alleyway after another. The Watch's shouts carried over the canals and the roads. They were far too close. I couldn't seem to take a full breath. If we were caught, the children would be returned to their father. Phoenix, Star, and I would go to prison for theft. Our lives would be over.

At pier five, I broke away from the group and approached a sailor standing next to the skiff that belonged to Captain Dhalmar, a skiff that would take passengers to his ship a short row away on the far side of the bay. Sounds of the boating party carried on the night breeze—laughter, the clinking of goblets, and the murmur of conversation. They were far enough away though. More than I could say for the approaching sounds of the Watch.

I had no time for niceties or a convincing story, so I held out the ring and swung the bag forward so the sailor could see the payment.

"All this for a quiet trip to Laqqara."

"How many?"

He looked over my shoulder and squinted at my group. They were clustered near a storage shed at the first section of the dock.

"Five."

"She will eat too." The sailor pointed at Emerald, who was growling and covering the coins inside with her wings.

"I'll share my portion with her. Not a problem."

Tilting his head, he studied my hands. "Why does a rich, pretty lady want to get on a filthy ship like Captain Dhalmar's?"

"When I said *quiet*, what I meant was I don't talk to you and you don't talk to me or anyone about this trip."

"For that amount," he said, "I think I can come up with an agreement. I'll have to talk to the bosun first though."

I shook my head. "No time for that."

He waved me off and turned away. "Deal's off. I'm going to lose my place if I let you stowaway. Go on with you."

"But—"

"Go now, lass, and I'll do my best to forget your description if the Watch comes asking questions."

I gritted my teeth. I only had two possible ships in mind for our escape. Spinning, I pointed toward a tight alley between two storage buildings. I lifted a hand to Phoenix, Star, and the children, indicating they should wait there for me. They did as I suggested and disappeared into the alley. Maybe I'd have better luck with choice number two if I started wheeling and dealing as one person instead of having the group behind me looking like too much trouble.

Leaving the pier, I headed for another alleyway, this one

nearly as close as the one where the others were staying back. I didn't like this shortcut but it would get me to the next pier quickly and keep eyes off me.

The alley blocked out almost all of the starlight, and the wind that had risen in the last hour drew up dirt and spun it in the air. A metallic scent curled through the dark passageway. Rain was coming. A lot of it. Masdam was known for the occasional horrible sea storm. We stuck out in the waves like a lobster's claw, and though the spot was great for waterway trade, our position put us right in the path of at least three powerful systems a year.

I adjusted the bag of stolen items on my back. Emerald grunted in annoyance. Glancing behind me and then before me again, I prayed to the Old Ones. The pier I aimed for wasn't too far off now. Just around the corner.

Something pushed me from the back and I stumbled forward, almost landing on my face but catching myself. My bag was ripped from my back, and a reedy male voice shouted a curse as he threw my sack over his shoulder and ran.

Heart pounding, I took off after him.

That bag held every gold piece, ring, coin, and silver bobble we had gathered over months of work. The thief had taken it all—even Emerald.

At the back of the man's hooded short cloak, smoke rose and a flicker of light showed. Emerald was burning her way out of the bag. The thief smacked a hand toward the dragon.

"I'm going to hunt you down, you little shit!" I hissed, fully aware I could draw the Watch to us if we were too loud.

From the way the attacker's voice had sounded and his slender, small shape, the man stealing my pilfered goods couldn't have been more than thirteen or fourteen.

He slipped around a corner and disappeared down a space where the alley branched into two, and my chest went cold. I had lost him and I had no time to search because the Watch was coming.

Cursing into the rising, chilly wind, I turned and hurried back to Phoenix, Star, and the children.

My face told them the story I couldn't bear to utter.

✾ 15 ✾

ZAVI

Zavi let the storm drench him and he didn't cower at the massive strikes of lightning. He deserved the world's wrath. If he hadn't had his brother to save, he'd have wanted the lightning to end him.

The theft of Lina's bundle had been too easy. A word to the rough barkeep at one of the dockside taverns and Zavi had a name. Luuk. Zavi had caught the young man right after Luuk had nabbed a woman's coin purse. Taking the purse from the young man, Zavi had threatened to shout for the Watch. Luuk had caved, and once Zavi had promised a bag of coins and jewelry with no take of his own, the young man agreed to rob Lina.

Zavi hated himself, but the deed was done. He truly wished she hadn't involved those children in this mess. Now she had the Watch combing the streets for her. It had been twelve hours. Through the wild wind and lashing rain of the storm, Zavi had kept his eye on Lina's group—well, except for Lina, who had hurried home. She seemed to be pretending all was well while her people made their way to a run-down warehouse.

Once the storm had passed and none came for the hideout's occupants, Zavi started toward Lina's house. Her street was wide, as were all the wealthy merchants' streets. Bleekerspath, they called it. In the older Deigs tongue, a *bleeker* had been a linen bleacher, so this hadn't always been a row of finely plastered and wood-timbered houses. Maybe, long ago, this had been a road full of those struggling to escape poverty, those desperate for escape like Lina was.

As the stars glittered overhead, he climbed the downspouts of Lina's home. Grasping a stern-faced gargoyle set at the top of the piping with one hand, he tapped her window.

She appeared shockingly fast and he nearly lost his hold.

Checking once over her shoulder, she raised the window and glared out at him. "What are you doing?"

He climbed over the sill and eased past her into the room. "I'm here to help you escape."

The chamber was exactly what he'd imagined her gilded cage to be. Lace, pearls, fine paintings, and silks—all the trappings of wealth in Masdam.

"What?" Her tone cut like a blade.

Her eyes were puffy and ringed in dark circles. He had done that to her, had stressed her so much that she obviously hadn't slept a wink.

"I heard that the Watch was on the lookout for a woman who had stolen something from Master Gerritsen, and if I'm not mistaken, the children hurrying toward your hideout were wearing his sigil."

"Their sleeping gowns," she muttered, her nose wrinkling.

"Should have thought of that. How do you know about our hideout?"

"I followed your friends to make sure they weren't caught."

"I... Thank you, Zavi."

Oh, how he hated himself.

"So why are you here to help me, a kidnapper?" she asked.

He raised an eyebrow and looked down at her. "You're no kidnapper."

"You don't know me well enough to say that."

"I think I probably do. When you steal, you only take from those whose demeanor begs for punishment. You don't lift anything from good folks."

She just glared.

"Phoenix's ex-husband is probably another version of your father or Drukker."

"You've got that bit right," she said.

He shrugged. "So you only saved those children from a nightmare existence."

"Not if they get caught." Her eyes were wild. She truly cared for these children and her friend. It was admirable and her devotion made him adore her even more. "Then he'll punish them for going along with my scheme," she said miserably. "That or they'll be dead when the Watch tangles with us."

"That won't happen," he said.

Looking up and shaking her head, she sighed. "I remember having confidence. It was so nice."

"You'll find yours again. I'm guessing since you are locked in your room," he said, "and no one has seen you all day, you must be trapped. What happened to your plan?"

Self-loathing chewed his heart and he fought a wince. Her eyebrows drew together as she studied his face and he cleared his features, hoping the weak candles and watery moonlight wouldn't let her read his expressions so easily.

"I was robbed." She held out a hand. "Before you say it, yes, I know. Ironic."

"I'm never certain if I am using that word correctly," he said.

Her lips shifted into what was almost a grin, but then the corners of her mouth dropped and sadness seemed to pour over her. She nearly drooped with it.

"I have trapped Phoenix and her children," she said. "Star is no better off. We ran that horse right off a cliff."

Zavi rubbed his chin. "Um, what?"

She waved a hand. "Oh, it's a saying we have. Phoenix, Star, and I. Never mind." Leaning on a wall that had been stenciled in yellow flowers, she crossed her arms. "I don't know what to do. I am to be married in a month. Or jailed, depending on how this plays out with the Watch. The king's army will come for Star shortly thereafter because her three years of off time will be over. She can't go back to the border wars. She just... I won't let it happen. I can't." She swallowed and the agony in her expression made Zavi's heart shudder. "And Phoenix, well, you know what she must flee and what she fights to save."

Her family. He did know. He knew exactly how wanting to protect one's family felt and the desperation in one's soul when that action was nigh on impossible.

"We will slip out this window together," he said, eyeing the moonlit opening, "and go to the hideout to make a plan."

Lina crossed her arms. "When you say *plan*, you mean stealing from Rietveld."

"Yes."

She exhaled in a rush. "Insanity."

"I will help you," he said. "Your friends will be part of it as well."

"No, we can't."

"Lina, you have the perfect in. No one in the high-class circles knows you are in trouble yet and you can visit his ship easily. We will steal enough to get you to the stars if you want."

Rolling her eyes, she snorted. "Sure, bard, sure. But hells, what do I have to lose? Let's do it."

Ah. And there it was. He had succeeded. The clever lady thief and her crew were now with him. Perhaps in a matter of days, he would be free of this curse and he would finally remember everything. His stomach twisted. How bad would that information be? Would he realize there was nothing he could do for Emiel? That his brother was already dead? His heart knocked against his chest like another version of him was trapped inside and dying to get out.

"I would ask why you are so keen to rob the most dangerous man in Masdam, but I have a feeling you won't tell me the truth. I assume your human blood allows you to lie?"

"It does. I will tell you everything at the old warehouse hideout before we plan. Deal?"

"Agreed."

He wished he could toss her over his shoulder and carry her down the outside wall, but that wasn't going to happen. Not with the stitches healing on his side. This climbing was probably going to open one up. His Fae blood meant he healed faster than those who were fully human, but his wound still needed time.

"What do you need to do before we leave?" he asked.

"Change my clothing."

He knelt at Lina's door, eyeing the handle. "I'll pick this just in case we need a backup plan for escape."

"Good idea. If we don't get out the window, we can leave through here and go out the back door, off the kitchen."

The lock was a stubborn one, worse than he'd expected. Or maybe it was the peony scent of her distracting him and making his movements clumsy.

He heard shuffling and glanced back only to see her tugging her skirts free. A grin pulled at his lips.

"Stay focused on your task, bard." Her chiding words didn't match the delighted mischief in her gaze.

"I'm very good at multitasking," he said. "I think we should see what I can accomplish."

She laughed quietly, dismissing him with a shake of her head. The thick braid of her autumn-hued tresses hung over one shoulder as she tried to undo her corset strings.

His blood went hot, and he turned back to the lock and nearly growled in frustration as the pick slipped once more. He removed a bumper key—a key with no real teeth that could knock a lock open—from the pouch at his belt.

"Will you unlace me?" Lina said behind him.

He swiveled to see her arms at her sides and her cheeks bright with annoyance.

She bared her teeth. "I can't go about with this thing pinching and holding me like a Laqqaran choking snake."

A flash of vulnerability showed in her eyes and his heart thudded, pushing him to take her in his arms and comfort her. He set the bumper key on the blue and gold carpet that covered the hardwood flooring.

"I will do whatever you order me to do, Moth," he whispered.

Spinning, she gave him her back. He took up the corset laces and began loosening them. The back of her neck looked as soft as satin and his lips ached to kiss her there, to linger and breathe her in. As his unlacing reached the halfway point of the corset, she inhaled and exhaled with what seemed like incredible relief. His hand strayed to her shoulder, and without really thinking about it, he drew the tip of his thumb along her skin. Goosebumps rose in the wake of his touch and she gasped lightly.

"You aren't finished with your task," she said breathlessly.

He gripped the laces and quickly loosened the corset further. She grabbed a black tunic from where it hung over a carved wooden screen, slung it over her head, and wiggled out of the corset, using the tunic to cover herself.

Grinning, he said, "I would have thought we were past that."

"Just unlock the door and let's get out the window."

"Aye, my lady." He bent to bump the lock. With one strike of the blunt key, the mechanism gave way.

Lina pulled on boots that came to her knees, ending at a pair of trousers that somehow made her look even more stunning than that corset.

He started out the window. "I'll make sure no one is around."

"The Watch could be around the corner." She leaned over him to spy the street.

"It'll be fine. Trust me."

He slammed his eyes shut and his hands froze on the gargoyle's wings. She shouldn't trust him. He didn't want to hurt her; he wasn't the worst of the worst. But he certainly wasn't putting her needs first. He was all but forcing her into this Rietveld heist.

But he had to do it for his brother. The memory he'd had of Emiel, of the blood and the scream... Recalling the warped images and the feeling of dread turned Zavi's stomach. If this were only about Zavi, maybe he would have acted differently or taken another path to uncurse himself, but Emiel could be dying and Zavi could be his only chance.

Pushing his guilt and worry for Lina aside and forcing his brother's face from his mind, he jumped down from the house's exterior.

Voices came from Lina's window and he looked up to see her standing with her back to him. Was it her maid?

Gods, don't let it be her parents.

He needed a distraction and needed it now. Good thing he was big on backup plans. He had just the thing...

As he dashed into the street, his side sent out a whip of agony and he grunted, going still until the pain subsided. From the hedge, he pulled the three fireworks he'd bought at the Eastside market, shoved their pointed ends into the soft ground, then used his flint and striker to light them. Before he made it to the shadowed wall across the street, pops and bangs erupted. Shouts and a scream told him a neighbor's infant was awake and that Lina's household was rushing to see what was happening. The front door of her family's manor house swung open and out came Lord Casparji, followed quickly by Lady Casparji, two male servants, and a maid, from the looks of her uniform.

His work was finished for now. He hoped Lina had made it out the back door.

As he rushed through the dark, Zavi plotted. Where would Rietveld keep the safe on his ship? His quarters? A protected berth behind the goods he was shipping? Would it be hidden or guarded?

They would have to be prepared for any one of those issues.

His side burned as if the cursed artifact sensed he was working hard to rid himself of its magic.

Emiel's face blinked to life behind his eyes. This time he saw more of the only family member he knew of. His brother was a barrel-chested man. He raised a goblet and toasted another hazy figure in the memory.

Rietveld.

The memory of Rietveld's evil grin bashed through Zavi's mind like a charging bull. He had been right to suspect the powerful merchant. Rietveld had done something terrible to Emiel, and Zavi had to learn the truth. Maybe it wasn't too late. He strained to see more in his mind's eye.

Pain lashed through Zavi and he fell to the ground.

He woke, unsure of the time, and hurried to the hideout, doing his best to dodge attention.

16

LINA

Zavi leaned on the table and gave us a measured look each as he clasped his hands. He'd rolled his tunic sleeves past his elbows and the tendons and muscles of his forearms were stupidly distracting.

"Last week," he said, "Rietveld's smallest vessel, a slick little beauty, brought in blue garnets."

I tensed. He sounded like a pirate now. That love of a ship and that easy tongue...

Star's mouth fell open. "No. Truly?"

Nodding, Zavi sat back in his chair and raised his eyebrows. "Truly."

"What are blue garnets?" Phoenix asked.

I poured some fresh water into two cups and handed them to Bram and Sanne. "Drink up. When you are in a situation like this, you need to take care of yourself as best you can."

They ignored me and continued batting a tiny ball of spun

wool back and forth. Shoulders slumped and eyes red, they looked absolutely miserable.

"Mother is going to be killed for real this time," Sanne whispered, her words stunted with occasional whimpers.

Phoenix hugged her tightly. "No, I'm not. All will be well. Just you watch the bard and our Moth. They will see us through."

Bram's lower lip trembled, but he held off crying. He rubbed his sister's back and gave his mother a brave smile. "And Emerald will escape, right?"

Star nodded. "Of course she will. She is a dragon."

Gulping down the scream of frustration and fear climbing up my throat, I paced the floor. "We need to know everything about this ship, even beyond what it holds. We need the guards' schedule, the sailors' regular activities, when they plan to sail. Everything." I looked to Zavi. "Can we even trade these rare gems for coins to bribe a captain? Or will we be picked up by the Watch the moment we try?"

"If you have even one of those stones," Zavi said, "you can hand it to any slightly off-the-books captain and you'll be in Laqqara before you can say *piss off, Drukker.*"

I had to chuckle despite our terrifying situation. Phoenix covered her mouth, eyes dancing with mirth as Star shook her head and smiled.

"Piss off. Piss off. Piss off," Sanne chanted. At least she was looking more cheerful.

Phoenix leaned down from her chair to run a hand along the little girl's curly hair. "Darling, please save that phrase for the ship. Only sailors talk like that."

"And pirates," Star said, eyeing Zavi. "Where did you hear about the garnets?"

Originally, she had teased me about him, almost encouraging me to dally with him. But now, she watched him with narrowed eyes. What had changed her mind? Maybe it was the fact that he was pushing us into this heist.

"From a guard who works the night shift at Rietveld's flagship," Zavi said. "I slipped some goblinbloom into his mead."

"Father smokes that stuff when he sends us to bed early," Bram said, anger cutting his tone.

How were we going to watch that ship for long enough to know everything we needed to know to steal the garnets? If we had someone aboard, that would work, but the Watch was after us all even if they didn't know my identity as of yet. They still had my rough description and the full descriptions of Phoenix and her children.

"Can you get on board and find out where the garnets are and how we might lift them?" I asked Zavi.

"I can't. I think Rietveld knows me."

"It's time for you to tell your tale, bard." I sat at the table and stared him down. He was so painfully handsome with his inked hands and fingers, those high cheekbones, and that tousled hair peeking from the scarf he wore tied at the base of his head.

"I was a pirate, as you can see." He held up the hand with the pirate inking. "But I remember none of it. Not the sailing. Not the sea. None of my crewmates or what my position was or even what ship I might have lived on for years. I did have one memory of Rietveld." He swallowed and his face paled like he was in pain. Clearing his throat, he continued, "I believe he put a memory stone in my side to make me forget something important."

He was cursed. But how did breaking onto Rietveld's ship end in a solution for him?

"A curse?" Phoenix asked, her voice awed.

"Yes. A memory curse. I visited an apothecary who removed it temporarily to study it. She told me that I must find the missing piece of the emerald stone, put them back together, and only then will my curse end. It will kill me if I allow it to continue festering in my side." He touched his lower ribs and his Fae fangs showed briefly as he winced.

I let out a slow breath. "So Rietveld has this missing piece with the blue garnets in a safe on his favorite ship? How do you know that?"

"I don't know it for certain, but it's a good guess."

Star sipped her watered wine, set the wooden mug back on the table, and ran her finger along the cup's worn edge. "It would be wise for him to keep his most valuable items in his most well-guarded, strongest safe. But why is he keeping this supposed safe of amazing items on his ship? Why not keep it at one of his well-guarded homes or shops where he can have as many of his crew members as possible to watch it?"

"Maybe he doesn't trust his entire crew," I said.

Zavi glanced at the children and rubbed his stubbled chin. I supposed because of his Fae blood, he never grew a full beard. I recalled the feel of that stubble on my neck, the way it scratched me lightly as his tongue...

I cleared my throat and crossed my legs. "Plus keeping a low profile has its benefits when you have something incredibly valuable. You must have been important to Rietveld if he spent gold to curse you—and to curse you in such a rare way. He could have simply tossed you overboard or drummed up false charges and had you imprisoned. Why a memory curse?"

"I don't know," Zavi said. "Honestly, if I'm wrong and the piece isn't there, at least I'll live out the rest of my days in luxury far away from the man."

"You plan to go with us if we succeed?" Star looked from him to me.

"If you don't mind the company. I will split with you once you are safely in Laqqara."

"It can't hurt to have another person to watch our backs," Phoenix said.

"I do know how to fight," Zavi said.

"I noticed that when you clocked Drukker at the dance," Star said, a hint of appreciation in her voice.

"And I probably know how to sail if it comes to us needing that," he said.

"Unless that was wiped from your memory as well," I said. "Not to be overly dark-thinking, but we can't rely on that."

"No, you can't. I haven't tried, nor do I have any recollection of working lines or anything of the sort."

I opened my mouth to add to that, but a bump sounded at the door.

Zavi was up and had his dagger ready before I could draw a breath. Gods, he was fast.

We remained silent as a horrible scratching sound ran over the door. The doorknob rattled.

"What do we do, Moth?" Phoenix whispered. Bram stood beside her, very obviously trying to not be afraid, while Sanne cowered under the table.

Zavi went to the door and set his hand on the knob. "I'll push them into the street. Can you all escape out that back window? I'll hold them off. Does that work for you?" He looked at me.

"Thank you." I stood, keeping my movements careful and trying not to scrape the floor with my chair. "Meet us at the De Groot warehouse when you're certain no one is following you." But if it was the Watch, how would he avoid being arrested? He'd be vastly outnumbered.

A quiet clicking came from outside the window that we had covered with rags. Sanne burst from under the table and ran toward the window.

"It's Emerald! Emerald! It's her!" she shouted, loud enough to call every Watchman from here to Saxonion.

Phoenix pulled the rags away and a small winged shape filled the square of glass.

My heart lifted as Phoenix raised the window enough to let Emerald crawl inside.

"Stones, but you gave us a scare," Phoenix chided Emerald.

The dragon flew to Star and landed on her shoulder while the children jumped up and down. Bless them, they were keeping their voices as quiet as they probably could in their excitement. Their laughs reminded me of a boating party I'd attended as a child. My father had tied a magical seeing glass to a string and set it into the water so we could watch the funny-looking flatfish swim in schools beside the ship. He still had that seeing glass in the display case at home.

"What are you thinking about?" Zavi asked me, his mouth tipped up at one side like he enjoyed the face I was making.

I had the sudden urge to kiss him and feel his tongue on mine. His arms would feel wonderfully warm around me. It was so odd; I almost trusted him. Not quite, but nearly. Despite his Fae blood and his pirate past. He had proved he cared about me—at least, he cared more than anyone else outside this room. Would his kiss taste like the wine he was sipping? Did he smoke a pipe when he was at home? Where did he spend his nights?

I shook off my curiosity and want, and I tried to focus on the task at hand. "I was considering attaching a seeing glass to Emerald and asking her to fly over Rietveld's small ship for us."

Bram's hand found the back of my chair. "What is a seeing glass?"

"It's a sphere of magical glass that shows its surroundings in a mirror made from the same materials. A spell was cast when both were made that linked them. It's an Unseelie magical artifact."

"And quite illegal," Star said.

"Yes. Father likes to break the rules to show off his wealth, but gods save anyone else who breaks the law. Unless of course, it benefits him." I waved Emerald over and the dragon soared from Star's shoulder to land on the table near my wine. She sniffed my knuckles in greeting and I patted her head. "Do you think you could fly over a place for us?"

"How much do you think she understands?" Zavi asked Star.

"Most of it," Star said. "She'll need to see the ship and have a person point at it, I'd guess."

Zavi made a humph noise like he was impressed. "Where did you learn so much about them?"

"In military training," Star said. "We worked with them in field exercises pretty regularly until the species stopped migrating through the area. It became difficult to find them, and the use of their breed died out. Now the military only uses mountain dragons and even then only in the far north."

"I'll break into my home tonight," I said, "and get the glass and mirror. Hopefully, he won't discover it missing and use the trace to find it."

"Trace?" Phoenix asked.

"A lot of the valuable items my parents own have a magical trace set on them. Another piece of illegal magic Father purchased. That's why I don't steal from him. If he notices an item has gone missing, like the silver candlesticks last year, he'll speak a spell and see the location of that item. He caught the sailmaker's son trying to sell them off by pier two."

Zavi whistled.

"Let me nab the seeing glass and the mirror," Star said. "You'll be distracted."

"But I live there," I said. "I know the layout better than anyone."

"You can draw a quick map. I can handle it," Star said.

"I think Star is right," Phoenix said. "Let her do it. If they catch her, she'll have a better chance of escaping."

"Why? Because you don't think I can fight my parents? That I'll hold back?"

"You aren't the fighter that Star is," Phoenix said.

I growled. "All right. Fine. I'll give you a map."

While Phoenix dug up a dinner for everyone—potatoes, a loaf of stale bread, and a few pieces of dried venison—I drew Star a map of my home, the hall where the display glass stood, and a few lines of escape for her, depending on if she ran into staff or not.

Star left quickly and we waited, the children dozing off on the bedding we had in the back. Phoenix lay down beside them while Zavi and Emerald joined me by the fire.

"Should we put that out in case the Watch comes snooping around?" Zavi jerked his chin at the flames.

I shrugged. "It would be stranger for them to hear noises of habitation with no fire on a chilly night like this, right?"

"True."

Zavi's chair and mine touched and his knee brushed mine, though he didn't seem to notice.

"Do you regret it?" he asked, his focus on the fire.

"What?"

"Our kiss." His voice was smoky and quiet. It was a voice made for night, for tangled bedding, for dreams.

My body heated as his gaze slid to my face. His eyes were a simple dark brown, but they burned my skin in the most delightful way.

"I do not," I said quietly.

"I'm glad. I worried I might have pushed you into something you didn't truly want."

"When I am out on the streets as Moth, no one pushes me anywhere." If I kept saying it, maybe it would become truth.

His grin broadened, a smile that warmed my body further, especially as he ran his hands along the thighs of his trousers. I wanted to smooth my palms over the muscles in his legs and over the flat surface of his stomach. Would it be unwise to suggest we go outside and find a forgotten ruin of a warehouse to continue my journey into learning the pleasures of the body?

Were his thoughts running the same route as mine?

A wrinkle appeared between his eyebrows as he turned to face the fire again, the light licking his long throat and the edge of his jaw. I glanced at his elbow, the one that had struck Drukker in my defense.

"It doesn't hurt. The elbow," he said.

"Oh. Good. And your side?"

"The memory stone? Oh, that hurts all the time, but only terribly when I try to remember anything."

"How long did the apothecary say you have to live if it remains inside you? Why can't you toss it in the ocean?"

"When she removed it, I grew so ill that I blacked out. The curse demands that the stone remains where it was placed until it is whole again."

"That's terrifying."

"It isn't cozy; that's for certain." He rubbed a knuckle over his chin, a bemused look bringing out a dimple in his cheek and making his eyes glint.

What had those eyes seen in his former life as a pirate? Forgetting everything would drive me mad.

"What memories do you wish for the most?" It felt like a very intimate question and I worried for a moment that he would be upset that I'd asked. He'd helped me from my parents' house, so I had no desire to add fuel to the fire that was his life. But curiosity gnawed at me...

His eyelids shuttered for a moment, then he seemed to peer through the hearth fire and into another world. "My brother."

He had a sibling? "How do you remember him if all of your memories are gone?"

"I get flashes of memories sometimes. Bits of faces and the touch of a place in scent or weather or feel. I have sensed the dip and roll of a ship's deck in my mind. I saw my brother's face and I knew. Emiel. I know his name somehow. And he's in trouble. Or was."

"You have to get your memory back to help him? What did you see?"

"Rietveld and my brother on a ship. I was there and..." His fists clenched on his knees and the muscles around his jaw tensed beneath the faint stubble there. "Rietveld did something terrible. I know it like I know my own hand. There was blood."

An image of Star and Phoenix bound and gagged appeared in my mind. I imagined Rietveld chuckling as his men threw them overboard and their bodies disappeared into the dark depths. A chill swept through my bones and I set a hand on Zavi's shoulder. The muscles under my palm tightened.

"We will get that piece back," I said. "I'll help you find your brother."

"He might already be dead." The chill in his words told me he was holding back an avalanche of emotion.

"If he's not, we will get to him." No use pretending death wasn't a strong possibility. I'd seen enough of Rietveld's cold business practices to realize shedding blood was a regular part of that man's schedule.

A slow breath left Zavi, his body moving under my hand as he stared into the fire. "Thank you," he said. "I don't deserve your kindness or your loyalty."

"You don't know if you do," I said with a grin. "You could have been a person who gave all to the poor and helped old women cross streets."

"A kind pirate?"

I marveled at the fact that I was smiling as we spoke of pirates. I'd always been so afraid. Ever since that night... A memory of darkness, shouts, and a quiet, low voice came over me, pulling the heat of the fire from my body. I remembered looking up into the eyes of the pirate holding my arm in a vise-like grip. Eyes as green as grass on a spring morning. So lovely. So dangerous. I tried to pull away, but he only held more firmly and dragged me toward a skiff.

"Lina?"

I blinked and there was Zavi's earnest face, his eyes wide with concern.

I waved off his concern. "I'm fine. I had a memory of that night."

"When you were nearly kidnapped?"

"Yes."

He stood, took the cup I'd been using from the table, then handed it to me. "We are a pair, aren't we?"

I sipped the wine and let its alcoholic warmth soothe my mind. "What do you mean?"

Shrugging, he stared into the fire "I'm tortured by memories I can't grasp and you are injured by memories that won't let you go."

"Maybe knowing you will drive away my fear of pirates."

"I hope so." A strange tone threaded his words, something like pain or grief.

"Why do you say it like that?" I asked.

"I don't know how this job will go, but I know for certain I shouldn't have pulled you into it."

"You just finished talking me into the robbery." I had to chuckle. "Don't undo your work, bard."

The edge of his mouth lifted and he shrugged, sitting back in his chair with his knees wide.

I wanted to ask him more, but the corners of his eyes showed fatigue and stress, so instead I went about tidying up the hideout, keeping my hands busy so I wouldn't fret about Star.

After two hours, I was about to explode.

"We have to go after her." I was doing my best to pace a rut into the floorboards. "The Watch has her. No way she's taking this long and all is well."

Phoenix stopped my progress and set her hands on my forearms. "Star is fine. Give her another hour." She glanced across the room at her sleeping children as Emerald hopped off Sanne's folded arm and flew toward us. "She might have had to wait until your father's guards grew tired or complacent."

"True. Yes." Drawing away from Phoenix, I started my pacing again. "He most likely set even more guards after my escape."

Phoenix sat with Emerald in her lap. She patted the chair beside her and raised her eyebrows at me expectantly.

Zavi leaned on the wall near the door. "Definitely more guards, but I can go check on Star if you'd like."

"In an hour," I said, finally sitting beside Phoenix, who appeared mollified. "Then we take action. But would you mind slipping out and making certain we don't have eyes on our hideout?"

Phoenix bit her lip. "You don't think anyone around here knows about us, do you?"

"I don't know, but that's the problem. We don't know."

With a quick bow of his head, Zavi cracked the door and slid through. His movements somehow didn't make a single sound.

I shook my head. "What I wouldn't give to have Fae grace."

"You like him."

"I don't."

Phoenix snorted. "Don't even try to lie to me, Moth. He is the flame that draws you. I don't blame you either. He has a good air about him."

"Air? You judge males on their scent?"

"That's not what I mean and you know it. Stop being obstinate or I'll box your ears like you're one of my own."

I grasped her hand and squeezed it. "I am one of your own. Box as you see fit."

We laughed quietly and talked of strategy, stroking Emerald and feeding the dragon bits of dried meat.

Neither Zavi nor Star returned for over an hour.

17

ZAVI

The night swallowed Zavi whole as he circled the old warehouse that served as Lina's hideout. Rain misted from the black sky to highlight the cobblestones' edges and dripped from broken doorways and leaning walls that looked ready to fall into the street.

A rat scurried across a drainage pipe and someone coughed from a dark window three doors down. Zavi crept toward the window, keeping his back against the warehouse and his movements silent.

And there he waited, silent and ready.

After what felt like ages, the shuffle of boots carried from the opening and into the night. Two men. No, three.

"Stop hacking like an old hag," a rough voice whispered in a hiss.

"Shouldn't have brought him. He's always as loud as a well-paid whore."

Chuckles filled the window and Zavi touched the hilt of his dagger. He could be in that window with their dead bodies at his feet in moments. The third would most likely have enough time to call out though and that was what stayed Zavi's hand. That and the possibility that the Watch would find the bodies before Zavi, Lina, and the others had the chance to do the Rietveld job. More noise, more trouble. Not a good idea.

These weren't Watch men, but Zavi would have bet his hammock that they had been paid by the Watch to be here. That told him a few things, one of which was that the Watch didn't truly suspect Lina was in this area but neither did the Watch think it was impossible for her to pass through. The hideout was secure for now, but Lina and the rest of them would have to find another way out of the hideout to avoid being heard by this lot.

Maybe through the roof?

If the children weren't involved, that plan would have been fairly easy, but with one so small as Sanne...

But Phoenix had to bring her children because the moment they set out on this heist, they would have to leave. There wouldn't be time or distractions enough to stash them somewhere. No, after the heist, the women would have to run and run fast if they were to escape.

He prayed he would find that artifact and be strong enough to help them do just that. Aiding them in their flight would maybe ease a fraction of the guilt crushing his heart.

But all of that depended on what he remembered if—no, when—he uncursed himself. His brother had to come first.

Zavi hurried through the tight space between the building and the one that stood beside the hideout warehouse. He had to catch Star on her return or the men hiding would call the Watch down on her immediately. His tunic snagged and ripped. Pausing and cursing silently, he tugged the torn fabric off the rusted peg that had grabbed him. He remained there for a while, watching.

A shape passed by the opening between structures. The person strode confidently. It was her.

He squeezed free and ran for Star. She whirled, took hold of his mistreated tunic, then threw him to the ground. His breath left in a gust that made him dizzy.

"Friend, not foe," he whispered.

She put a knee on his chest, compressing his ribs painfully. "Friends don't creep up on friends. Not sure if you know that, bard, or should I call you pirate? I know you are keeping something from Moth, and I want you to spill your guts."

He edged her gritty boot away from his throat. "Another Fae hater, are you?"

"No. I loathe liars."

"I told Moth everything. Now, there are three men keeping an eye in that building there." He cut his gaze toward the back of the building beside them. "I thought perhaps you didn't want to dance right by their window and ruin everything."

She released him and he stood quickly, following her as she strode in the opposite direction. "Thank you."

They kept quiet until they had rounded the corner and slipped into the hideout from the western side of the row of dilapidated warehouses.

Lina ran to Star and hugged her tightly. "You scared me. I'm furious."

Star grinned and patted Lina's back as Phoenix waved then went to the children, one of whom was stirring with whispered questions.

"You still good with the bard being in on this?" she asked Lina in a whisper. "You trust him?"

Zavi pretended not to hear.

"I do," Lina said. "Rietveld might have his brother." Her gaze held a quiet fury on Zavi's behalf and it made his chest ache.

He rubbed the spot where Star's boot had been moments ago.

"Ah." Star took a dull brown crockery cup from the shelves by the far window and set it on the rickety table under the shelves. "That is the information he was keeping to himself. Rietveld is an enemy. Not just a target."

"Correct," Zavi said. It didn't make sense to argue it now. He had been false to Lina when he'd first broached the topic. It was better that they focus on that small crime of his rather than begin to wonder about the thief who had taken their stolen goods and forced their hand. In fact, he needed to clear that possible avenue right now. "You could go after the thief who took your hoard instead of hitting Rietveld with me."

Lina frowned, a wrinkle appearing between her coppery eyebrows. "You know the goods are already sold and scattered by now."

"I want to know you are truly in this with me with no backup plan."

Star bent and retrieved a dusty wine bottle from beneath a stack of moldy crates. She uncorked the bottle and poured her glass, filling it to the brim. "Well, do you want to hear how I did or are we going to chitchat all day?"

She downed the entire cup, then pulled two items from the large bag slung across her body.

A mirror with a gilded frame and something wrapped in soft leather.

Lina unfolded the leather to reveal a sphere of blown glass. "You did it. You amazing woman, you did it."

"I am pretty fantastic." Star poured another cup.

Phoenix approached and sighed over the magical items. She brushed a hand over the sphere and shivered.

"Feel the power, do you? I've wondered how much humans can sense," Zavi said.

Phoenix nodded, a curl coming free from her braided and looped light hair.

Lina took the mirror and eyed Emerald, who was flying circles above the large table in the center of the room. "I can sense it too. Emerald, will you come here and do us a favor?"

Would the dragon truly be capable of this job? If Rietveld's men spotted the creature, they would shoot the dragon down with an arrow in a heartbeat. But like with the rest of this heist, Zavi, Lina, and her crew wouldn't know what would succeed until they tried.

Please let this work, Zavi prayed silently.

18

LINA

The mirror shivered in my hands like it felt cold, as if it were a living being. Fighting revulsion, I swallowed and traded a glance with Zavi, who grimaced, seeming as uncomfortable with the magic as I was. My reflection, pale and wide-eyed, faded to show greasy-haired sailors and bustling merchant men rolling carts toward the docks. The sunrise showed in the mirror, bouncing off a puddle from last night's mist and showing a slice of the morning's pinkish hue. Emerald, with the seeing sphere tied to her chest, flew over the water then, showing us whitecaps and a bobbing gull sitting in the bay beside a large ship I didn't recognize. Our view shifted until we were high above a smaller craft with tied blue sails and orange-painted railings. A bronze bell gleamed as Emerald soared over the boat.

"That's the one, right?" Phoenix asked. Both her children leaned on her, their gazes trained fiercely onto the mirror.

"It is." I blew over the silvered surface to dislodge a spot of dust. "Hopefully, Emerald will circle back. We need to see the guards stationed there and watch when they change up."

The mirror's scene changed from the craft to the open sea where the horizon pulled the sun from the dark line of the ocean's lulling waves.

"Back to your mission, dragon," I muttered.

Emerald made a sharp turn, and Sanne gripped her stomach, moaning a little.

"Too much moving about," she said, leaving our huddled group at the table to instead lie back down on her mountain of ragged pillows.

The boat came back into view and, with it, the pier and the guards. A group of three shifted their weight from foot to foot, hands clasped or crossed at their chests. Each was armed with a sword and dagger, which hung near the orange sashes at their belts. Two were big men and as they lifted a crate onto a wheelbarrow for a struggling merchant's servant, their grace and power were obvious. Good fighters. But the third ran his mouth more than the others and he did nothing to help nor did he seem to be watching the crowd passing the boat's plank as was his duty.

"A weak link in Rietveld's chain, hmm?" Zavi leaned and cocked his head as he studied the image the magic provided.

"You're reading my mind," I said.

"You know that isn't a magic a Seelie Fae can do."

"Who knows what is in your blood? You might have Unseelie hiding in there."

He chuckled, which surprised me. "Could be. I wouldn't mind some of their powers."

I tapped the mirror and looked to Star. "You could start with that guard."

She nodded and cracked her knuckles like she was ready to fight immediately. "Yes, and then take on the other two."

"So you think force will be necessary? Not just stealth?" Phoenix asked.

I shrugged. "I'll have to think on it and get everyone's ideas."

Emerald soared higher and we watched as the guards switched out, the three replaced by five younger men who had a military way about their movements.

I chewed the inside of my cheek. "The heavies for night watch and these ex-soldiers for daytime watch, then?" I looked to Phoenix, Star, and Zavi, wanting their opinions.

Zavi tapped a quick rhythm on his knees. He wore rings on most of his fingers—some gold, most a simple metal. They highlighted the size of his hands and his movements reminded me how dexterous he was. Those hands had been on my hips and in my hair. Warmth stirred between my legs at the memory of our reckless moments in the alley.

He noticed my staring and lowered his chin, his gaze going hot under his thick black lashes. "Or Rietveld is changing out his guards because he is about to sail."

My heart cinched even though Zavi's tone had been so relaxed. "If they plan to sail today, we have five hours until the tide turns."

"Not enough time," Star said.

A light rain started, droplets blurring the mirror's display, and I blinked. When I opened my eyes again, the image showed Rietveld swinging open the door of the captain's quarters. He raised a meaty hand to greet one of his sailors, his bosun perhaps, then took a few steps over to a raised wooden box affixed to the deck. He removed a brass key from a red velvet bag tied to his belt.

"What is he up to?" Zavi frowned at the mirror and glanced at me.

"That's the compass box," I said. "I don't know why it would be locked on a ship like that."

Rietveld raised the collar of his sea cloak against the inconsistent rain and glanced toward a cluster of sailors at the far end of the ship, then over his shoulder at the man I assumed was his first mate, who was looking oceanward with a spyglass. With quick movements, Rietveld lifted the compass box lid.

"But he didn't use the key," Phoenix said. "It was unlocked."

Star crossed her arms and made a humming sound.

The image shimmered as if Emerald had been buffeted by the sea wind. A glimpse of the horizon showed patchy clouds between swathes of golden light, but the view remained fuzzy. I had been holding the mirror, but I rested it on the table in hopes of clearing the magic image. Rietveld was there, his form slightly blurry. He reached into the compass box with the brass key, then the sunrise pierced the light rain, cast a rainbow of watery light, and obscured our view.

Phoenix grabbed my arm and edged so close to the mirror that her breath fogged the shiny surface. "What did he do? Did you see? I think there's a compartment at the bottom of the box. He might be using the brass key to unlock it."

I eased her back and looked closer. "It's clearing. Hold on. Ah, he moved away."

Rietveld stood beside a sailor as Emerald wheeled away to show the men on the main deck. The image blurred again and then the dragon was flying the seeing sphere over the outer ring of the warehouse district, where rain barrels stood against stacked crates and workers milled about the various buildings.

"She's coming back," Phoenix said.

"Do you think Rietveld has your curse piece in there?" I asked Zavi.

"It's not a bad guess," he said. "What else would be that small and still important?"

I shrugged. "The blue garnets?"

"I'm not sure. I would think he'd keep those in his quarters."

"So he acts as captain on his own ships?" Star asked.

Gods, that compass box was right out in the open. Stealing from it would be impossible without significant exposure. "When it pleases him," I said, finally answering Star's question. "At least that's what my father has said in the past."

The tension in the room made every sound too loud.

"What do we do?" Phoenix looked out the window for Emerald, then returned to warm her hands by the fire.

Everyone went quiet, all of our minds churning.

A few minutes passed before Emerald tapped on the window. We gathered her inside, released her from the heavy weight of the sphere, and fed her a scone Star had stashed in her pocket.

Phoenix, Star, and Zavi took up chairs at the table, but I started pacing again, the plan forming in my mind. "I'd love to get on board at night to avoid a crowd seeing us, but then the heavies will be there. We'd have to fight them. Could we do it without causing a ruckus?"

"Not possible," Star said, feeding Emerald the last crumbs from her palm.

I clicked my tongue against the roof of my mouth. "We can't make a scene. The Watch will be on us in seconds. We'll have to infiltrate during the day. I can pretend I've come to ask Rietveld for help."

Phoenix frowned. "You mean you'll tell him the Watch is actually searching for you?"

"Yes. I'll ask him for help."

Zavi studied my face. "What kind of help? For the record, I like this idea. This is what I meant about you having an in with him."

Nodding, I continued planning out loud. "Tell me what you think of this. Maybe I can simply ask him to call off the Watch and speak to my father, to help ease my punishment for my reckless behavior. He isn't a man of rules, as we all know from his business dealings."

"That's for sure," Star said.

"So he might find it endearing that I wanted to escape," I said, "if only for a day."

Zavi rose and leaned against the wall near the fire. "I don't see Rietveld as ever finding anything endearing. I wish I could remember..." His lips pulled away from his teeth, showing his Fae fangs, and he put a hand over the place where the memory stone hid inside his body.

A shudder halted my pacing. "Don't try to recall anything now. We need you alert and ready to do the job."

"What jobs will everyone have?" Phoenix asked.

I took a deep breath and summoned some courage. "I'll get Rietveld's attention from the landing and he'll welcome me on board."

"Sounds so easy when you say it like that," Star murmured, raising an eyebrow.

I snorted. "Right. Once I'm there, I'll tell him someone is following me. Hopefully, Rietveld will send at least one of his guards to check out my false lead."

Zavi crossed his arms. "So we will have fewer eyes on us as we try to sneak on board."

"Yes. Star," I said, "you can lead the guard away and perhaps even create some noise around the corner to draw more of them away. Zavi, can you swim?"

"Like a fish."

"Good. You can swim to the ship. You'll be able to get on board somehow, right?"

"Thanks for all that detailed direction, Moth."

My flat look told him to stop whining. "Your blood gives you the ability to climb quite well from what I recall. The drain pipe at the house never even shook under your weight."

Phoenix grinned. "Someday we need to hear all of your stories."

Heat rose into my cheeks as a story I would *not* be sharing came to mind—Zavi's hands on my hips and his hot breath...

Star rubbed at her left shoulder. She'd been cut deeply there during a skirmish in the north when she was young and freshly recruited into the Deigs unit of foot soldiers. "What's after that?" she asked. "I mean, if we aren't all stabbed and flung into the sea by then."

Phoenix sighed. "Someone is definitely getting stabbed."

Star chuckled darkly, and Zavi raised his eyebrows at her nonchalance.

"After that," I continued, "Zavi goes to the hull and gets into the more expensive stuff stashed behind the basic goods.

There is a slight chance his artifact piece is in there and not in the mysterious compass box. And there is a very good chance that compartment holds gold, which is what the rest of us need."

Zavi nodded. "Done. I'll load up and then..." He looked at me, the side of his lips tucked up in a grin.

"Then I get into the captain's quarters because of course he will offer me a steadying drink. I'll knock him out the way you've taught me, Star. Zavi, you slip past the sailors and meet me there to pick any locks that might be in the way."

"Slip past?"

"Yes. Phoenix is going to make it possible with one of her signature moves."

Phoenix was rubbing her hands together already. I had to smile. She loved explosive distractions. Her work would make Zavi's fireworks look like child's play.

I set my hands on the back of Star's chair. "That's the basic plan. Should work perfectly."

Star twisted to give me a knowing glance. We had worked together long enough to know what the other was thinking.

"But..." Zavi broke away from the wall and stared at each of us in turn. "There are so many holes that I don't even know where to start."

"We work better on the move, bard. Don't muck up operations with too much detail. You are here because we allow it."

"What about the compass box's mysterious contents?" Star asked, glancing at Zavi with concern that actually appeared genuine. She was starting to like him and I was glad. It would make our team work better together.

"We will get to it," I said. "Don't worry. I have an idea. Plus we have a Fae pirate with us."

He sniffed and crossed his arms again. I would have bet he knew how the sight of his muscled forearms and biceps weakened my resolve. Bastard. "I *do* have superior speed and strength."

I lifted my cup and finished the wine. "Really, it's just the lockpicking. We're rubbish with locks."

Zavi snorted, a grin tugging at his full lips.

Phoenix nodded. "It's been a weak spot for us, sadly. But now you're here and all is well." She grinned widely and clasped her hands together.

Turning, Zavi watched Emerald roll around on a few copper coins someone had dropped. "I'm going to end up as fish food, aren't I, dragon?"

Emerald looked up at him and snorted sparks. He laughed and bent to scratch the little beast's chin.

This plan might work.

It had to work. With all the ruckus we'd be making, we would be caught if things didn't go exceedingly smoothly. I swallowed and tried to chase my fears away with thoughts of Laqqara's shoreline—the red sand, green succulents, and winding roads leading to cities where women were equal with men. Sophia's kingdom.

The place I'd always thought of as my true home.

I blinked and realized Zavi was watching my face. Something tender swept across his features and he handed Emerald over.

"The dragon ate one of your coppers. I hope that's not the end of the little scaled spy."

Phoenix and Star were bedding down beside the children,

whispering ideas about how to get Phoenix's explosives on board.

I took Emerald and ran a hand down the smooth, dry scales of her side. Small spikes rose from her spine, each one shiny and rounded at the tip. Made for defense, not for attack. I opened my palm and the dragon set her head there. A clicking sound issued from her throat, tickling my wrist.

"I just hope we don't get them all killed," I whispered to Zavi.

"I won't let that happen."

His gaze told me he was serious, that he would put himself between danger and my friends. But something dark lurked in the lovely spark of his eyes. I sighed and twisted away, pretending to fuss with the dragon. I liked the bard. Very much. But I still didn't completely trust him.

"You might not recall the man very well," I said, "but I know more than I wish I did about our mark."

Zavi's eyes glinted with interest. There was something about that sparkle in his look that drew me in despite my reticence. There was a genuineness to his gaze, an intensity.

I continued in a quiet voice so the others wouldn't hear. "One morning when I was sneaking to the kitchens to grab a freshly baked roll, I heard my father talking to one of his messengers. The ones who run notes and orders all hours of the day. They go places he refuses to and sometimes do more than any messenger should. Well, I listened, frozen on the stairwell so I wouldn't be caught and thrashed for disobeying my set schedule."

"Your family is just a joy, hmm?"

"Delightful. Yes," I said, my voice sharper than I'd intended. There was something about Zavi that drew emotion from me. "So his messenger had a tale to tell about one of Father's suppliers. The man supposedly shorted Rietveld when the cinnamon came in and gave a larger portion of the spice to a competitor. Rietveld had the spice trader strung up by the halyard of the very ship we are about to rob. His most prized vessel. The trader's organs had been removed while he still lived, with everyone looking on. Rietveld fed the trader's insides to the sharks in the bay even while the last of the man's life leaked from his body."

Zavi swore like the pirate he was—quick, quiet, and as foul as an autumn storm. He gripped my hand and looked dead in my eyes. He said once again, "I won't let that happen."

"It's nice and all that you think that, but even with your skills and ours, every last one of us could end up offering our guts up for the fishes."

He laughed, too loudly really, and covered his mouth, glancing back at the children.

"What is funny about this?" My glare melted as I studied the wrinkles at the edges of his eyes and the way he could hardly keep his laughter from booming across the room.

"You're so blunt," he said. "I don't know why, but it is delightful."

"You think it's delightful when I basically call you an idiot?"

"I truly do."

I snorted. "Well, I'll do my best to keep tossing condescension your way, then."

"You aren't afraid of me either, which I like."

"Should I be afraid?"

His glance touched my cheek briefly before he focused on

the fire. Heat shot through my body and gathered low in my belly.

"I think you could take me," I said.

"Take you?"

He rubbed the back of his neck and smiled, his dimple showing deeply in his slightly stubbled cheek. "The ways I could go with this conversation..."

My body wasn't cooling down, that was certain. I never thought I would miss an alley, but at the moment, I did. Very much. "The place next door has a loft half exposed to the sky. What do you say we pick up where we left off?" I had no idea what I was doing, but damn if it wasn't fun.

"I hope you mean to the north and not the south because while I would adore participating in what you're suggesting, I don't think the Watch's hired hands would allow us to do as we wished for very long before they took action. The not-fun type of action."

A laugh bubbled from me and I caught Star's look from across the room. She had one eye cracked open. Everyone else was sleeping soundly as the rain pattered on the tin roof. With a wink, she turned away from us, all but giving me a thumbs up.

❧ 19 ☙

ZAVI

O nce again, Zavi found himself scrambling up things not meant for climbing, and all for his firefly. Of course, she wasn't his. Not by a long shot. But in his own head, in his heart, he could tell himself pretty lies. Gorgeous falsehoods like Lina might come to love him at some point and that they would break his curse and live forever in the wild sands of Laqqara, sunburnt and laughing. She was using him for pleasure and he was fine with it. He wanted more from her, but it wasn't as if he could expect more. Until they secured the missing curse piece from Rietveld, Zavi was living on borrowed time. He couldn't build a new life until he could remember his first one. Plus, if Lina ever found out that Zavi had been behind the robbery that had set her on this path of thieving from Rietveld, she'd never forgive him. No, he had to satisfy his heart with dalliances and keep his eyes on the goal—saving Emiel if he was still alive. If they were both alive by sunrise two days hence.

Lina climbed up the half-broken fire ladder outside the

neighboring warehouse like she was born to sneak about in the dark. Quiet as a whisper, she made it to the top, then turned to grin down at Zavi. He followed, fully silent, and spread his cloak on the dry plaster and clay tiles of the warehouse's roof. A rough rectangle of planks shielded them from the rain and they sat close. He wasn't exactly nervous, but his heart beat faster than normal. Maybe it was because he was starting to really care for this woman. He'd steered clear of relationships up until now. Well, as far as he could remember. This whole sensation was new.

Lina stared past the shelter to the stars peering through a scattered break in the cloud cover. "Do you think my plan will work?"

The scant light from the struggling moon drew silver lines over her pert little nose and heart-shaped lips. He wanted to kiss her.

"I do."

"So my talk with the others went well, you think?"

"Yes."

"Really? Because I could have said more. I rushed it a bit."

"Like you said, your group likes to think on their feet and leave details to the scenario."

She nodded and crossed her legs.

"Why would you want my opinion?" he asked, honestly curious.

"You're not a simple bard. Somewhere in there, you have the experience of being a pirate, and based on the fighting I've seen you do and the stealth you've shown, a good bit of what you knew is still present."

It was a good point. He wasn't sure how true it was though. He didn't feel like a pirate. He already missed uneventful evenings in the tavern, he longed to strum a lute, and he had so enjoyed just being alive when his mind was distracted from the curse.

"What are you thinking now?" Lina broke into his thoughts. Her gaze seemed to be trying to peel back his layers. "Do Fae think in the same patterns that humans do? I wonder in what ways you differ from humans."

Zavi flicked the tip of his pointed ear and lifted a lip to show a fang. "Aside from the obvious."

"Yes, apart from your interesting looks."

"Interesting. Hmm. I'd hoped for a better adjective, but I'll take what I can get."

She grinned and shook her head. "You're incorrigible."

"So are you."

"Completely." Her grin widened, and her face lit up with the glow that only she possessed, the luminous energy of her, the light that had him calling her *firefly*.

He turned and eased her down, her smile going sly as he crawled on top of her. "Now, what exactly did you have in mind? Or would you like me to use my imagination?"

Her lovely lips turned up and she reached up to tuck a lock of hair behind his ear. Her fingertip brushed the pointed tip and a pleasant shiver rode down his spine.

Her eyebrow lifted. "Like that, do you?"

She did it again and her tongue touched her lip as she did so, making it all even better. Old Ones save him, but she was enticing. His body was lit up from end to end. He caught her hand and kissed her wrist, nipping at the soft skin with his teeth and making her inhale sharply. His free hand went to her throat and her eyes shuttered briefly. Having the chance to give her pleasure made him feel like the luckiest male in all the realms. "This isn't about me. This is about you. Tell me what you want."

"But I like seeing you swoon at my touch, Zavi."

Desire shot through him at the sound of his name on her lips. "Say it again."

She grabbed his tunic and slowly pulled him closer, setting her mouth against his ear, her lips almost touching the point. Shivers danced under his skin and he grew as hard as a century-old oak.

"Zavi," she whispered.

He was going to lose his battle for control if he let her run this show. It was time to take over. No way was he allowing her to bring him to the peak before she'd even had any fun.

Taking her wrists, he pinned her down and ground his hips against hers. She moaned lightly and her body arched toward his, her warmth pressing against his length. The friction was divine. He swallowed and looked away for a moment, trying to think of terrible things instead of this glorious moment with Lina. Cold nights alone on the sea. The week he'd had nothing but moldy bread to eat at the ruins. Once his body had calmed a fraction, he faced her once more.

"What's wrong?"

"I am having difficulty going slow. The Fae side of me can be rather insistent when it comes to physical encounters."

She lifted her eyebrows. "Oh?"

He smiled down at her ferociously gorgeous face. Due to her inexperience, she didn't quite understand. He had been new to this once too and recalled the nerves he'd had.

"What I mean is that part of me longs to ravish you quickly," he said. "That part of me is incredibly insistent."

She snickered. The vile, adorable little thing was enjoying

his discomfort. "I thought Fae males were known for their stamina."

His blood roared at the insult and he dragged her hands over her head, keeping her pinned tightly. He licked the base of her throat in that delicate crescent of skin above her collarbone. She tasted like salt and honey. "You could destroy all of the Fae realm with that dangerous mind of yours and this decadent body."

"My body isn't decadent. It's not that much different from any one of the women in Masdam."

He laughed quietly against her soft skin. "I beg to differ." Rising up to watch her expressions, he added. "I have looked. I have sampled."

A wrinkle appeared between her eyebrows and he had to grin at her jealousy. He liked that very much.

"Don't worry," he added. "None have enchanted me like you. I swear it on my brother's soul."

Her features fell and she wiggled free of his hold. Of course, he allowed it, shifting his weight to one of his elbows. He didn't truly want to pin her. He wanted her to do whatever she wanted in every way.

She licked her lips and sighed. "I am sorry that Rietveld wronged your brother. And you. We will figure this out."

Between kissing her fingers and rolling a fraction to press lightly into her hips again, he whispered what his heart was singing: "I don't deserve you."

The truth of what he'd done crawled up his throat, ready to scream and ruin everything. Should he let it out? Of course he should. But would he?

He shut his eyes, wishing all of this was different. Perfect, like it could be in another scenario where she hadn't been his mark and he hadn't had a curse set on him that endangered his only living family.

Would she forgive him?

He mentally shook his head at himself. He was beginning to sound like a broken wind chime, clanging the same note over and over again.

"Talk to me," Lina said, lifting herself up onto her elbows. Her coppery hair spilled over one shoulder and caught a dusting of moonlight.

Sitting up and resting his forearms on his knees, he sniffed a half-laugh. "I'm the shame of all Fae males now, for sure. Giving up a good rucking for a chat."

A chuckle made Lina's body vibrate against his side. "You're not only those bedroom eyes and big...ego."

He laughed quietly then, only keeping the sound muffled to remain hidden from the Watch. "Well, thanks."

"You're welcome. Now, tell me what is bothering you so much. Is it our plan?"

"I'd be a madman if I weren't at least a little bit worried about the heist," he said. "But no, that's not everything."

Her fingers laced his bicep, her grip far too small to encircle his muscle. She was such a lovely blend of strength and delicate beauty. "I'm trying to trust you. I really am. Tell me what's bothering you."

No. He couldn't. If she was still attempting to believe he was who he said he was and not like the pirate who had tried to kidnap her years ago, telling her that he'd orchestrated the theft of her hoard would only ruin what progress he'd made. He'd keep it to himself until they were finished with the heist and had Deigs' shores far behind them.

All right. He was through waffling. That was his decision. He had to put Emiel first and break this curse to find him.

"I just hope the children don't get hurt during our shenanigans."

Lina's eyes softened, then she lay back on the ground again. "We won't let that happen. You said so yourself that you would protect them."

He turned and resumed his position, half on top of her with one elbow supporting the bulk of his weight. "I will do my very best."

"That's all any of us can do, as the saying goes. Now, stop this blathering and kiss me properly, bard."

Grinning, he set his mouth on hers gently. He teased her bottom lip with his tongue while his hand snaked down her stomach. She increased the intensity of the kiss, drawing her tongue over his in a less than experienced way, then nipping at his lip. The heat of her body reached his palm through the clothing that he wanted to rip away. She lifted her tunic, untucking it from her belt and giving him access to her bare flesh. His fingers found her breast and he cupped the amazingly soft skin there. Her back arched and she whispered his name. He drew one thumb over the top and she let out a moan against his shoulder.

Desire, more powerful than anything he'd ever felt, suddenly washed over him. He wanted to devour her, to treasure her, to claim her. As his mate.

He pulled away, panting slightly, and her eyes widened.

"What's wrong? Did you hear something?"

This was not okay. It was one thing to have some fun with her and give this woman the pleasure she asked for, but it was completely wrong to claim her as a mate when there was deceit between them. Besides, there was no way she'd want to mate with him officially. It was like humans getting married. It was for life. They barely knew one another. Why was his heart pounding and his blood demanding he take her now? He looked down at his hands; they were shaking.

"I, I, yes. I heard something."

She was up and crouching, easing her way toward the edge of the roof, before he had the chance to process why. She was looking for what he heard. He shook his head harshly, trying to clear it.

One word echoed in his mind.

Mate.

No. He couldn't think of her as his mate. If he did, he'd never be able to leave her side, not without horrible pain. And Lina needed complete freedom. Damn the Fae side of him for being so wild. That part of his blood oftentimes didn't care about anything but procreation and security.

"I see movement," Lina whispered from where she peered into the dark street. Her tunic was still rumpled and halfway untucked at her small waist.

"How many shapes?"

"Two. One is rather large and I think I've seen him before."

"Lago. Yes. I've seen him meet with some of the Watch at The Last Dock. Got into a brawl while I was tuning my lute a month back. The loser didn't get up."

Lina bit her lip. "Yikes. Well, maybe we should get back to the group. In case they find it and we have to fight our way out."

Zavi nodded and they hurried toward the ladder, keeping their footsteps as quiet as possible. The rain helped cover some of their noise. Lina pointed toward the ladder on the far side of the roof, its handrails sticking up like masts of a ship.

He met her gaze and gave her another nod. They would lead the group up here and down that ladder if their hideout was compromised.

20

ZAVI

After a few hours of sleep but before sunrise, Lina woke the crew and got everyone eating and prepping for the heist. They discussed more elements of the plan, including signals and timing.

Zavi watched her lead, a pride that he had zero rights to feel glowing inside him.

Once everyone had set to their work, Moth tossed a heavy sack at him. It hit his chest hard, and if he hadn't been formed partially of Fae blood, he'd have fallen back on his arse.

Lina put her hands on her glorious hips and raised a copper eyebrow. "Show me what you know, pirate."

The sack was filled with locks in every shape and size. There were even a few tools inside.

Zavi looked up at her. "If you have all of this, you've practiced. Do you really even need me?"

"We have discussed this. I'm rubbish at it."

"Me too, remember," Phoenix said, raising a hand and half

listening to Sanne whisper a story she'd made up about Emerald, the Fae King Lysanael, and his human wife, Queen Revna.

Star paused in sharpening a viciously shiny throwing knife. "Also me. We weren't just being humble earlier. I haven't been able to hear very quiet noises since my injury. As you know, hearing is oftentimes the key."

Zavi grinned. "Key. I get it."

Lina rolled her eyes. "Locks. Show me." Gods, she was gorgeous when she was demanding things. "I want to feel better about your part of tomorrow's gig."

Setting the sack on the floorboards near the fire, Zavi gave her a nod. "As you wish, Lady Moth."

Star snorted and sheathed her sharpened knife in a pocket sewn onto the leather vest she wore over her tunic. "I like that. Lady Moth."

"Do you, Lady Star?"

"Oh, don't you start on me. You charmed me enough at the point of my blade. We are good. For now."

"Point of your blade?" Lina frowned, then shook her head. "You know what? Doesn't matter. Focus on the job." She pointed at the sack.

Phoenix chuckled. She was wearing what she deemed her "very special dress." Zavi had seen her slip several bits and bobs that looked alarmingly like fuses into tiny pockets sewn into the folds of the sleeves and into the bodice. She tugged a ragged tunic over Sanne's head, and Zavi recalled the part of the plan that involved disguising the children as beggars so the Watch would have a harder time spotting them during the wait for the signal.

The first two locks Zavi pulled out were too simple to even waste his time with, so he placed them aside. The third was an old double spinner model set into a bronze doorknob, and though it was older than the dog he needed to go check on, it was a good challenge for a proper picklock. Lina ruthlessly stood over him, glaring as he worked with the picks she'd included in the mess.

The tumblers were rusted and stubborn, but he shifted one then the other and held up his accomplishment for her perusal.

"Nice. Another." She sat on a stool beside him and the firelight painted her delicious lips so that he was near salivating to crush her mouth to his again. She kept her eyes on his hands. "Focus, bard."

He chuckled and went back to his work on the fourth lock.

"Star fell during a pirate attack on the north coast," Lina whispered, her gaze on the lock. "She nearly died. The injury affected her hearing."

"Did you know her then?"

"No. Not until years later."

"I hope I get to learn all of your stories," Zavi said quietly as the fourth lock gave way. His heart pinched at the revelation. He hadn't meant the words to come out so serious.

When he looked up again, she was studying his face, but she didn't reply, so he dug around in the sack and retrieved lock number five.

"Where did you find this?" The bronze lock was a convoluted tangle of gears and switches, with two keyholes. If it had five fewer parts, it would have been a padlock. But this —it was ridiculous. "A circus? A joke shop? An octopus's lair?"

Star and Phoenix had wandered over to watch his

attempts at the lock, which required not only two keys but also a number combination.

Lina stared at him. "I stole it from the shipping guild's office." She blinked. "Where Rietveld runs the show."

Zavi's stomach fell. "Fantastic."

He tried using a bumper key on the first keyhole at the same time as he worked a pick into a mysterious opening at the top of the contraption near the shackle. The tumblers on one side of the metal monster clicked like he'd done something good, but the shackle didn't so much as budge when he yanked on it.

So he tried another strategy. And another. And yet another.

"I need to do something with my old dog. At my place," he said, while using two picks on the second keyhole. He paused and looked around for something to shove into the open space on top. If it had a mechanism that bolted shut when the other part was unlocked, perhaps he could block that tiny bolt by jamming up the opening.

"Dog?" Lina leaned back against the corner of the hearth. The neck of her tunic shifted a little to show the top of her cleavage. It was a very nice distraction. "I really hope that's not a metaphor for *wife*."

A laugh crept out of him in the midst of his frustration with the damned lock.

Star's hand appeared under Zavi's nose. She was holding a box of wooden bits and bobs. "Any of this useful?"

"Actually, yes," he said. "Thanks"

She gave him a smile. "No problem."

He selected a rounded piece that looked like it had once been part of a bucket handle and rammed it into the opening.

"Resorting to a good stabbing, hmm?" Lina said, leaning toward him to look.

Phoenix lifted her arm and Emerald flew down to land near the crook of her elbow. "Stabbing always makes you feel better."

"Definitely," Star said, going back to sharpening weapons near the back room.

With the opening jammed, Zavi wiggled the pick in the second keyhole.

The shackle fell open.

21

LINA

The sun rose, and soon I was donning a traditional Deigs corset and gown, thoughts of strategy whirling through my mind. If we failed today, we were as good as dead. It wouldn't be a quick death either. Rietveld would make us suffer.

Phoenix's hands were quick with my braid, and I watched as Star helped the children pack stale rolls and dried fruit into the bags they would have on their little backs as they waited for the signal to come aboard or to run. Emerald bounced over the countertop near the sink, nudging a teacup with her snout with seemingly no goal but to make noise.

"Please hush, Emerald. The Watch isn't gone just because it's morning. And the city noise will only cover so much."

The dragon looked up from the overturned porcelain and let out a puff of smoke.

"Don't give her any lip, beastie," Star said over her shoulder.

The dragon lowered her head in submission. Star was obviously her mother.

I hated that Zavi wasn't back yet. He'd returned home to see about his dog. A smile tugged at my lips as I imagined him baby talking the mutt he had spoken so fondly of late last night after everyone else was asleep.

Phoenix tapped my back once. "All done. Everyone ready?"

"As ready as we can be," Star said, adjusting Sanne's bag over the girl's shoulder.

I straightened my back and put on the mask of calm I always wore when setting out on a job. "We are going to fool them all, and before sunset, we'll be gone from this prison forever."

Sanne raised her arms and began to cheer, but Bram grabbed her and hugged her, shushing his sister gently.

Star went to the door, peeked out, then turned and nodded.

"If Zavi doesn't get back in time, we move without him," I whispered. "Plan two."

"Got it." Star pursed her lips like she wanted to say more.

I slipped out, praying to any god who might listen that the Watch's eyes weren't on our door. I couldn't very well climb out a window in all these layers of lemon and cream silk. Walking as quickly as I could without drawing notice—the fine dress and the fact that I was unaccompanied was jarring enough—I aimed for the docks and Rietveld's ship. He would be there now, checking the boat and discussing the upcoming sail with the crew. I knew shipping schedules like I knew my own menstrual cycle.

If the Watch did nab me, it might all still be okay, but this heist would be far easier without more bodies. My mind whispered, *This is impossible. You're going to get them all killed.* I shoved that thought down and stomped on it with a pair of imaginary boots.

The streets were coming alive. A man in a ratty apron pushed a cart of small green apples. A woman leaning on a warehouse wall that had once been blue lifted the hem of her moth-eaten dress to show her ankle to a cluster of sailors, who smelled like a brewery. Gulls called overhead; one careened toward the street to snatch a dockworker's oatcake. The man grabbed for the bird, but, of course, he missed and cursed the gull's retreat. A young man with a mop of blond hair clomped toward me wearing shoes that were clearly too large for him. He bumped my elbow and tried to lift the small purse tied to my belt, but I knocked the back of his hand sharply with my knuckles and he released the knot before he could undo the string.

"Not today, darling. Best improve that technique." I winked and continued on.

The street gave way to the docks, where sailors and merchants milled about, yawning and chuckling as they did business. Sea salt and the scent of fresh fish blew through the chilly air, and water licked at this kingdom that had held me in its wicked grip my whole life.

Either way, I'm done with you soon.

Drawing my face into a worried grimace, I approached Rietveld's floating beauty. Sides painted a sunny yellow and a stormy blue, the ship bobbed gently in the sunrise-hued bay and raised its figurehead proudly. The figure was carved to look like one of the Fae's powerful dragons from the Shrouded Mountains. The dragon's glass eyes glittered as I drew the attention of the guards. Rietveld's large form moved on deck, his crew gathered around him in a half-circle.

"What do you want, my lady?" a guard with a chin like a pork chop asked, nicely enough if one ignored the leer.

"I must, must speak to Master Rietveld. He is my only, my only—" I forced a hiccup and pressed my eyes shut like I couldn't stand to say another word. I wouldn't cry because Rietveld knew enough of me to see through that. He had observed the headstrong girl I'd always been and had heard plenty of excuses from my parents. Rietveld would know I was a fake if I tried to weep all over everyone, so I played it all subtle-like.

"You can't speak to the master now, my lady. Maybe come back in two days when he's returned."

"He's sailing out? I must speak to him before he leaves. I must."

The other guards looked behind me and beyond, clearly seeking my chaperone. Big jaw took my arm, not so gently, and turned me away from the gangplank, whose pale pine boards reached from the dock to the ship in one solid pathway that my feet needed to be on. Now.

Timing was everything.

I shoved past Big Jaw and his cronies and started up the gangplank, making sure my slippers smacked the boards as loudly as possible. "Master Rietveld!"

Rough hands pulled me back and off the plank. The ship bobbed as a swell from a larger vessel rolled through the bay. The boat fenders popped up and down, the old knotted and tied bunches of rope guarding the craft from damage against the pier's side.

"Let's get you back to your father, my lady. Where do you live?" Big Jaw passed me off to the most muscled of the group. "Messton will take you there. He's a good one. Don't fret now."

Damn. This was not going well. I was going to have to be louder, which would draw the wrong eyes.

"Master Rietveld! It's Lady Lina Casparji!"

The guards dragged me away from the pier.

Not even step one of this plan could go smoothly? I gritted my teeth and slammed my heel onto the overly muscled man's foot.

22

ZAVI

Zavi had very little time to tie up his life in the ruined castle he'd called home here in Masdam. Lina and the others needed him at Rietveld's ship in less than an hour.

The chill autumn wind bent the branches of the oak standing in front of the old castle's crumbling gatehouse. He hurried past the broken-down great hall and up the cracked stone steps to his room. Wolfling stood waiting at the threshold, his crooked tail wagging in an uneven pattern and his tongue lolling. Zavi leaned down to scratch him properly behind the ears.

"Morning, Wolfling. Thanks for holding down the fort. I brought you a gift, but you have to do something for me first." The strip of dried venison would be tempting to Wolfling since the beast mostly lived on dropped crumbs around the bakery and the occasional less-than-smart rabbit who got a bit too close to town.

Wolfling licked him across the nose, then began snuffling

under the edge of Zavi's cloak.

Zavi gently pushed him back a step and began to gather what little worldly goods he had. He'd have to leave the lute. No place for that while climbing around a ship and trying to not die.

"I'll miss you, friend," he said to the well-worn instrument.

A bone-handled knife the size of his forearm went into his belt and he grabbed the small stash of coins he had in the top drawer of the cabinet by the hammock. He could possibly use the amount to bribe a guard if need be. A pair of fingerless kidskin gloves sat beside the stub of a candle that used to light Zavi's late-night reading habit. Sliding the gloves on, he read from a sheet of parchment he'd started studying the night he'd met Lina. It was from the bookseller two streets down from the guild house.

The passage detailed the history of piratical events in the Masdam area and its Kruid Bay up until two years ago. He'd only been half relieved when he hadn't found his name on it in the neat lines of ink. It would have been revealing to know what possible crimes he'd been a party to as a pirate, but it would have been horrifying as well. There were details on shoreline attacks of warehouses, the taking of vessels leaving the bay, accounts of ransoms demanded after abductions, and instances of killings at the wharf for what appeared to be the fun of it, with no treasure in evidence as motivation for the crimes.

But what if his name wasn't even really Zavi? What if one of these listed pirates was actually him? Or his brother...

He shook off the thought, finished taking this and that from the room and tucking things into pockets and small bags on his belt, then called Wolfling to follow him out of the ruins.

"You know Widow Arend, Wolfling, don't you? She's the one who tended to you when I was sick last summer."

Wolfling grumbled and huffed, trotting to keep up with Zavi's long strides.

"Now, don't be like that. You can't come with me. I will miss your smelly self more than I should, but we can't have you along. You'll bark at all the wrong times. I just know it."

A lump formed in Zavi's throat. Wolfling had been his only friend and he actually would miss the creature a ridiculous amount. But the dog would be safe with the widow.

The widow's house, a two-story plaster and wood monster at least a hundred years old, appeared beyond a row of high hedges. Widow Arend was digging up bulbs in her garden, her hunched back stronger than most humans' healthy ones. She turned and beamed as they approached.

"Bard!"

"Good morning. How is your garden coming along?"

"I have decided to move my bulbs and I'm probably murdering them all with my old hands and my rough ministrations."

"I doubt that. Your flowers bloom brighter than the guild house's."

She waved a hand. "Flatterer."

He bowed shallowly. "I've been called worse."

Wolfling circled Zavi's legs, his usual signal that he wanted very much to leave and go back home. Zavi ruffled the dog's floppy ears.

"Now, how I can help you? Good neighbors are good even out here in the near wilds," the widow said.

They hardly lived in the wilds—more like a stretch of rocky ground between the ancient town walls and the farmland that kept the city alive.

"I appreciate your heart, and I am here to inconvenience you, it's true. Could you adopt old Wolfling? I must leave for a long stretch of time and I don't think I'll be returning."

Definitely not returning. Not after going up against the most dangerous man in Rietveld.

The widow stood slowly, hand on her knee, but Zavi didn't aid her because the one and only time he had, she'd smacked his offered hand away with surprising force, informing him she had no need of physical assistance. She ambled over to Wolfling and rolled her knuckles under his chin. He sighed almost like he wished he didn't enjoy it.

"He'll be stubborn about this, but I want to know he's in good hands," Zavi said, ignoring the pinch in his chest.

"Of course I'll take him. I love the mutt. He keeps the vermin away when he's here and eats the rabbits who try to take my cabbages."

Zavi crouched to rub Wolfling down once more and to look the animal in the eyes. "I'm sorry that I'm leaving, old man. But you'll have all the bunnies you want here." He gave the dog a quick kiss on his ugly head. With a sniff, he rose and gave the widow another bow. "Thank you very much. I hope the Old Ones bless you."

The widow gripped his arm, her fingers so wiry and strong that he was fairly certain she would leave bruises. A grin pulled at his lips.

"You take care of yourself, bard. You aren't the person you were before."

He blinked and started to draw away. He'd never told her

about his missing memories.

"Ach, don't look like that." She released him. "I don't know your secrets. I'm just saying that you aren't that anymore," she said, pointing to his pirate tattoo. "And I know that truth like I know the ground I've been working for fifty years."

A breath left him and he felt lighter despite the sadness of leaving his best friend. He took her hand and kissed it.

"You are a gem, Widow Arend. A gem beyond price."

She giggled, a hint of the young woman she had once been in her eyes, and she held Wolfling with a touch to the head as Zavi left her garden for the last time.

It was time to risk all and get Emiel back.

A flash of memory hit him. He doubled over beyond the widow's hedges, hot, thorn-sharp pain lancing through his side.

His brother's face washed over his thoughts. He had a scar on his chin, which showed white in his dark beard. A scar from a skirmish with a northern lands pirate crew during a raid on the outer islands near the Shrouded Mountains.

He'd been that far north with Emiel.

The memory blurred and then all Zavi saw was blood. So. Much. Blood.

A shiver rode up his spine, and he worked hard to stand straight and walk on. He'd had the dragon tattoo inked on him while up there. Damn, there was so much he didn't know! He walked slowly and looked at his hands. How much blood had he spilled with these hands? How could fingers that fought also play the lute? Exhaling roughly, he sped up. His brother, Lina, and her crew all needed him today. He had to get to the docks and end this curse once and for all.

23

LINA

The guards whirled me around so that I couldn't even see the ship any longer as they dragged me away. Well, I guess this was it. We were finished before we'd even started.

"Stop." A deep voice I knew well had the guards frozen in their tracks.

Rietveld.

Never thought I'd be so glad to see him.

He stood on the gangplank, motioning for them to bring me on board. I exhaled and glared at the guards as I internally summoned up the mask I needed to manipulate Rietveld and keep him distracted as the plan went into play.

They brought me to him, and he seemed even taller than I knew he was. He had this whole air of being absolutely ruthless, something in the way he stood and glanced this way and that, like no one else mattered. The ship bobbed beneath my feet, and my palms grew damp, something that hadn't happened to me in ages.

"To what do I owe this honor, Lady Lina Casparji?" He jerked his chin and his men scattered, hurrying back to their stations.

His beard brushed the embroidered collar of his sweeping cloak; there wasn't a spot of dirt on him. I didn't trust such wild tidiness on a ship. It could only mean too many staff members had been threatened within an inch of their lives to keep their master at a godlike level of perfect appearance. It spoke of cruelty.

"You may have heard I'm in some..." I stopped, swallowing and looking at the sparkling water of the bay and the broad ocean beyond. I set my chin as if I was almost too proud to say what came next. "That I'm in some trouble."

"Aye. That I did. What's it to do with me? Where is your father?" He was no doubt confused as to why I walked alone. Turning back to me, he said quietly, "I can send a man to your father and get this cleared up for you. I would do this as a favor to your father."

There was no subtlety in the way he said *favor*. He wanted Father to owe him.

I licked my lips slowly like I was thinking hard. His gaze shifted to focus on the movement, and his eyes widened for a second. He desired me. Good. That would make this less impossible.

"You have been in the world. You know what I don't. What I'm not permitted to learn," I said.

He crossed his arms, untrusting, but his body remained angled toward me.

"I was hoping I could discuss my possible futures with you. In a way that no other men in my life will do. True possibilities."

Pursing his lips, he ran a hand over his beard. "Interesting invitation. Your father would not like it."

"I can't let others limit my potential. I am a woman, but I am a brave one and one who doesn't care for a mundane life beside a domestically minded husband."

A snort of laughter came from him and he glanced toward the gangplank where his guards were gathered and gesturing.

Big Jaw was missing. I smiled. *Way to go, Star.*

If I had Fae eyesight, I could probably have seen Star at the end of the alleyway they'd nearly pulled me into. She was likely standing in the shadow of the warehouse, using that whistle she'd dug up during a military mission in Veilbury, the place where the Unseelie King had supposedly roamed before returning to his realm. The whistle was runed and many people found the whistle's quiet song impossible to resist. When she played the whistle—which she did very rarely— men especially were drawn to her and their minds were even sometimes fogged. I couldn't hear the music over the sound of the ship, the gulls, and the water, but I would have bet she was using it now.

"If I were to listen to your ideas about the future," Rietveld was saying, "how would that help you? Are you asking for advice? Or are you going to ask for money at some point?"

I made myself smile despite the way his cold eyes and emotionless features twisted my stomach into knots. "See? This is why you are the best one to talk to. You get to the point. You don't fret over manners and play around the conversation."

"When I cut, I aim for the jugular."

Fear grabbed my chest and squeezed. I kept my breathing

steady. "I know. I don't want to waste your time." I set a hand on his chest, then bumped his body with mine as if the water's roll had unsteadied me. I ran my fingers down to his belt before drawing my hand away with two keys I'd nicked from his cloak pocket. One was light, one heavy.

"Then don't." His voice was soft, but it held a promise of pain if I did. "Tell me what you're thinking now and I'll give you my honest opinion. I might even give you money if you intrigue me enough." His gaze slid down my body. It wasn't only business ideas swimming around in his mind.

I swallowed the bitter taste at the back of my mouth and turned slightly, making sure to brush a breast lightly over his forearm. The tip of his tongue touched his lip and he locked his gaze on me.

I was playing with a very dangerous creature here.

Only Zavi was scarier than him. Or he had been before I'd learned more about him and seen his gentle way with the children and with Emerald.

"Master Rietveld! What is that woman doing?"

I pointed at Phoenix, who had grabbed one of the guards by the shirt and was attempting to shake him. Tears flowed from her eyes. She was so, so good.

"I can't believe you!" Phoenix shouted into the shortest guard's surprised face. "Got yourself under my skirts, then left me. I will tell my boss about this. The brewer will kill you! The fines will be hells to pay, I promise you."

Fighting a laugh, I watched Rietveld march down the gangplank and order her taken to the ship's brig. The guards —with Phoenix in tow—passed by and a snippet of Rietveld's hissed whisper carried on the salty breeze.

"Get the madwoman down there before the Watch comes. I have a pretty package I'd like to keep for myself and I don't care to lock horns with the brewer. Man's a pain in my arse."

They dragged Phoenix below deck.

Just as planned.

Once Rietveld had finished giving orders, I rotated away slightly and wiped at my eye as if I were still on the verge of tears. I sniffed loudly and straightened my back like I was so proud but also incredibly sad and desperate. Rietveld had to be eating this up.

A gull cried out in four short bursts. Time to get Rietveld into his quarters.

"Can we go someplace private to talk? I worry that the madwoman drew some attention."

He studied my face, then took my arm and walked me through the door to the captain's quarters. The beeswax-and-ink-scented room was dark, dimly lit by the rising sun washing over the portholes. This ship was too small for grand windows, but the furnishings were fine—leather chairs with bronze buttons, a large walnut desk and chest of drawers, and a series of oil paintings featuring sirens bobbing on lightning-washed seas.

One of those paintings likely hid a safe, and hopefully, one of the keys I'd nicked from Rietveld would open it.

A face appeared in the porthole behind Rietveld's head. Zavi.

"...and I think your father would approve," Rietveld was saying, facing away from the peeking intruder.

The ends of Zavi's black headscarf whipped in the wind as the pirate bard winked at me. He disappeared from the porthole's thick glass and I schooled my features and focused on Rietveld. I hadn't heard a word he'd said.

A series of pops and bangs sounded outside.

Rietveld pushed past and left me alone in the cabin. I went straight to the middle painting and shifted it sideways. No safe. I tried the next one up. Nothing. The one below the first piece. No safes in sight. Damn it all.

As shouting and the bumps and bangs of a scuffle went on outside the door, I hurried around the desk and shoved Rietveld's heavy chair aside. I tugged out the middle drawer of his desk and searched for a false bottom. Nothing.

Sweat beaded along my hairline. I needed to get out there and help. And if we didn't find the blue garnets, or at least some large score, we were doomed.

Where was Rietveld's personal stash? He had to have a safe here somewhere, right?

Bracing a hip against the desk, I shoved it forward a bit and a glint of something metallic caught the scant light. I bent and moved a small crate of ink bottles. And there, on the floor, was a tiny door—like a small trapdoor of sorts, latched shut with a padlock. I fished out the keys I'd nabbed and tried one. No luck. I tucked it back into my pocket, then worked the second into the lock. A crash sounded outside the door. The fight was ongoing. It seemed like Rietveld had gone out there ages ago, but in reality, it had been only a minute. Breathing to keep myself calm and my hands steady, I turned the key and the lock unlatched. I threw the little door open to find a tiny velvet bag and a stack of gold coins.

I couldn't stop smiling.

Pocketing both, I shut the door with a foot and hastily rounded the desk. I cracked the door to see Star battling

Rietveld and the last of the sailors and guards still there and standing—four large men whom she was keeping at bay with kicks and swipes of her largest dagger.

She was toying with them.

"Finish it and let's be done with this," I said. "I've got the first part of our mission completed."

Rietveld left the fight and lunged for me, rage burning in his eyes. I whipped out the velvet sack and held it over the ship's side.

"Ah, ah, ah, Master Rietveld. I'd think twice."

He lurched to a stop, eyes going wide and his nostrils flaring. "Lying bitch."

"I do love a good fib. Now, we have a deal to make. Will you call off your men?"

I leaned around to see behind him. Star had one man by the hair and another frozen with a blade to his throat. The third was missing and I assumed he'd gone overboard by her hand or foot.

"Oh, never mind. It seems my associate has taken care of that particular problem."

"Your other associate," Rietveld hissed, laying on a sour tone, "is stuck in the brig." With a flick of his thick fingers, he threw something into the bay. "And now, you have no key to get her out without me. The only copy is at my gambling establishment."

Chuckling, I covered my mouth. "A good effort, but you're lacking information," I said, still holding the sack over the side.

"I'll just call the Watch."

I let the sack slip down a bit in my grip and he jerked as if to grab it before stopping himself. "I don't think you will. In fact, I believe you and what's left of your crew will calmly disembark and keep your lips sealed shut until I toss this to you as we shove off from shore."

"You won't toss shite, you lying bitch."

Zavi popped up from the gangplank like a jack from his box and Rietveld's lip curled.

Zavi leaned on the railing and crossed his arms. "I'd have thought a man like yourself would have better vocabulary. Really, I'm disappointed." Turning slightly, he kicked the planks into the water. A splash sounded. "And sadly," Zavi continued, "I'm afraid you aren't going anywhere until you tell me what you did with my brother."

Zavi stilled in the way that predators do before striking. He was lethal. The hairs on the back of my neck and along my arms stood on end, warning me. But Zavi remained where he was, his eyes flashing with what looked like pain.

His broad chest moved in a deep breath, then he stalked toward Rietveld, never once blinking as his boots knocked along the deck.

Oh, no, no, no, no, we weren't doing this. The Watch would be here any minute. Our plan was only halfway completed. We didn't have a plan for a confrontation between Zavi and Rietveld. I knew that would be too explosive, too risky. We had wanted to keep this quick and be gone before Rietveld had a chance to lay eyes on Zavi—or vice versa.

But now, Zavi was circling Rietveld like a lion ready for a filling meal.

❀ 24 ❀

ZAVI

Zavi's heart beat so fast and so hard that his teeth rattled. This was the man who had stolen his life and his brother. Here was his nightmare, and Zavi wasn't about to go the peaceful route if he could get Rietveld to talk.

Rietveld smiled and Zavi had a dagger at the man's throat in the blink of an eye. He pressed the blade to Rietveld's skin. A line of blood ran down the front of Rietveld's tunic, staining the pale blue wool and gold-thread embroidery along the neckline.

"Where is Emiel? Where is the curse piece?"

White teeth flashing, Rietveld grinned like a madman. "It's infuriating when someone gets in the way of one's business, isn't it?"

"Is that why you cursed me? Because I disrupted a business deal? That's why you wiped my memory and left me for dead just outside the city walls?"

"I should have simply run you through, but it has been

rather entertaining watching you squirm on my hook." Rietveld's gaze cut to Moth and Star, who had come up beside her. "Do they know who you really are? I would guess they don't." He laughed, and Zavi's knife cut the side of the man's neck. But Rietveld kept on chuckling like the blood running down his front didn't matter in the least.

Zavi moved the knife to hover at Rietveld's groin. "Enough of your games. Tell me where the curse piece is and what you did with my brother, or I'm going to start relieving you of body parts."

Finally, a hint of fear showed in the man's eyes, but his focus shifted to the dock, only a few feet off, since the ship remained tied up.

"Zavi." Lina's voice held a warning.

Zavi turned to see the pier crowded with enemies. The Watch, Lina's father—Lord Casparji—and her horrible fiancé gathered with bows and swords drawn.

Lina's fiancé, Drukker, stepped forward out of the shadow of the large black-cloaked Watch member. "Unhand Master Rietveld before we come aboard and we might let you live."

Zavi looked to Lina and Star. What did they want him to do? He had an idea, but it would be very, very messy. His Fae blood roared in his veins, and that more feral side of him demanded action.

Lina jerked her head toward the compass box, but before she could finish mouthing whatever idea she had, her father and two Watch members had tugged the ship close and the lot of them were boarding, swords flashing. An arrow zipped over Zavi's and Rietveld's heads, and there was no more time to plot and strategize.

Zavi knocked the heel of his boot on the deck three times.

The deck exploded in a flurry of splinters and light. The compass box, which they guessed held the curse piece, dropped below deck, into the brig where Phoenix would be prepared and waiting. Rietveld stumbled backward, but Zavi caught him long enough to hit him in the temple with an elbow and knock him out.

Letting go of his fear of his skills, Zavi let his Fae side take over.

He grabbed Rietveld and threw him over the side, moving as fast his Fae blood allowed. Strength surged through him. He whipped around and cut down a slender Watchman with two quick cuts of his knife.

Star and Lina kicked and used the heels of their palms to strike at two others. Lina's man went down groaning, but Star's Watchman was a better fighter and she had to keep at it.

Zavi shot a foot into Lina's father's gut, driving him backward. The awful excuse for a person dropped into the bay with a great shout.

Lina spat into Drukker's face, then kneed him in the stones. The man doubled over, cursing her name. Zavi bumped the man with a shoulder and sent him into the drink too.

Blood boiling, Zavi whirled and struck another man, another, and another, until the deck was littered with those knocked out or dead.

Shouts from the pier erupted, announcing more Watchmen and most likely some of the king's men too, and Lina gripped Zavi's arm. "Can you get us out of here?"

"I can." He began barking orders, hoping Star, the newly freed Phoenix, and Lina understood his commands. They untied the ship, dumped attackers into the water, unfurled the sails, and pushed off. Arrows would fly soon. They had to clear the bay and get into open water. This was a fine vessel and would move fast, but whatever ship the Watch and the king's men ended up on would be quite capable of catching up. Zavi had to get this craft going quickly and gain enough distance to at least put them into the dangerous strait that ran between Deigs and Saxonion, just before the border of Laqqara—where all of Deigs got their spices and where Lina had told Zavi she planned to find her freedom.

A memory of Emiel flashed through his mind's eye. Blood. The sea beyond, dark and glittering. Rietveld's cold eyes. In this blurry memory, Zavi watched the crime lord take hold of someone and shove the person at his brother.

Fire shot across Zavi's stitched side, then slithered over his stomach and into his very bones. Black spots swam in front of his eyes and he gripped the ship's wheel to keep from falling over.

A volley of arrows hit the mast, the deck, and the sail. He ducked, heat lancing the tip of his pointed ear as one arrow nicked him. But they kept on.

"Everyone alive?" he called across the deck.

Lina, Star, and Phoenix called out, "Aye!"

They cleared the bay and entered the wide ocean. A salted wind blasted his cheeks and he inhaled deeply, savoring the scent of the sea. The sandy slopes of the kingdom's edge ran southwest, marking the direction they needed to travel. He set a course for the strait, but he couldn't completely leave Deigs yet because there was always the chance Emiel remained there, trapped somehow by Rietveld. But they did have to get away from the Watch and the king's men. Once he broke the curse, he'd know what exactly to do and how his brother fared. At least, he hoped he would. Pain punched him again and he gripped his side, wincing at the curse's powerful magic.

Lina, with her wind-tossed red hair pulled into a thick braid and her eyes shining, drew him away from the helm. She shoved what was left of the compass box into his hands. "It's too much to hope they'll give up or that Rietveld dies in the water. Get that thing out and uncurse yourself before you die and leave us floundering. I know boats, but I'm not a sailor. We need you to get out of this alive. Plus, I've grown fond of you, bard. I'd rather you stay alive. At least for now."

He swallowed the guilt of arranging the robbery of her stash and forced a smile through the two types of pain he was currently experiencing. The men at the pier were still attempting to fire arrows, but the ship was far enough away that the volleys fell into the water. But a ship would be on Zavi and the rest soon, if it wasn't already. He couldn't spot one moving away from the piers yet, but it wouldn't take too long.

Sitting on a barrel labeled watered wine, he tore the box's lid away, tugging it from its battered hinges. The whole thing smelled like Phoenix's explosives. Inside, a broken compass lay beside a complicated wheel lock that appeared to be guarding a false bottom. He could have smashed the box further, but what if he damaged the curse piece? Not worth the risk.

Holding the box close, he turned the dial and listened for clicks, but the noise of the sea and the children who had finally emerged from their hiding spot made that job nearly impossible. A bark sounded and Zavi sat up straight only to see Emerald flying low over the deck and Wolfling bounding toward him with Sanne and Bram in tow.

Sanne pet Wolfling's head as Zavi held the box between his knees and leaned close to the dog's snout.

"I've never been so happy to smell something so rancid," he said, laughing as Wolfling licked his jaw. He kissed the old monster on one crumpled ear.

Sanne lifted Wolfling's other ear. "When Star had us hide in the cargo hold, I thought your dog would bark and give us away. But he was so good!"

Bram reached over his sister to scratch Wolfling's scruff. "It's true. What's his name?"

"Wolfling. How did you find him?"

"When we were waiting on you, he came to the hideout," Bram said. "Mother told us he was likely your dog and had followed your scent there. Lina gave him and Emerald a piece of roast she nicked from the butcher shop."

Lina looked over her shoulder and grinned. "You owe me a breakfast, bard."

"If I get this open, I'll owe you more than that and might live to actually pay back my debts." Zavi turned back to Wolfling. "I hope you were polite when you left Widow Arend."

Wolfling barked.

"Don't be sour with me, dog. You're the one who promised to stay and came anyway." He scratched Wolfling's throat roughly and Sanne watched with shining eyes.

"Can you really talk to him?" Sanne asked. "Because

you're, you know." The little girl's gaze went to his pointed ears.

"No, but I like to pretend."

"Pretending is for children. Not for you."

"You see, that's the great thing about being an adult," Zavi said. "You can decide what rules to break and break them to your heart's content."

Phoenix had walked up and now put a hand on her hip. "But there will be consequences when you break rules, whether you are a child or an adult. Isn't that right?"

He chuckled. "Indeed. Sometimes the punishment is worth it. Sometimes not." He'd meant to joke, but his tone had fallen flat as his mind twisted around a question. What rule had he broken to be cursed as he was? What had he done to anger Rietveld?

"Come on, love," Phoenix said, gently pulling Sanne away. "Let's give the bard some time to work on his puzzle box."

"Good luck!" Sanne waved as she pranced away ahead of her mother.

Phoenix tugged an arrow from the deck, then waved an impatient hand. "Let him work, Bram. Come on."

Bram and Wolfling joined Sanne and they ran a circle around the deck with Emerald soaring over the dog's head.

Zavi went back to the lock. The wind eased off and the ship slowed, which was bad for their progress but good for noise level. The lock clicked at the twenty-two on the dial. After a few more moments of turning the cool brass knob, another click sounded, this time on the number five. The final click was set at either three or two. He tried one combination of those numbers and rotations, then another, then another, until he began to forget what he'd tried and what he hadn't.

Lina shouted his name. "Am I on the same track? I haven't gone off too much, have I?"

He eyed the sun and the lay of the cliffs. "You're doing well."

Again and again, he worked the dial. Backward two turns before stopping at the second number, then forward to the last. No, that wasn't right. Forward once then backing up to the second number...

The lock refused to budge.

The sun began to set and a black slash on the sea behind them said they were being chased. They would have to enter the strait before he could uncurse himself. He would have to sail those dangerous waters, because he was the only one with the proper experience. It was incredibly troubling that the fighting and the sailing remained whole and strong in his mind while his own brother was little more than a ghost to him. Shivering, he shook off that thought.

No, not a ghost. He lives. I would know if he was dead, wouldn't I?

25
LINA

"Zavi!" My voice was hoarse and my throat raw. "I never thought I'd say this to anyone ever, but it's time to be a pirate again."

Blowing out a breath, he stood and handed me the compass box that he hadn't yet unlocked. "I wonder if Emerald could melt the lock without damaging the piece."

"It's a thought. One we will deal with once we are safely through this nasty spot and not smashed on the rocks."

"I don't remember sailing this, but it's as if my body does." He squinted at the sun beaming through the clouds, then barked some orders. Eyeing me again, he grinned. "What's that look for?"

"I like it when you are all commanding."

"That surprises me."

"Why?"

"Because of the awful males you've dealt with. I'd have thought you wanted the rest of the ones you must interact with to leave off the ordering about."

"You're not like them." I bit my lip, realizing it was true and not just a light conversational piece I was throwing into the wind. Zavi wasn't like any males I knew. Not even a little bit. He cared for the children. He followed my orders during the job, well, mostly. And he'd been vulnerable with all of us, telling us about his plight and about his brother.

Zavi's eyes twinkled. "That's the best compliment I've had in ages. Now, get your arse to work!"

I glared but couldn't quite keep from smiling. "Eh, now, watch that tone."

He winked and my heart stuttered. Ugh. I really did like him far more than was wise. I had a life to build and no time for romance.

I called for Phoenix, Star, and Bram, and we set to doing what we could with the sails and lines, Zavi giving us tips and adjustments as we rolled through the increasingly rough waters. Hours passed and still no sign of a ship following us. It wouldn't be long though...

The pale sand of Deigs' southern coast lined the white-capped water to the southwest and the current was doing its best to drive us into the rocks that hid there. All my life, my father had bemoaned this part of the trip to Laqqara—the deadly Dragon Skull Strait. It had claimed one of his ships and lost a king's sum of saffron and cinnamon. We'd had little to eat that year despite the wealth my family had mustered up over the centuries.

My old childhood friend, Sophia, and I used to make up stories about it. We'd both been through it—her more than me though since she had a home in Laqqara and traveled with her family seasonally to arrange trade deals. Once the kidnapping happened when I was fifteen and Sophia was twelve and she was killed by the pirates, her family never returned to Masdam to see my father or arrange deals. I'd heard they had gone back to their ancestral home. I truly hoped that had been accurate gossip because it affected my future.

The wind whistled over the sails' lines and drew my focus back to the present. Water splashed over the side and Emerald lifted from Star's shoulder by the bow to fly higher.

"It wouldn't be bad if we had that seeing glass up and working again," Zavi called from his spot at the helm. "Did that treasure make it into the bags the children brought?"

"Oh, it would help you spot outcroppings?"

"Yes, and more."

I waved a hand and hurried to get it from the captain's quarters, where I'd stashed all of my personal items. Back on deck, I motioned for Emerald and she came quickly, her gaze darting this way and that as I tied the glass to her like we had earlier. She seemed to understand what we needed. Dragons were such a wonder!

Rushing across the wet deck, I delivered the looking glass to Zavi. He held it aloft.

"Are dragons always this clever?" he asked.

"I think so, if the stories are true. When you get your memories back, you'll have to tell us if you have some dragon adventure stories in your past."

"I hope I do."

The mirror showed a blur of black and Zavi must have seen it too because he shouted new orders to Star and Phoenix. Sweat bloomed across Zavi's forehead, making his dark blond hair stick to his tan skin. His tattooed fingers gripped the mirror and the ship's wheel and so help me if I didn't wish for us to be done with all of this silly survival stuff so that I could have those hands on me.

"Is my sailing prowess earning me points right now?" he asked above the crash of waves and the snap of the sails.

"It is."

"Are you silently coming up with ridiculous metaphors like *he can sail my strait anytime* or *I wish he'd batten down my hatches? Please say yes.*"

I snorted a laugh.

"We might die," Star called. "Can you please show the appropriate level of fear? If not, Phoenix is going to start worrying you've both lost your wits."

Zavi and I chuckled in unison and warmth filled me. It was so odd to feel both incredibly frightened and completely at ease.

I couldn't help but grin at the vicious strait that was trying to murder us. I was here, free, laughing with whomever I chose, and doing exactly what I wanted.

I was finally free.

Zavi hissed, his white teeth flashing in the darkening night. "I need that sun to stop blinding me in the mirror. This is less than easy, I'm afraid, despite my experience."

"It wouldn't be called Dragon Skull Strait if it were."

"That's the name?" He whistled. "I wonder if that rock there extends. It almost looks like the skull of a ridiculously large mountain dragon lying down in the water. I feel like there is something jutting out; my gut says there is."

"Mountain dragons don't get that big, so I'm guessing it's simply a fun name, but maybe you're right. I hope you're right."

I wondered if he would balk at my calling it fun, but he

grinned wickedly and turned the ship's wheel, his muscles straining under the rolled ends of his tunic sleeves. Nope, he thought it was fun too.

As we sailed into the tightest part of the strait, all conversation died and I held my breath, unable to tear my gaze from the churning water and the rocks that glistened like glass under the afternoon sun. They would slice this ship into threads if we sailed too close and the freedom we'd fought for would end before it had a chance to truly begin.

The ship dove over a wave and leaned harshly to port. Sanne shouted from belowdecks, her shrill young voice cutting through the smashing waves. The current pulled at the ship like a great hand beneath the water. A bang echoed from the hull and Zavi's eyes widened as he steered and watched the mirror.

"Higher, Emerald! If you can hear me, higher, please!"

I looked up to see the dragon flying higher, her seeing glass reflecting the piercingly bright sun.

"Great job!" Zavi eased the ship's wheel in a direction opposite to what I would've tried in his shoes.

The ship shuddered and lurched. Wolfling's barks carried on the wind, but I didn't turn to see if the dog was on deck.

The strait poured into the undulating sea and it was over.

Zavi exhaled loudly and the hand holding the mirror dropped to his side. He glanced my way. "We're through."

I leapt up, shouting and cheering. Star and Phoenix joined in and soon the children were on deck with the dog, singing and doing a makeshift jig near the bow.

"I think it's time for a party," I said.

Zavi handed me the mirror as Emerald landed. "But I need to get this curse piece free."

"Are you in pain right now?"

"No."

I put my hands on my hips. Fear flitted through his features, tightening his eyes. He was worried about whether or not the piece was there at all. Understandable. And worried what his memories would hold. He needed some time to breathe.

"Maybe your mind needs a break from thinking," I said. "Just a few laughs and a little dancing. That's all I ask."

"And a cup of wine perhaps?"

"Definitely."

As the sun set, Zavi found a cove off the coast—a wild and sparsely wooded area that didn't appear to be claimed by Saxonion or Laqqara. We brought the sails down and dropped anchor. Wine and what little food we'd stashed in the children's bags were brought out for a humble feast.

I sat near Zavi on two low crates beside the helm. We shared a cup of wine, handing it back and forth.

"What is your favorite food?" I asked.

His smile showed the point of one of his fangs. "Oranges."

"Fancy."

"I'm a fancy fellow. What can I say? I have been living in a castle for a while now, so it makes sense my tastes run rich."

"A castle?"

"They're ruins actually. On the outside of town."

"I do remember you mentioning something about that. Next question. Besides the obvious pirate tattoo, have you found out what your inkings mean? Perhaps by asking around or from a memory that slipped through the curse?"

He held out his hands and studied them, tilting his head

this way and that. The edges of his full lips turned down as if looking at them saddened him.

"It feels so wrong not knowing the reason why my own hands look the way they do."

"I bet. It has to be incredibly frustrating."

"Frightening, too," he said, a world of pain washing over his gaze.

I longed to touch his cheek and tell him it would be all right, but it was possible his life would never be all right.

He cleared his throat and fisted the fingers that were painted with black swords, skulls, arrows, and water. "This hand probably denotes prowess in battle."

"What do the water drops mean?" I asked.

He regarded me with one dark blond eyebrow lifted. "I think that's blood."

I grimaced. "Oh. Right. That's...intense."

Blowing out a breath, he nodded and held up the hand with the dragon inking. "I'm guessing I either had a nickname that revolved around dragons or that I spent some time in the Shrouded Mountains with the Mist Knights."

"That would be amazing."

"And scary."

I huffed a laugh. "Yes."

Finishing the wine, I scooted closer to him. The warmth of his body was pleasant and I liked how I could feel the vibration of his voice when I was leaning on him.

"Is it my turn to ask questions?" He leaned back and snatched another bottle of wine we'd found in the cargo hold. With his teeth, he uncorked it, then he poured a measure into the cup.

"Ask away."

"To our escape." He downed a swallow, then gave the drink to me.

"To our escape." I lifted the cup and drank.

"First question," he said, his voice low and serious. "What is your favorite thing to do when you aren't nicking shiny objects like a raven?"

"I enjoy dancing."

"I did see that at the Port Day celebration."

I nodded. "I also love reading."

"Really?"

"What? Don't I look like someone who reads?"

He held out his hand. "Settle down, now," he said, grinning. "I meant no offense. I just haven't seen you with a book."

"Since we met, I haven't had tons of spare time."

"What types of stories do you enjoy? Or are you into researching facts and histories?"

"Oh, not that. No. Phoenix loves that sort of thing, but I adore romances."

"Ah." He gave me a sultry look. "For the naughty bits?"

"How else is a sheltered Masdam lady meant to learn such wonderful things? I can't very well question Phoenix and Star about all of my many curiosities."

"I think you could."

"I'd rather see how things play out in a scenario than just discuss them over the dinner table."

Chuckling, he leaned his forearms on his spread knees. One of those knees brushed mine and our thighs met, sending heat coursing through me. I downed another gulp of wine.

"You always surprise me," he said.

"Is that good or bad in your opinion?" I don't know why I cared. I never cared what men—or males, as Fae men were called—thought. Especially Fae males. But Zavi was different, and I couldn't help but lower my defenses a little with him. It was such a beautiful night and Phoenix, Star, and I were well on our way to achieving our dream.

"Good. Very good," he said. "Now, how did you and Phoenix become friends?"

"I used to buy bread with Mother at the bakery where Phoenix worked after her husband threw her out. She made these amazing little knots of chocolate bread."

"Why did he throw her out? Besides the fact that he is a horrible person."

"She found out he had a mistress, and he decided he might as well make the mistress his wife. But," I said, taking a sip, "he is alone now. The mistress had enough money to leave Masdam. Although I'm sure that woman was awful, sleeping with a married man and all, but she inadvertently inspired us to plan for our own freedom. I'd already befriended Star, who had been keeping an eye on the bakery at night. She had to drive off a group of younger lads who had decided knocking off unmanned shops was a fun evening activity. Star and I wanted Phoenix to join our life of stealing from foolish men."

Zavi chuckled. "You are so very good at it."

"Thank you kindly." I tipped an imaginary cap to him. "One night, we invited Phoenix to join us. She refused the first five times we asked, but she eventually gave in because we are the most fun."

"And the most annoying," Star said from where she was cutting up an apple for Sanne.

Phoenix grabbed Star's hand and dragged her into a dance of sorts. She sang a tune, then looked to Zavi.

Star pretended to die from Phoenix's singing, sticking her tongue out and making Bram laugh and Wolfling bark. "Why don't you find an instrument and sing us a real song, bard?" Star asked.

Oooh, yes. I pulled Zavi to his feet. "I like that idea. I bet there's one near the hammocks belowdecks."

My heart was like starlight, shimmering and floating high in the night sky. This was what life was meant to be.

❧ 26 ❧

ZAVI

The lute they'd found was far finer than the one Zavi was used to playing, and its mellow sound carried over the dancers in a swirl of well-rounded notes. He hoped his voice would be a welcome addition to the jaunty tune.

"To the gardens,

to the sea,

to the fields where the sun shines free,

Come with me,

sing with me,

be with me where the sun shines free..."

Lina's red braid whirled around her waist as she spun near Star and Phoenix, who each kicked up a foot in time with the song's beats. Wolfling leapt up at Emerald, who blew sparks at him, the two playing like old friends. Sanne and Bram held hands and danced in a circle.

Zavi could almost forget about his troubles for a while.

The ship following them had disappeared after the strait, so they were most likely safe for the time being. His mind did need to relax for a bit, like Lina had suggested.

The gorgeous woman eyed him mischievously and stepped away from her friends. She stomped dramatically as Zavi lowered the pitch of the song and sang its last notes.

"To me, my love,

to the green,

we go to find the fire between,

you and me and me and you,

only now for the heart beats true."

He set the lute on a coil of rope and took Lina into his arms.

"You smell divine," he whispered into her neck, inhaling that peony and honey scent she had.

She was soft in his arms, pressing her curves against him and waking his cock. "You do too. Can we maybe talk for a bit in the captain's quarters?"

"If you keep rubbing against me like the sweet kitten that you are, there won't be as much discussion as you might hope for."

Taking his hand and leading him away, she laughed. "Let's see how it goes, hmm?"

Behind them, Star strummed the lute, the tune growing into a familiar reel. The rest had taken up dancing again and he was glad that he and Lina would have their privacy amidst the distraction.

With only a pale sheen of moonlight strewn across the bed, he was glad again for his Fae eyesight because Lina had already started to undress.

"Am I supposed to join in or just enjoy the show?" he asked, his voice rough.

The moon-white skin of Lina's long neck and bare shoulders, the soft curve of her lips—it all nearly undid him right then and there. He swallowed, trying to steel himself so he'd last longer than two glorious minutes.

She kicked off her slippers. "Will you unlace this?" Turning, she shifted her braid over her shoulder, baring her back to him.

He undid her corset and loosened it, exposing more of that glowing skin of hers. He set his mouth at the base of her neck and dragged his lips to her shoulder. He was rewarded with a quick gasp and goosebumps that trailed along her skin.

She eased her dress off, then stood and looked at him. Only a dagger strapped to her thigh and a half-length shift covered her maddening body.

He knelt and set his lips over the curve of her breast. She inhaled, her chest moving him slightly, then she tugged at his tunic and cloak, her desire obvious. Complying, he removed cloak, belt, and tunic, leaving only his trousers and boots. But that body of hers called him back before he could finish undressing. Bending close, he kissed her sweet lips, exploring her mouth with his tongue. His heart stuttered as she welcomed the kiss, drawing her own tongue over his. Blood rushed through him as well as that Fae urge to claim her both in word and deed. Forcing himself to hold back made stars dance before his eyes.

"I probably want you more than you realize," he whispered, wishing she could read his mind so he wouldn't have to voice this incredible need, this desire that he knew would never go away, not even if he had to break away from her.

She set a hand against the hard ridge in his trousers and grinned into his cheek. "I don't know. It's pretty obvious."

He laughed into her hair, then undid her braid, loosening the thick locks so they fell over her shoulders and breasts.

"You're the most beautiful thing I've ever seen, firefly. You absolutely glow."

Taking his face in her hands, she pressed a closed-lipped, rather chaste kiss to his lips. Something about it felt...reverent. "I'm so glad to have found you."

Afraid to say more, and worried the spell of this moment might break, he focused on giving her every bit of pleasure he could.

Her shift slipped from her shoulders with one quick tug, and then he was on his knees again, licking his way across her nipples and making her gasp and arch toward him. His cock strained against its confinement. She joined him on her knees. With torturously slow motions, she unbuttoned his trousers, then she slid her cool fingers around him. He hissed and drew back, the world growing fuzzy. Fire blazed through every inch of him.

"Is this all right?" she asked.

He opened his eyes—he hadn't realized he'd closed them —and looked at her genuine, petal-soft features.

"It's so much more than all right," he choked out. "It's the absolute best damn feeling I've ever experienced."

Her smile lit the room, then her gaze turned delightfully wicked and she blushed furiously.

She stood, putting him at eye-level with her perfect feminine form. "I don't know what I'm doing, but I've heard of kissing in other ways."

He gripped her thighs and, using his teeth, tore off the dagger and its strap. The weapon clattered to the floor. The ship tilted as she dug her fingers into his tangled hair as he kissed his way from the indent of the dagger strap to the apex of her thighs. His tongue darted into the velvet darkness there, and he hummed, lost in the scent of her, the feel of her, and the amazing fact that he was about to take her in every way she wanted. She moaned and held his head and her body quaked in his grip. He felt goosebumps shiver down the backs of her legs as she let out a small cry.

Suddenly, he couldn't wait to have her.

He stood abruptly, gathered her up, and set her on the chest of drawers, which were at exactly the perfect height.

"You're sure about this?" He certainly hoped so or he was going to be horribly uncomfortable for a very, very, very long time.

She kissed him, her fingers grasping the sides of his head and her thumbs rubbing across the sensitive tips of his ears. "So sure."

He shuddered, his body quivering with the need to be inside her and to claim her as his own. She wouldn't be his, not really. He knew she wanted freedom, and he wanted that for her, but maybe he could claim this one moment in time.

He pulled her legs higher around him and eased himself into her. There was no greater sensual delight and he fought hard for control. She groaned and gripped his shoulders, urging him to go on. Gently driving into her warmth again and again, his body trembled and demanded urgency, but he continued slowly and steadily. She felt like pleasure itself, the exact definition of the word. Heat, devotion, longing, acceptance... This astounding woman with her bravery in fighting those who would chain her down and her clever mind and her laugh. Life existed only in the way she held him and waited for him to claim her.

"Zavi," she said, breathless. "Pick me up. I want to be in your arms."

Letting go of the way he normally hid his Fae speed and strength, he lifted her and held her so that she could take her pleasure on him with her own movements. She gasped, then she rocked her hips forcefully as they spun into what felt like one being, joined in body, soul, and heart.

Once they were spent, he laid her gently on the bed. He spread her hair all around and marveled in its many shades of ruby, garnet, dusk, and dawn. Peppering her with kisses, he slid a hand down her smooth stomach until he stopped to draw circles on her hip.

He was utterly, completely, and totally content.

"We can talk now, if you want," he said, grinning down at her.

"I'm not sure I can find the words."

He kissed her temple and inhaled her scent. "I understand that. There are no words to adequately describe how much I want you." How much not only his body but his heart and soul wanted her too.

Her lovely mouth turned up with a smile and she twirled her finger in his hair.

"I want to talk about us," she said, her tone shy and tentative. "About what might be. But I worry you'll find someone in your memory once your curse is broken. Perhaps you are sworn to and love someone else. I'm selfish to take you tonight, knowing that. A villain for doing it, really."

Remaining propped on one elbow, he ravished her with kisses and flicks of his tongue. His hand studied the soft rise of her breasts, the dip of her belly, and the fluttering pulse at the base of her neck.

"If this is villainy," he said, "then I vow to be the worst criminal in all the realms."

A laugh made her move against him. "You didn't even take off your boots."

"There wasn't time for that."

She nodded. "It did feel like that, didn't it?"

"I couldn't have waited for proper shoe removal. Not tonight. Maybe for our future trysts, I'll consider it." He hadn't meant to say future. His stomach tightened. What would she say back?

"But perhaps that was part of why it was so very good."

He chuckled and scratched his chin. "Well, I guess we should experiment to see for ourselves. What do you think?" Wrapping a hand loosely around her throat, he kissed her hard.

She snagged his arm and drew him on top of her, linking one leg over him. "Yes. I do think the subject is worthy of exploration."

Leaning to the side, he toed off his boots, then tugged his trousers off. She moved to her stomach, shifted her weight to her elbows, and cupped her chin in her hands. The shape of her round bottom stirred his Fae blood into a frenzy, and he fisted his hands in an attempt to restrain himself.

A laugh danced through her eyes. "You are very pretty, you know that?" she said to him.

"I prefer dangerously seductive."

Her eyes closed halfway and the tip of her tongue touched her bottom lip. "You'll need to convince me of that."

He growled, low in his throat. "Not a problem."

Even if he couldn't mate fully with Lina, from this moment, he knew she would forever be the main feature of every single dream.

27

LINA

He was the most thrilling and gorgeous male I'd ever laid eyes on. He was here, stalking up the bed as I watched him over my shoulder. His slightly slitted pupils were so fascinating and I finally allowed myself to be thrilled by the dangerous beauty of them. I had to be in some sort of fantastical afterlife. We must have perished in the strait and this was my heaven.

And that growl curled my toes.

Taking me under the arms, he lifted me and set me against the sloping wall of the room. The wooden boards pressed into my chest, but I didn't mind with Zavi hard against my back. I rolled my hips to press harder into his length. Another growl rumbled through him, vibrating across my back and making my mouth water.

His breath stirred the air beside my ear and his lips grazed my earlobe. I shuddered, want coursing through me like the beat of a song.

"You want dangerous?" His voice was low and made the hairs on the base of my neck rise.

Definitely. "Yes," I whispered.

Winding my hair in one fist, he bumped my knees farther apart. He slid into me, more easily this time, and he was far less careful. Starting slow, he worked into a fast pace. Every push of his hips sent a wave of pleasure through my entire body. I was dissolving. He yanked my hair back and nipped the side of my throat as he thrust forward again.

"I want to claim you, Lina. Let me be the fire you want, Moth."

I set my palms against the wall and shut my eyes to focus on the pleasure. "But fires burn."

"True. And I might draw you into my curse," he said with a gruff voice, his movements changing to an agonizingly slow rhythm that had me at the very precipice of shattering.

We were playing with words as well as with our bodies, but an underlying drive to flesh out our fears came to life between us—bright as the flick of a flint in the darkness. But I trusted him now. I believed in him. It didn't matter that he was Fae and male. He was Zavi, and I wanted him to be mine. Not just tonight. But always. I wanted his quick tongue, his kindness, the way he was ready to dive into any adventure.

I wanted him. "If you are my curse, so be it. I will die in your fire and savor the feel of the burn."

He pressed his head against mine. "Lina. My mate."

I set a hand on his sea-salted cheek. "Zavi."

Increasing his pace, he rocked his hips hard into me until we both fell from the precipice and burned as one.

❧ 28 ☙

LINA

After a quick doze delightfully tangled in Zavi's arms and legs, I woke him and sent him off to work on that compass box again. I washed in the leftover water I found in the ewer and went through a stash of deep red Laqqaran-style clothing Bram had brought in his bag. I slid on the type of tunic and loose trousers that Laqqarans usually wore, and I made my way to the deck where Star, Phoenix, and Bram were busy following Zavi's distracted orders on how to get the ship out of the cove and into open water.

I joined Phoenix near the mainsail.

"He's smitten, Moth. I hope you are good with having him tag along on our Laqqaran adventure for the long term. Do you think the Ofandrus family will have an issue if he joins us there?"

"I have no idea what to expect. I was too afraid to write to them."

Father would have found that letter, no doubt, and made

my life even worse. The family we planned to stay with until we had our feet on the ground were old friends. I had no idea if they still lived where they once had, but it was our best shot at finding a safe place to figure out our new lives. I had been to their ancestral home three times during my childhood. Hopefully, my feet would remember the way.

"I did it!" Zavi called over the rush of waves. He held up the box. "But there isn't just one piece. There are two."

Bram manned the helm as the rest of us hurried over to look. Inside the half-broken false bottom of the compass box, two emerald triangles sat side by side, one lighter than the other.

I touched Zavi's shoulder. "Any ideas on who else Rietveld might have cursed?" I didn't want to say out loud what I was thinking.

"My brother, of course." A world of pain crossed over his handsome features and I wished I could ease his agony.

Star crossed her arms. "Well, let's get your memory back, shall we?"

ZAVI MOVED THE PIECES FROM PALM TO PALM WHILE Phoenix secured a needle and thread from our stash. Star burned her best dagger over a candle to make certain it was clean for the cut she'd have to make in Zavi's side.

I held the ship's wheel while Bram, Sanne, Wolfling, and Emerald each held a corner of a blanket from the captain's quarters and laid it out in the most complicated way possible.

"Thank you," I said. "That will be a perfect spot for the surgery."

"Plenty of light, at least," Phoenix said as she arranged the needle and thread on a square of parchment.

Zavi sat beside her and stripped off his belt and tunic.

Star walked up with her knife, her eyes studying Zavi's face. "You ready?"

Sanne had wandered over and taken her mother's hand.

"Have you done this before?" he asked Star.

"Yes. On the battlefield. I can't promise you'll have as neat of a scar this time."

"The apothecary two streets from the Guild Hall did it for me last time."

Wolfling whimpered and curled up beside Zavi. He ran a hand over the scruffy dog's side, then lay back with his hands behind his head.

"That apothecary is a legend," Star said as she eyed Zavi's old wound. "You'll heal faster because of your Fae blood, right?"

"Yes." Zavi gazed at the cloudless sky.

The sunrise had bled all the dark shades of night away but left no color in its place. The sky looked like a scraped page of parchment.

"I really hope the water stays calm," I said quietly.

Star cut him open and pulled out the memory stone. Despite the blood, the object was darkly beautiful with its deep green color and expertly carved runes. I held a fold of linen at Zavi's side as he lifted the darker of the two pieces and set it into its slot on the artifact.

A blast of gold light blinded me. Sanne shouted in alarm and the sound of Emerald's squawk penetrated the morning.

When my sight returned, Star was already stitching Zavi back up and Phoenix was wiping blood from his side. The complete memory stone lay on Zavi's flat and muscled stomach. And though his fingers twitched, showing the blast of power hadn't killed him, his eyes were shut fast and moving side to side under the pale skin of his eyelids. Like he was dreaming. Was that how his memories would return, in some dream state? How long would he be out? We needed him to get us safely to Laqqara.

I held my breath.

"Is he dead?" Sanne asked, leaning toward Zavi.

"No, love, he's just recovering from his curse," Phoenix said.

Zavi stood in a flash of Fae-quick movement. He opened his eyes.

Gone were the dark eyes I'd admired. In their place were fully slitted Fae eyes as green as spring grass.

29

ZAVI

A chill swept over Zavi's eyes and head like someone had splashed him with icy water. He looked around, his sight blurry and voices from the past screaming in his ears.

Lina stumbled back, Phoenix catching her and Star reaching out but missing.

"It's you," Lina said, her color gone from her lovely cheeks.

Images of ships, lightning, a group of both Fae and humans surrounding him and singing, and countless swings of his fist and sword overtook his mind.

"Wh-what is..."

His brother walked beside him in a memory.

They each had a girl gripped by the hand, young girls, the daughters of wealthy men whom Rietveld hated.

"We can't do this," past Zavi said to Emiel.

His brother exhaled roughly. "But it's just for ransom money. He promised they won't be hurt."

"We are already hurting them. Look how scared they are and rightly so," Zavi argued, keeping his voice very low as the girls tried to shout around the gags in their mouths. "I'm not doing this."

"But he will kill us," Emiel said.

Zavi gritted his teeth. "We'd deserve it."

"True, but I still don't want to die. What can we do?"

"Let's take them to him, act like the obedient, gold-hungry pirates that he thinks we are, then when he orders us to take them to the holding location, instead, we will help them get back to their families and we'll take our ship and get out of this horrible place."

"No way he won't send an assassin after us," Emiel whispered.

"We will be with my crew, brother. No one will get close with my crew around."

Emiel blew out a breath between his teeth as they passed through a crumbling warehouse. "I'm still not used to the whole pirate king label you have these days."

"I will never be used to it, so you're not alone."

In the darkest part of the old dry dock warehouse, Zavi bent and gathered the girls close.

"We have a plan," he said, keeping his voice quiet and steady. The poor things were beside themselves and he hated himself for the millionth time. "Trust us, and we will take care of you and make sure nothing bad happens, all right?"

Zavi's memory fogged.

A new memory bled into place.

He was on one of Rietveld's ships, docked in Masdam, and Rietveld was holding the yellow-haired girl. Zavi and Emiel had blindfolded the girls so Rietveld wouldn't see them as a threat to his part in this. The other girl—the slightly older redhead—was bound and sitting in a chair inside the captain's quarters. The door was slightly ajar and unlocked since they had surprised Rietveld in their efforts to undo this kidnapping.

Rietveld handed the yellow-haired girl off to Emiel. "This one will die because of your betrayal."

A muffled cry came from the red-haired girl in the captain's quarters. She couldn't see them, but she must have heard Rietveld.

But Emiel was going to do his best to save the yellow-haired girl. Zavi knew that. The girl's friend didn't, sadly.

In current Zavi's head, the memory grew hazy and time flexed, going too fast.

He couldn't grasp what was happening.

Everything cleared again, and past Zavi was on deck with Rietveld, who was headed for the red-haired girl.

Maybe if he distracted Rietveld, the girl would have time to run.

Zavi was going to suffer for this. He'd already been threatened with death when Rietveld had seen him whispering with the girls. Rietveld knew Zavi had betrayal on his heart.

Stones, but he missed the days of being on the open sea, pillaging wealthy trade ships and drinking the nights away with his men. He wished with every part of him that Emiel had never tangled himself up with Rietveld. Zavi had been forced to join in the schemes to find a way to help his brother escape the crime lord. Zavi might have been the king of the seas, but Rietveld all but ruled the cities and the powerful nobles there.

Past Zavi shouted, "I'll set the Watch on you, old man!" to

Rietveld before running for the side of the ship and diving into the cold waters of Kruid Bay.

The churning water of the memory morphed into voices and faces as it switched to new memories. They were jumbled as they spun from one moment to the next.

Current Zavi opened his eyes. Nausea swept through him. He caught himself on the railing and dropped to one knee. He was going to be sick.

"It's you," Lina hissed. "Those green, green eyes. You tricked me." Tears flowed from her eyes and her voice had gone thick. "I try not to think of her, of Sophia, of the dear friend I lost." She folded in on herself, her eyes shuttering, and Star gathered her close. But Lina straightened and took a step toward Zavi. She bared her human teeth. "I knew Fae were horrible and pirates even worse. Why did I trust you? Why are you here tormenting me? You are the reason Sophia is dead!"

"I'm trying to remember." He got to his feet only to see Star glaring alongside Lina. "Red hair. A merchant's daughter. Old Ones, save me, but you're her, aren't you?"

"Damn right, I'm her. And the blonde girl was Sophia, my dearest friend!"

Chest caving with guilt and worry and a thousand other emotions, Zavi started toward Lina, but she held out her hands.

"Don't you touch me," she snapped. "Don't even talk to me. You're a Fae pirate, and I want nothing to do with you ever again."

She was the little red-haired fifteen-year-old he'd kidnapped years ago. Being half-Fae, he didn't age like humans, and so their aging process sometimes confused him.

Lina was the redheaded girl, and the yellow-haired younger child had been Sophia.

He blinked, trying to remember what had happened. His head swam with memories he couldn't parse. He bent over the railing and vomited, the movement tugging at his stitches. When he turned back around, Lina was gone and only Star remained.

"You say one word to her and I gut you in your sleep. Tell me what to do to get this ship to Laqqara. If we need more hands, we will have Phoenix and Bram do the work. We will make for the first true port, then we will never see you again. Agreed?"

"I have to remember my brother. What Rietveld did..." But he couldn't remember anything except Emiel's human eyes—they'd been in an orphanage together and Emiel had been the only one willing to play with a half-Fae boy.

"Emiel?" Zavi shook his head, but the memories were too garbled to understand. "Lina!" Gripping the railing, he worked his way toward the door to belowdecks, where Lina had disappeared. He held himself up but just barely. "I didn't want to kidnap you or your friend," he rasped, head spinning. "Neither did Emiel. We tried to stop Rietveld. We..."

A cloud rose in front of his line of sight and he knew no more.

30

LINA

There was no way I could return to the captain's quarters, not to the place where Zavi and I had promised ourselves to one another. *Mate.* His whisper echoed through my mind. Belowdecks, I found a crewman's hammock near the brig, crawled into the smelly thing, and lay there to think.

For the first time in my entire life, I had started to trust a man, a male. And a Fae at that! Pressing my fists against my temples, I took a shuddering breath. My heart sat on one side, and on the other side was betrayal. I was being beaten up, bitten by the sharp teeth of the lie. The truth held me tight and bled me dry.

How could the person who sat by the fire with me be the same person who had killed my best friend? A small voice inside my head tried to say that he wasn't the same, that the past was the past, but the flashes of memory from that night pushed that voice into a dark, faraway corner.

Those eyes. They had haunted my nightmares for months

after I'd escaped from the kidnappers. From Zavi and his brother. I could never recall how I had ended up running down my street and back into my house. My fear had long ago blacked out most of the event. But I'd never seen Sophia again. The pirates had killed her at the older man's order. It had been Rietveld. I'd never known because I'd been blindfolded at some point during the kidnapping. The order of events tumbled in and out of place and I couldn't come up with a full memory of the event.

Zavi had shouted something as I'd made my way to this hammock. I'd been drowning in shock and hadn't processed it. What had he said? That he and his brother had tried to stop Rietveld and they hadn't wanted to kidnap us?

Bull shite. One either does the job or one doesn't, and they certainly did.

"Why didn't you save her?" I spoke the question aloud as tears rolled off my cheeks.

Grasping the well-worn fabric of the hammock in my fists, I ground my teeth together. I wanted to hit him, to hurt him, to make him feel as scared as I had been that night. I wanted him to suffer loss like I had when Sophia never turned up again and my parents refused to even discuss it, barring me from all contact with the Ofandrus family. I'd not only lost my best friend, but Zavi, Emiel, and Rietveld had also stolen away my second family, a group of adults and children who were far kinder to me than my parents.

Squeezing my eyes shut, I took a slow breath. We needed Zavi to get safely through the sea to Laqqara, so I couldn't destroy him yet. But I would get revenge for Sophia and for myself. He was a liar, a criminal, and a pirate, and he wasn't getting away with this, no matter how he had been cursed.

I rolled out of the hammock and began pacing, ideas forming and dissolving in my head. It was easier, and far less painful, to plan a murder than it was to obsess over each of Zavi's words to me in an effort to figure out what was real and what had been a lie.

I'd never felt more alone than this. A shiver shook my bones, and I swallowed against the dryness of my throat. Would Star and Phoenix understand why I could not allow one of Sophia's murderers to live?

Could I actually injure Zavi?

Did I have the steel in my soul to do the job?

My blood ran through my veins like frost.

Yes. Yes, I did.

My tears returned but these ones were hot and angry. I wiped my cheeks roughly and kept on pacing and plotting. I couldn't give in to the fear.

But he was up there. And he had called me *mate*.

Bitterness touched the back of my tongue and I forced my tears to dry up. I wouldn't let him crush me. Not now, when I was so close to what I'd always wanted—true freedom.

I'd also get something I hadn't realized I wanted so badly. Revenge.

❧ 31 ☙

ZAVI

avi woke up tied to a barrel of what smelled like sardines. The barrel's ribs pressed against his spine. His ankles were bound and both feet were asleep due to the tightness of the knotting. Wolfling slept beside him, snoring impressively.

Star was at the wheel. She was the only one on deck.

The enormity of what his mind was recalling with every second threatened to make him pass out again. So much history. So much blood on his hands.

With the deadly fighting skills he had, he'd known his past was dark. The tattoo, of course, had been a very obvious clue.

Although he'd tried to hold off bloodshed during his crew's raids, and he only boarded and pillaged the wealthiest, those with plenty to spare, he had still done terrible things. Killed innocents, even if it had been accidental. Stolen. Kidnapped.

His job with Rietveld was the first and only he'd worked with the bastard though. He had tried to undo the job once he'd seen the girls and had only taken it in the first place to save Emiel, but it had still happened. He had slipped into Lina's house via her window and nicked her like one did a pretty gold coin. Emiel had crept into one of the great hall's windows and taken the blonde, Sophia.

Hadn't Emiel managed to save Sophia? Lina believed her friend was dead, and perhaps that was true.

He set his head back against the barrel and tried to relive that night, to find out how exactly the rest of the job had gone. What had he done after he'd jumped into the one-mile depth of Kruid Bay, the deepest bay in the world, the same one they'd just left?

Shutting his eyes, he worked on remembering that cold swim. Hazy images rose up in his mind's eye.

"Where did you go, Emiel?" he whispered, his lips cracking.

He had climbed out of the water and onto the starlit pier, two piers down from the one where Rietveld had been docked in another of his trade ships. Not knowing where Emiel was, Zavi had searched for him in all of their usual haunts. Emiel hated Masdam as much as Zavi did, for many of the same reasons that Lina did as well—too many cocky males with too much coin to throw around. It was a city rotted with corruption. Every time he made landfall, he ended up in a sword fight, which was not his idea of fun.

The streets of the city spun through the rising memories, but the only thing completely clear after that search was the memory he'd seen part of earlier.

Rietveld had caught Emiel and sent a message to Zavi to come get his body. When Zavi arrived at the ship, Rietveld had a knife to Emiel's throat. He smiled and punched Emiel hard. A tooth had gone flying and blood had splattered across Emiel's chin and cheek.

"Watch this so you know what's about to happen to you," Rietveld said.

Two of his men grabbed Zavi even though he couldn't do anything with that knife poised to cut his brother's artery. Rietveld had another of his sailors rip the side of Emiel's tunic, and then Rietveld cut him open.

And placed a familiar object in his side.

A cursed magical artifact missing one triangular piece.

Emiel had been cursed too.

"Where is the other piece?" he shouted to Star.

She ignored him.

"It's my brother's. I have to find him. He tried to save Lina's friend. Please, believe me, even though you have no reason to. I swear it. I'll swear on anything you want me to."

"Pirates hold very little respect for anything besides gold."

"Then give me gold to swear on."

Star rolled her eyes.

"We didn't want the girls to be hurt. If we hadn't taken them, Rietveld would have hired someone else. It was better that we did the job. He had sworn not to hurt them."

"If you were working with him, you'd have known that wasn't true."

"I wasn't. I was the king of the *Ghost*." His ship had been magnificent. Broad, sleek, and as uncatchable as the creature it was named for.

Her mouth fell open. "You were a pirate king?"

"My memories say so."

"But the *Ghost* was the most feared ship in the northern hemisphere."

"Aye. And I'm not proud of what I did to create that reality. But I'm not that person now. My time without those memories…" How could he explain something he didn't understand himself?

Star was studying him. She was listening. Thinking.

"Please keep the piece safe until we get to Laqqara."

"You aren't giving the orders around here anymore."

"If I'm doomed, why would I help you sail through the next rough spot? I should just give you the wrong tack and delight as we all go down with the ship."

"Oh, you definitely seem like a better person, talking like that."

"Desperation turns everyone into a monster."

"Fine. I'll keep the piece on me. For now." She took it from a pocket on her vest and held it up for him to see. Sunlight danced across the etched runes.

"Thank you."

"I'm going to free you so you can sail." She knotted a rope around one section of the wheel. The other end was secured to a barrel. Then she approached him. "If you make even one move I don't like, I'll cut off one of your fingers and feed it to the sharks. Every time you piss me off, I'll take another finger." She untied him and stepped back.

"You would have made a truly frightening pirate."

"Shut up and sail," she said, pointing to the wheel.

Wolfling licked his hand and followed him. "Is Emerald belowdecks or off hunting fish? We could use a better look at that spit of land. I don't think we're far from the Eastknife current."

Star left, presumably to find Emerald and the magical artifacts he'd requested, and he was glad for the hush of the sea and the dog at his side. More than anything, he wanted to storm down the stairs and grab Lina and explain everything.

But he couldn't remember it all.

Would his full memory ever return?

And the other question cutting him like a rusted blade was this: where was Emiel? He racked his brain. He recalled watching Rietveld's healer sewing up Emiel's side as Rietveld slipped the piece into the small bag at his belt. Then they had done the same thing to him. Nausea flooded Zavi at the memory. The way that magic had felt. The way it had tasted on his tongue. His Fae blood made him very good at sensing magic and that meant when a dark force was set into his body, he suffered far worse than a full human would.

Before Rietveld's men could curse Zavi, right before they inserted the artifact to his bleeding side, he had strained to see around the men to view his brother.

Emiel's eyes were vacant, his color faded, and he watched Zavi like he would a stranger.

"I'll make use of him in Ashrahl," Rietveld was saying to his foreman as they looked Emiel over.

The memory went dark.

Ashrahl. The most northerly port city in Laqqara, the seat of the spice trade, and a place where Rietveld was just one of the many crime lords. A dangerous place until you were well away from the city proper.

Emiel could be in Ashrahl. Zavi took a slow breath. He would speak to Lina somehow. He had two days to attempt to explain that he wasn't who he had been. That he hadn't known. That he had been as surprised and horrified as she was that he was her kidnapper.

Star reappeared and set Emerald up with the seeing stone. She handed him the mirror.

"You still want us to dock in Ashrahl, yes?" he asked.

"Yes, it's still the first port we come to in Laqqara, right?" Star studied him.

"It is if you don't count the small landing area right at the border."

"That would set us in the wilderness. I agree with Ashrahl as our landing spot."

He nodded. "You can get anywhere in Laqqara from there. Plenty of caravans to join, horses to buy, supplies."

Nodding, Star lifted Emerald and helped her launch into the air with the extra weight. "That works for me."

"And the others?" he asked. What was Lina doing right now? What could he do to fix this?

"They'll agree. It's the simplest plan and we need to get rid of this ship as quickly as possible to bury our trail." She was keeping their end destination a secret from him.

He rubbed a hand over his face. "Can you just tell Lina something?"

"No."

"But if I can explain that I was as shocked as she was and that Emiel—"

Star tilted her head. "Which finger do you like the least? I'll consider starting with that one."

She had her dagger out and at his hand in less than a second. She wasn't as fast as him, but she wasn't that much slower. He didn't want to fight her. He might lose, plus he liked her, and she meant so much to Lina.

He shut his mouth, swallowing the words that longed to spill out. Star sheathed her dagger, then went to the railing and crossed her arms. She watched Zavi like a prison guard.

THAT NIGHT, WHILE STAR MANNED THE HELM, PHOENIX found him on deck. He had been staring at the moon, his mind wandering between how he could fix the tear between Lina and him and what Emiel could be doing for Rietveld in Ashrahl. Would either of them listen to him? Words had always come easily to Zavi, but now they abandoned him.

"Eh, I think we should gather what we can carry and sell off from the ship," Phoenix said. "We can divvy it up. Even though you don't deserve a single coin."

"I don't. I won't take more than I have to in order to find Emiel."

Phoenix nodded. "Your brother."

"Yes, he's working for Rietveld in Ashrahl, where we are going to dock."

"Star mentioned some of that. Well, it's not up to me. We let Moth lead our jobs. She has the quickest mind of the three of us and so she makes the decisions after we voice our opinions. And she's going against both of us, demanding that you get your fair take from the ship."

Did he dare to hope she didn't completely loathe him? That maybe she was considering the fact that he could change? "Did she say why?"

Phoenix tucked a fallen strand of flaxen hair back into the knot of thick hair at the base of her neck, then she nodded. She still hadn't looked him in the eye. "She did."

"And?"

"I don't have to tell you shite, pirate."

"Phoenix. I tried to help the girls. I'm not that person anymore anyway."

She met his gaze then and the anger in them reminded him of a mother bear he'd had an accidental run-in with near the forests of Saxonion.

"So you simply decided to stop being a pirate king? You have no desire at all to go back to your crew on the *Ghost* and to take up working with pigs like Rietveld so that you can make all the gold you want? Sure. Just like that."

"Yes. Exactly like that. Although, I do think some of my crew would leave the business as quickly as I would if given an out."

Her head tilted to one side and she looked him up and down. "As they say, actions speak louder than words." She turned on her heel. "Follow me. Any funny business and I'll blow your cock off with my extra powder while you're dreaming."

Zavi chuckled. "I deserve as much. I know."

Phoenix had changed dramatically since he'd met her, and he had no doubt the presence of her children was the cause. Though he'd only known her for a short time, he'd seen it clearly. The circles under her eyes were fading fast, and there was a spring in her step that hadn't been there before. Her smiles came more frequently now. Not for him at the moment, of course, but nonetheless... And she appeared more focused when working on what was in front of her. Her mind was settled, it seemed. Despite his anguish, he was very glad for her. He hoped her horrid former husband would die a terrible death.

They sorted the coins and property deeds hidden in the wall beside Rietveld's desk. Zavi's healing memory had reminded him that the man had a penchant for stashing things in walls. The entire time they counted gold, silver, and copper coins, thoughts of Zavi's time with Lina in the room tore at his heart. He felt shaken and pulled thin. Like being ripped away from her had stolen half of his soul. His mate hated him. And there was little he could do about it. Her childhood friend was dead, and it was almost directly his fault.

Phoenix broke the silence as she poured a handful of tallied coppers into a small linen pouch. "Tell me your side of the story."

"You want to hear that from me?"

"I know she's not ready to hear it, but I want to know what is going through your head and how much I need to loathe you."

"Just for transparency here," he said. "I do have the ability to lie. I inherited at least that much from the human parent I never knew."

"You didn't know your parents?"

"No, I grew up in an orphanage with Emiel, who is not my brother by blood."

"Oh. Huh. Well, spill it. What truly happened that night? Do you remember it all now?"

"I don't remember the last bit, but I've got most of it cleared up." So he told her the awful tale, how he had to rescue Emiel from his bad decision to team up with Rietveld, how Zavi hated the man, the way they'd tried to get the Watch to come after Rietveld. He only recalled going after the Watch, so he still wasn't sure why Rietveld had escaped that trouble.

"Most likely Rietveld had the Watch paid off."

"A good guess."

"But you only remember leaving the girls on the ship?"

"Emiel took Sophia. He planned to help her escape, but I don't know what actually occurred. I don't remember seeing Lina again that night or ever thereafter."

"Are the memories still coming back? Also, why did Emiel take up with Rietveld to begin with?"

He looked around the room as he tried to dig up the memory. "He had smuggled some gold across the border for some noble fellow who wanted to avoid kingdom taxes. But the tax man caught him returning; the tax man was in Rietveld's pocket. Rietveld demanded that Emiel pay off his debt by nabbing the daughters of two wealthy men who had more money than Rietveld wanted them to have."

Phoenix nodded and glanced at the door.

"Is someone there?" Zavi asked. He had heard a crack of the wood, but ships were noisy like that.

"No, I don't think so," Phoenix said, standing. She wiped her hands on the Laqqaran trousers she wore. They'd brought Laqqaran clothing in order to blend in a bit. "Let's move on to the cargo hold, shall we?"

Did she believe his side of the story? Did it matter?

Phoenix led him toward the opening to belowdecks.

Lina was down there.

Before he left the sunshine of the deck, he wove a mask of coldness for himself. Shoving his emotions deep inside, he followed Phoenix. He couldn't push Lina. Not yet. And not only because her friends would eviscerate him, but also because he honored her rage. He wanted to show her that he accepted the fact that he had been her nightmare. He wouldn't argue. Not yet.

Lina's scent danced through the salty air, and his blood rushed through his veins. His heart beat hard in his ears and he fisted his hands. Phoenix preceded him down the worn steps. Lina stood belowdecks, half of her in dark shadow. She turned. Emerald was perched on her shoulder. The dragon bumped her cheek with her tiny snout and Lina's beautiful fingers drew a line down the dragon's back. His hands ached to grasp her hips and pull her close. Her scent attempted to unravel his mask and he fought to keep himself from running to her and burying his face in her hair and covering her with a thousand fierce kisses. Some parts of him staunchly refused to lie low, so he held his breath, keeping her scent at bay until they turned at the base of the steps and headed in the opposite direction of Lina, toward the cargo hold.

Needless to say, it was not a pleasant day. He had a feeling that it was only going to get worse.

32

LINA

Zavi had left a while back, heading back to the deck with Phoenix. I really wished he hadn't seemed so sad. His bowed head and how he fisted his hands in frustration made me forget who he was for a brief moment. Especially belowdecks in the dim, inconsistent light of the swinging lanterns hung along the walls, because I hadn't been able to clearly see his eyes. He had looked like Zavi, the bard who had stolen my heart, not the pirate king who had participated in the most traumatic moment of my life. I was glad he hadn't tried to talk me out of my anger.

I would have thrown the dagger hiding under my tunic right at his throat and he would have deflected it. Revenge had to wait until the right moment, when he was asleep, distracted, or beaten down.

Phoenix had suggested I listen in on their conversation in the captain's quarters. I'd told her thanks but no at the time, but I hadn't been able to stay away. I'd heard it all. He'd reported Rietveld to the Watch. Zavi and Emiel had tried to get Sophia off the ship before Rietveld had ordered her killed. But I'd also heard that Zavi didn't recall the end of the story.

Very convenient.

I didn't believe a word. He had fooled me once, but he wouldn't be doing that again.

I wondered what Sophia would say if she could speak to me from the afterlife. She'd always let me go first when we'd played pick-up sticks. When Father and Mother had snapped at me while she was visiting, she'd usually taken my hand. She'd kept me from folding in on myself when their verbal abuse had grown heated. Just her being there had held my parents off from the worst of their cutting remarks, slaps, and pinches. Father had wanted to look good in front of Sophia because he was negotiating spice trades with her family. They grew the best saffron in the world. At least, that was what Mother used to say.

Why hadn't my parents ever spoken of Sophia's family after the kidnapping? I had always believed it was because they were sparing me from the torture of remembering my lost best friend—not out of kindness, but so that I wouldn't come undone and miss my tea appointments and embarrass them. Maybe there was another reason though. Perhaps they knew more about the kidnapping than me and were hiding it.

But why?

Or maybe the Ofandrus family had cut all ties with us because they were so upset. That would make sense. They had lost a child, the promised heir of their entire business. And with the way Father used to not-so-gently suggest they instead have their younger son inherit, as was custom in Deigs, they were probably angry with him and ready to never see him again. He had all but outright insulted their daughter

—who was now gone. I could imagine that being completely horrible, like salt in a wound.

"Hey, Moth?" Star's voice carried down the steps.

"I'm here. Do you need me up there?"

"If you can, I'd love some help with the sails," Star said.

"Is..." I didn't want to say his name.

"No."

A sad smiled stretched my cheeks. I loved my friends so very much. They knew what I needed and I didn't have to utter a word of it.

Star, Bram, and I worked to set a course to sail around a troublesome spot. We would be in Ashrahl soon. I lost myself in working the lines and teaching Bram what little I knew of sailing. I heard Zavi's boots knock along the deck behind me once as he returned to the wheel, but I didn't look at him. I just couldn't.

One question turned over and over and over in my head as I went to open a crate of lemons. How were Zavi and my kidnapper the same person?

Using my dagger, I worked at the nails holding the crate, but they wouldn't budge.

How was this the truth of things? The kind pirate was the kidnapper. The one who'd helped murder my dearest friend. It was impossible. But it wasn't. It was true.

"You might want to take it easy on that crate, Moth." Phoenix stood beside me. I hadn't realized her boy had left and she'd taken up his spot. I'd been lost in memories, both old and horrible and new and agonizing.

Mate.

The memory of his voice uttering that word washed through my thoughts, as steady as the tide, the salty sting of the full meaning never truly leaving the shores of my heart. I wanted to murder him. I wanted to throw myself into his lean, warm body. I wanted to kick him overboard. I wanted to strip him naked and show him the extent of my feelings.

Phoenix set a hand on my arm. Her gentle eyes found mine. "Do you want to have a cup of wine with me and look out over the bow?"

I set the empty urn I'd been attempting to store away down in the crate. It was cracked near the mouth thanks to my angry handling. "Yes, please."

"Wine it is. I found a nice port in the hidden stash inside the captain's quarters."

"How did you find another hidden treasure trove?"

She dragged me toward a pile of old sailcloth where she had apparently set this bottle in question. "Zavi knew that Rietveld prefers tucking things away in walls."

"Ah. Right. Because they were pirates together."

"They weren't working together regularly. At least, that's what he said."

"I heard that part."

"I wondered if you had taken me up on that." She took two wooden mugs from the depths of the old sailcloth and poured out the ruby-colored wine.

I downed my entire portion in one go. "Keep 'em coming."

Phoenix poured more into my cup. "My pleasure."

We stood side by side and looked out over the waves.

"I can't believe it's him." I gripped the railing, knuckles whitening.

Warm fingers closed over mine. "It's horrible."

"I care for him, Phoenix. I truly do."

"I know. He cares for you too. More than cares, I think."

"I'm so angry. He took Sophia. She's dead. Because of him. I had nightmares every night for at least two years."

Phoenix slid an arm around me and I leaned into her. Star joined us, and I glanced over my shoulder to see Zavi at the helm. My heart lurched in my chest like it wanted to fly to him.

"Do whatever you want to him, Moth," Star said quietly. "We will help in any way you choose."

The deck was falling away from my feet and my head clouded. Phoenix held me tighter and Star moved the unruly wisps of my hair away from my face.

"I have to avenge Sophia. I don't want to, but I also very much need to."

Star patted my back. "He's a pirate. Death could have taken him ages ago. He's lucky he's made it this far. As far as I see it, the world won't be less without him in it to hurt anyone else. He is a liar and has proven he is capable of terrible crimes."

I turned to look her in the eye. "Do you believe that?"

Star shrugged. "Until he proves me wrong."

"Sophia doesn't get the chance to prove anything to anyone," Phoenix whispered, her tone clipped and fiery.

We drank the rest of the bottle together, and they helped me to the hammock because I refused the captain's quarters.

"Phoenix, sleep in there with your babies. Get a good night's rest," I murmured, half drunk and feeling like I was headed for the bottom of the sea. Maybe I'd wake up and this would have all been a bad dream.

Star and Phoenix bid me goodnight and I was left on my side of the ship alone.

Sleep didn't grace me with its presence. But anger did.

My mind showed me Sophia's frightened face as I had seen it that night when we were gagged and dragged aboard that ship by Zavi and his brother. Her eyes had been so wide, white all around, so bright in the darkness.

After hours of lying there, ruminating with my rage building, I slipped out of my hammock. We were nearly to Laqqara. Star could get us the rest of the way.

Ignoring the headache pounding in my temples, I slid my dagger up my sleeve and gripped the edge of the fabric to keep it there.

Don't worry, Sophia. Vengeance comes tonight. I was through with waiting.

The steps barely creaked under me as I headed for where I guessed Zavi was—on deck at the helm.

33

ZAVI

The sea was rougher by the moment, some far-off storm sending swells their way. But they'd be to Ashrahl before that storm made landfall, so he wasn't worried. The only thing he worried about at this very moment was the person creeping toward him with a dagger in her hand.

Lina.

She had to be in a state to think she could sneak up on a half-Fae. She was smarter than that. His heart ached. Of course, she was grieving the loss of the person she'd thought he was. And furious with him for good reason. She wasn't thinking straight.

When she got close, Wolfling let out a low growl. Zavi set a hand on his head and the dog quieted. Zavi looped the rope attached to the mast around the ship's wheel to hold the course. He turned and knelt, looking up at her and exposing his throat. Wolfling whined, then began to jump, but Zavi gripped his scruff and forced him to remain where he was.

Lina's lips pulled away from her teeth and her eyes were as fierce as ever.

"I had planned to reason with you," he said. "To argue my case and fight for you. Because I love you. I really do. But I can't bring myself to get in your way."

Her face mostly shadowed by the sail, she stared, her legs accustomed to the motion of waves and her stance unmoving. The sea spray misted his cheeks and put the taste of salt in his mouth. The dagger in her white-knuckled grip shook slightly. She wasn't herself and he didn't blame her one bit.

He shut his eyes. "Do it. I am guilty of so many crimes. I have blood on my hands. I'd thought to live for my brother and see him uncursed, but honestly, he was as bad as me. Not as horrible as some, but what does that matter? We were pirates. We deserve whatever punishment life dishes out. I arranged the theft of your stash. I hired that young man."

She stiffened.

"Yes, I'm guilty of it all. I organized the robbery to coerce you into working with me. In hopes that I could save my brother. But that's no excuse for putting you and yours in danger. I'm a criminal, through and through. I should have been honest and asked for your help. But now that I know who and what I was... I'd consider myself lucky to die by your hand, by the hand of one I was blessed to meet. So do it, Moth. Kill your kidnapper and end your suffering. I will not fight you." He held out his hands and waited for the strike.

The cold steel touched the skin below his ear and he forced himself to remain still.

Wolfling obeyed Zavi's earlier command, but a soft whine poured from him.

"I hate you," Lina said to Zavi. Her voice was as rough as the sea. It sounded as if she'd been screaming for days.

"You should."

"Do you remember Sophia's death now? Do you recall what happened to me or how I escaped? Have any more memories surfaced?"

"No."

She sniffed. "It's so convenient that you can't remember everything."

He cracked his eyes open and wished he hadn't. She looked like someone had torn her into pieces and done a poor job putting her back together. Her eyes were wild, her hair blowing every which way, her hands shook, and the grief tugging at her beautiful mouth destroyed him all over again. He had done this to her. He was the one who had torn her to pieces.

She pressed the blade to his skin and the heat of blood ran down his neck.

Wolfling whimpered and scooted along the deck to press himself against Zavi's knee.

"Take your revenge, Lina."

With a roar, she backed up an inch, flipped the blade, and threw it into the mainmast. "I can't bloody do it!" Tears flooded the tone of her voice.

Wolfling had started barking.

Remaining on his knees, Zavi held the dog by the scruff again.

Keeping her back to him, Lina shook. Her shoulders heaved, and she coughed. "When will we be in Ashrahl?"

"Less than twelve hours now unless I'm reading this weather wrong."

"Less than a day until I never have to see you again." She put a hand on the railing and watched the clouds skirt across the crescent moon. "Less than a day," she said, her words almost too quiet to hear, "and I never have to see those eyes again."

A blade sharper than the one she'd held against him sliced across his heart, making him wince. "I'm so sorry," he whispered.

They stayed in those positions for several long, terrible moments before she left the deck and went below, not once looking back. He finally stood and returned his attention to the helm and the swells.

"Rietveld, you horrible bastard, you did a fine job punishing me," he said to the wind.

He couldn't have imagined anything worse than hearing his mate long for the day she'd never see his eyes again and watching her walk away. The agony was more intense than anything the memory stone had set on him, worse than any battle injury or poison he'd taken from an enemy's hand. He'd lived long and hard, and still, this was the worst night of his entire existence.

But he certainly deserved it. That, and more. And the joy that crept in at the thought of Lina finding her freedom and living her dream? He pushed it away because it didn't belong to him. That joy has nothing to do with him at all. No, he was the villain here despite the fact that he loved her so very, very much.

I was a coward. A child playing at being grown. A real woman would have cut that monster's throat and dedicated the deed to their friend. His acceptance of the guilt shouldn't have moved me. It was a game. He was a Fae pirate. They were well known for their tricks and manipulative behaviors. I'd fallen for it. He was up there, alive, while Sophia's body rotted away in the bay somewhere, unburied and forgotten.

Loathing burned through my veins, hot and unrelenting. Sleep evaded me completely as I swung in the hammock. The swells tossed the ship ruthlessly, but the sun rose without a call for hands on deck. I locked my emotions down and started my day, going through the steps of prepping for our arrival in Laqqara's first port city with a mask of cold indifference firmly in place. I didn't crack a smile when Emerald landed on my shoulder and licked my ear. I shooed her away, not caring that Sanne gave me a dirty look. Bram whispered something in his sister's ear and they hurried to join Phoenix, who was counting coins once more in the captain's quarters. She was readying our take from the job. We hadn't even discussed what to do exactly with the blue garnets. We hadn't discussed much of anything.

After tossing the seeing glass and mirror overboard to confuse my father's tracing magic, Star had come to my hammock last night, but I'd pretended to be asleep to avoid any sort of talk. I was such a coward.

Now, Star and Zavi were drawing in the sails and bringing us into the bay. Phoenix emerged from the captain's quarters with the children and Emerald flew above, scales sparkling in the sun. At one point, I would have found that a particularly beautiful sight. I loved glittery, shiny things. But I couldn't summon any happiness.

My mask held me in stasis, steady and unmoving. It was the only way I could get through today. Once I was away from him, from the sharp tug of longing I felt to be near him, I'd let my mask fall away.

With the use of the nice levers Rietveld had installed, I helped Star lower the boat down the side of the ship. Soon, we were aboard the small craft with all of our bags stuffed to the brim. I rowed and so did Zavi. We moved in perfect time like we had when dancing on Port Day and also during our time in the captain's quarters. I pushed those memories down, down, down, and imagined my mask more firmly in place. I tried not to glance to the side to see Zavi's concerned looks or the muscles rolling in his strong arms. I barely noticed when he gave up his water to Sanne, who had accidentally left hers on the ship. The short trip to the dock lasted far longer than it should have, but then it was over and I was in Laqqara.

No celebrations yet. I had to get out of his sight, to flee the urge to throw my arms around him and tell him I knew he wasn't the person he had once been. No, I wouldn't let my mask fall until I was safely away from the only male I'd ever trusted, from the male I should not have trusted for even one moment.

Phoenix hopped out of the skiff and onto the dock first. Wolfling followed, with Emerald launching into the air above him. The sun was low in the sky and the air was even drier than I remembered from my childhood trips to this southern kingdom. I helped Sanne out, and Bram followed. Star, Zavi, and I unloaded our goods. Star handed what I assumed was the second memory stone piece to Zavi.

"We can sell the ship," I said to Star and Phoenix as we worked. Wolfling was chasing a ripped piece of burlap that rolled across the dock. Emerald dove at the burlap and stole it away. "I'll get a quote on the garnets if the jeweler my father once used is still in the same place a street away from the main market."

A tall, thin man in traditional Laqqaran red—his trousers wide and flowing like the ones we all had donned during the trip—approached with a friendly wave. "Good afternoon, travelers. Docking fee is ten gladecoins or the equivalent. I'm glad to see you have your red for safety."

"Have any flocks been spotted in the area lately?" I asked, eyeing the sky.

Phoenix handed him the money and he began to count it out.

"Not in a while." He lifted his fistful of coins and smiled. "Let's keep it that way, hmm?" With his free hand, he touched his shoulder, a Laqqaran movement that was meant to wish luck on everyone in the surrounding area.

Star discussed the sale of the ship with the man, then we thanked him and started up the dock.

Bram leaned close to Phoenix. "What was the thing he talking about?"

Phoenix's gaze went from Bram, to Sanne, to me. She wanted me to explain and probably to do my best not to scare the children.

"The Laqqaran ibisgon is a majestic creature," I said, glad for something to think about that had nothing to do with my past or the male walking right behind me. "But they sometimes get a little too close to humans. They can be aggressive. Red frightens them because it's the hue of their only predator, the southern mountain dragons. The dragons are never seen unless you're in a very rural area, but the ibisgon is fairly common."

The sounds of the city trickled into the bay area. Donkeys brayed, hawkers with melodious voices called out their deals, and carts knocked their way over the cobblestoned streets.

We stepped off the dock's sun-bleached wood and onto the dry, packed earth that led to the main road into town. I inhaled the scent of cinnamon, fresh fish, and the sage-and-rose perfume many Laqqarans wore. It was an aroma I associated with Sophia. When we used to braid one another's hair, that scent had permeated the air. A sign marked the beginning of the road. It pointed to the Saxonion border, the two largest Laqqaran cities—Leptis and Luxurium.

"Here is your take from the ship and the garnets too," Phoenix said, handing me a sack of coins and the small bag of raw gemstones.

I tucked them away in my trouser pocket. Laqqaran trousers had buttoned pockets that went much deeper than any typical pocket in Deigs. They were so much better designed.

Phoenix turned to Star and gave her a similarly sized bundle of coins, then she faced Zavi. "I think you should accept this," she said to him. "We don't want to owe you anything for the sailing."

"You owe me nothing." He scratched Wolfling's head and his throat moved in a swallow. "I won't accept even a copper of that."

Phoenix sighed and retied Zavi's portion to her belt. Star frowned at Zavi, then lifted her head as Emerald soared over to land on her shoulder.

Zavi looked at the ground, took a breath, then moved away from Wolfling to stand in front of me.

My heartbeat tripled its pace. His scent rose on the air—and it took everything in me to keep from falling into him and forgiving it all. Anger whipped through me. I clutched the dagger at my belt. What he had done was not forgivable.

Zavi's beautiful and terrifying eyes pinned me in place. A storm of emotions rolled through me—the ache of wanting his arms around me, the grief of losing what I'd thought would be another half of my heart, and the gnawing pain of knowing his past.

Star and Phoenix drew the others away, Star chatting about what they might see at the market.

"Lina." His voice was a whisper. "I'm sorry. I hope you find the freedom you deserve in this wild land. I wish you joy. Nothing we experienced was a lie. If I had known, I never would have..." He rubbed the back of his neck, then tore the scarf from his head of dark blond hair. "I never would have mated with you. I hope the pull isn't as powerful for you. I don't think it will hurt you because you aren't Fae."

I knew enough of Fae to know that when he said mated, he meant married, or very close to it anyway. I felt like I was falling from a high cliff and had no idea what type of landing was waiting for me.

"And because I hate you." The words left a bitter taste on my tongue, but I kept my mask in place and refused to show any feeling at all.

I turned on my heel and left him standing there.

I would never see the Fae bard—friend, lover, mate, nightmare—again.

Lina's words slammed through Zavi's mind, smashing his concentration and beating down his will to go on.

Hate. Because I hate you.

He could hardly breathe. His beautiful, fierce, life-loving mate hated him. The truth of it devoured his soul and left him empty, a cold wind where his heart had been.

Maybe an ibisgon would dive from the downy clouds and crush him into the cobblestones. He would welcome death.

Attempting to push the horror away, he studied the buildings he passed. The red gutters of the blacksmith's shop. A crate of braided hemp outside the roper's establishment. Dark bloodstains outside the back of the butcher's place. He tried to see things instead of recalling his conversation—if one could call it that—with Lina.

Now that a good chunk of his memories had returned, Zavi recalled the layout of Ashrahl. He'd been here numerous times. Often in disguise. Usually to help another orphan who had lived in the home where he and Emiel had once been.

And many times, the help they needed was to get out from under Rietveld's managers. The man called them managers because they did just that—they managed his affairs away from his home base of Masdam. These managers were terrifying folk with absolutely no code of conduct, not even a pirate's code. None were granted parlay or a fair split of takes or a chance to walk away from a job. No, once a person was caught in the web, there was no way out.

Zavi bypassed the main market and larger roads through Ashrahl and instead took the narrow alleys and a few rooftops to where he thought Emiel might be working. Emiel was a big man, and if Zavi had been in a manager's shoes, he'd have put him to work on either protection of a client or on street detail outside a stash house.

The day passed in a haze of returning memories and false hopes when someone looked a bit like Emiel. As he perched on the rooftops, the dust of the city rising around him, Zavi absorbed the onslaught of memories from childhood onward. He saw someone large enough to be Emiel, walking beside a noble in the streets below, then a recollection of a day spent sailing toward an isolated island where northern pirates had holed up broke his concentration. He lost track of another man in the alley who could have been Emiel as memories of a battle—dragon shrieks from the Mist Knights' mounts as they joined Zavi and his crew in fighting the northerners— flooded his mind. Emiel hadn't been in that battle—only the crew whom Zavi treated like family. A crew of misfits like him.

He and his crew had sailed all over, from the far north,

which was a grand mistake, to the distant south, which was delightfully bizarre. But he wished he couldn't remember all of it. Not the time when he had sacked and sunk a Saxonion trading vessel, mistaking it for a ship belonging to the horrible man who had once run the assassins' training facility in Isernwyrd. The trader in question had had the same colors as the assassin master. Zavi had killed innocents that day. He longed to go back and change the decision to order his crew to attack.

Another large man, this one in a hooded cloak, walked around a corner below Zavi's perch and he scooted closer to the edge of the tiled rooftop to get a better look.

That was when pain pierced his sides and he was lifted into the sky.

Gripping the talons that had held him, he felt blood slick around his fingers. He craned his neck to see what had taken him although he already had a terribly good guess.

Yes, it was an ibisgon. A hungry one.

Shouts rose from the streets below, where his blood dripped to the dry stones beside a cart stacked with tanned hides. The bird veered toward the side of town packed with taverns. Zavi reached for the dagger at his belt, but he couldn't get around the ibisgon's talons. The bird closed its hold on him even more and he cried out, pain burning him alive.

A squawk sounded and another ibisgon collided with his captor. The birds tangled in the air, and with feathers flying, they spiraled toward the ground. Zavi was jerked wildly as his captor held him fast with one massive foot. The birds shrieked and split from one another, and Zavi was dropped into the open air.

He fell into the cart of hides, his landing cushioned. His wounds screamed at him and he tried to sit up.

Someone's shadow fell over him and a voice asked, "Want some help?"

Zavi held his breath. It couldn't be, but it was.

Emiel.

His brother was right here, standing over him and offering aid. It was an absolute miracle.

Zavi smiled through the pain, his heart racing at the sight of his brother. Memories rose up in his mind's eye. Emiel loading his slingshot with a fig and shooting it at the headmistress of the orphanage. Both of them running down a dark hall, laughing as they went.

"Yes, good sir," he said to Emiel. "I would love to get myself patched up if that's possible. I will warn you though. I don't have much money." How was he going to broach the topic of Emiel's memory?

Emiel showed no signs of recognizing him. He looked over his shoulder as if checking for something or someone, then he turned back to Zavi. "I can handle it. Come as quick as you can or our hides will end up in this cart."

Zavi put an arm over the back of Emiel's neck and hissed at the pull on his wounds. "That sounds ominous. Have I fallen out of the pan and into the fire, as they say?"

A chuckle left Emiel. Stones, it was wonderful to hear that.

"I have a friend up the road a bit. I'll leave you with him."

They walked away from the cart and down the now empty street. Everyone had hurried indoors when the ibisgons showed up.

"You're part Fae, hmm?" Emiel asked.

"I am. Is that a problem? Have you had trouble with my kind in the past?" Maybe he would mention his memory issues on his own...

"No. I just haven't met anyone with Fae blood," Emiel said.

"That you know of."

He nodded. "I bet you'll heal up quick."

"Faster than you would, yes," Zavi said. "But I still need some attention."

"Just don't ask my friend any questions and don't give him much about you either, all right?"

Zavi nodded. "I can keep my mouth shut."

"Good, because my employer doesn't like strangers around his buildings."

Rietveld or a manager who worked under Rietveld? "I know a little about Rietveld."

Emiel halted and swallowed. He turned dark eyes on Zavi. "Don't get into his world if you can help it, Fae," he whispered. "He'll own you if you're not clever enough to run when you get the chance." He started walking again, taking most of Zavi's weight.

Zavi knew he had at least one broken rib.

"How did you know I work with him?"

"Lucky guess," Zavi said. "He's big on this stretch of water."

"He is. Now, that's enough talk."

Emiel knocked at a large door marked with a dark red sun. A wave of pain had Zavi sweating rivers down his back. After another knock, the door swung open to show a man with a long nose and a scar from his left eyebrow to the top of his head of short spiky hair.

"What now?" The man with the scar looked Zavi up and down. "The ibisgon got you?"

He waved them into the abode. Light filtered through wooden shutters, and a large circular table sat in the center of the main room. A female's voice and a child's echoed from one of the three rooms at the back of the place. Emiel helped Zavi up onto the makeshift surgery table. Stones, the pain was hellish.

"All right." Emiel rubbed his hands on his dark red trousers. "I leave you to it," he said to the scarred man. "Best of luck to you, Fae."

Zavi couldn't let him leave, not without at least trying to tell him the truth. He might never catch him again. "Wait. This is going to sound insane, but do you have a scar like this?"

He lifted his tunic, tugging the fabric away from the blood.

The healer lifted a hand to hover over Zavi's injuries. "Careful now. Don't make it worse."

Blood covered the spot where the memory stone had been, but the scar was still fairly visible. He looked up to see Emiel staring.

"I..." Emiel started. "I can't." He spun and doubled over, hand gripping his tunic where it covered his stomach.

"I know what that pain and nausea is, Emiel."

Emiel turned and steadied himself by holding the edge of the table. His face was pale. "How do you know my name?"

"Do you recall anything from your past?"

"It's none of your concern."

"Emiel. Why would I know your name? Why would I have

the same exact kind of scar you do? I'm not a madman. Will you let me tell you what I know?"

"No. I can't do this." Emiel pulled a handful of gladecoins from his pocket and tossed them to the healer. He flung himself out the door before Zavi could utter another word.

"You should try to be still." The healer was threading a needle, holding the bone and thread by the lantern hanging from the beam above the table. "This is going to take a while." He looked at Zavi. "Do you want a dram of Faewine? I have a low-quality blend in the back. Your friend paid me enough for a bit of it."

"Bring on the wine." There was nothing to do now but let the man do his work. He couldn't very well run after Emiel with his guts half hanging out.

Post wine, the chore of trying not to think about Lina became so much more difficult. Her face and voice shimmered across his semi-consciousness as pain blurred the edges of reality.

"Almost done," the healer murmured. "I'll wrap those ribs when we're through. You'll need to stay in bed for as long as you can to let them heal. Even with Fae blood, it's going to take a while."

But Zavi had no bed. "Thank you," he slurred. "Are you sure that was just Faewine?"

The healer shrugged. "That's what I was told. It might have some poppy in it too. You do look rather woozy."

Zavi woke up tucked into a narrow cot at the back of the healer's house. Wolfling stood over him, drooling profusely on the rough woolen blanket someone had given him.

"No," he said softly, rubbing the dog's chest, "you should

have stayed with Lina. I wish your nose didn't work quite as well as it does. I had hoped you'd be unable to track me."

Wolfling whined and twisted to look at the open doorway.

"What is it?" Zavi slowly swung his legs off of the cot and stood.

The front door of the house burst open and there stood Rietveld.

36

LINA

We bought some horses and made our way to the Ofandrus family's saffron plantation. My black mount was a steady girl with a white mane. I toyed with the coarse hair, braiding it this way and that as we rode toward our new life. Surely the Ofandrus family would accept us. Unless they blamed my family for Sophia's death.

The trip only took two hours, and the day was bright and lovely—a contrast to how I was feeling. I'd never see Zavi again. And that was good, right? Definitely. He was a major player in Sophia's death. He'd all but murdered her himself. So it was good he was out of my life.

Why did it feel like my chest was going to cave in?

The road curved in a westerly direction, the bend marked with a purple and red flag. This was it. I urged my horse to a trot, and we left the main road and headed onto the narrower path that the flag indicated. A stone wall led us along the way, and at a painted sign that said *Ofandrus Saffron*, we dismounted. An archway in the wall opened into the plantation. Posts stood next to the archway, so we tied our horses and did our best to dust ourselves off.

My hands were sweating. I took a deep breath, steeling myself. Would they accept us? Would they tell me why they'd never answered my letters, or would they just toss me into the road? Between the chaos of Zavi and the fact that I was about to set foot in the one place I'd wished to be for the last five years, I was a mess.

Phoenix set a motherly hand on my back and gave me a kind smile. She knew I was hurting.

Star gripped my shoulder and came close while the children climbed off the pony they'd shared. "When you're ready to talk, we are here. You know that."

"I don't want to talk."

"You need to," Star said. "You can't shove all these emotions away. I know you felt something strong for the bard."

"Please. Give me some time."

Star nodded and squeezed my shoulder briefly before taking her bag from her dun mare.

A tent on the far side of the entry road bustled with activity. People were shouting numbers and waving their hands over sacks of what I guessed was harvested saffron.

One woman lifted her arms and shouted, "Eh! This haggle is finished. He is the winner. We will have a new batch shortly."

She turned away from the disappointed traders and their murmurs of discontent, her brown cheeks shiny with perspiration and her hair stuck to her forehead.

I froze.

The woman's mouth fell open, then she ran toward me.

She hit me hard with a vicious hug. "Lina!" she shouted into my ear.

I couldn't speak. I couldn't get my hands to move to return the hug. She pulled away a fraction and studied my face.

"Lina? That is you, right? It's been, what, five years? Why didn't you write back? Why are you here?"

My heart lifted so high that I thought I might join Emerald, who circled above us.

"S-Sophia?" My lips were numb. "But you're dead."

She laughed and hugged me again. "I don't think so. I am far too sweaty to be a ghost."

Star, Phoenix, and the children had been quiet up to this point, but now they chuckled behind me.

"Do ghosts sweat?" Sanne asked.

"I can't believe this." Almost dizzy with this revelation, I looked Sophia up and down. At her pointed nose. The small birthmark on her temple, the one she used to call her lucky spot. "Your lucky spot." I reached out to touch her face, then pulled my hand back. "How? Tell me everything."

"I wrote to you. Didn't you get my letters?"

My jaw clenched and I fought to keep my voice civil. "Not a single one." My parents had kept this information from me, had let me think Sophia was dead. They had to know. They had probably read the incoming letters. Heat rose in my chest and I fisted my hands. To think that one's family was supposed to be a support. To care above all. They had watched me grieve over Sophia, not eating for days, not sleeping... Anger wasn't a strong enough word for the emotion boiling through me.

Sophia licked her lips. "I hate to be the one to say this, but your father is a monster."

"That's one of the reasons I'm here."

Sophia—Sophia! I could not believe it—waved at everyone behind me. The joy at seeing her alive and well eased my rage. My parents were in my past. This was now and I had my friend back. It was impossible, but here she was, right in front of me.

"We can figure it all out and swap stories while we are harvesting," she said. "I can't stay out here and just chat. This is the craziest two weeks of our year. Come on."

She linked her arm in mine and pulled me under the archway and onto her family's estate.

The old house sat in the center of a courtyard like it always had. A perfect square made from light brown bricks. A well stood near the front entrance, an outdoor kitchen had been added to the side of the house, and the stables looked much the same as they had when I'd been here as a child. We hurried past the kitchen and a small separate bakery to the back of the house, where the fields began. Saffron flowers bloomed across the flat land in a carpet of green and purple.

"It's gorgeous."

Sophia nudged me, and we started toward two large pale sheets of linen stretched across the ground where the fields began. People were everywhere—picking flowers in the fields, carrying baskets, going in and out of an outbuilding. Children ran here and there, carrying empty baskets to the fields and some squatting and plucking blooms alongside their elders.

"You were never here for harvesting, were you?" Sophia asked.

"I don't think so. I'd remember this." I couldn't remember most of my abduction, but I would recall this beautiful scene.

Joining two other women and three men, we sat with Sophia on the sheets. Saffron flowers had been strewn about and bowls of the crimson stamens sat beside each person.

"I'm throwing you into our harvesting crew, all right? I'll call for food and drink so you can refresh yourselves while you get down to work. Not a moment to spare during these two weeks!"

She showed us how to separate the flower and remove the stamen. We accepted a tray of hot tea, which was surprisingly refreshing despite the warmth of the sun on my back. It was autumn and the breeze was soft and cool. Sophia introduced us to everyone and we were encouraged to tell them about Emerald and how there weren't as many pocket dragons as there had been in Deigs long ago. We told them about Emerald's intelligence and the way she'd helped us through Dragon Skull Strait.

Phoenix helped Sanne work on her flower. "Won't your family want to know you have strangers here?" she asked, not looking up from Sanne's small fingers.

"Oh, no. I'm in charge of staffing for the harvest season. They'll just think you're yet another group I brought on to work. And, of course, Lina is no stranger."

"I feel like one." My hands shook as I placed a stamen in the bowl between Sophia and me. Emerald's small shadow fell over the pile of flowers near my knee.

"Will you tell me about what happened to you?" I asked Sophia. "Do you remember?"

"We have so much to catch up on. I can't believe your father kept my letters from you. I could strangle him."

"Get in line," I murmured, hoping I'd never see him again.

Sophia snorted a laugh and traded a heavy look with Star, who nodded. They both knew well how terrible Father was.

"Let's see. Where should I start?" Sophia asked me.

"What happened when the bearded pirate took you away from Rietveld, when Rietveld ordered him to kill you?"

Her throat moved in a swallow as she held up a flower and carefully peeled it apart. "Emiel was his name, I think."

"Yes," Phoenix answered for me. "He is Zavi's brother. The other pirate, the half-Fae one."

Nodding, Sophia accepted a fresh basket of flowers from another worker. She carefully spread the blooms over the sheet, adding to our task. "He told me his name. I remember looking up at him and him pronouncing it slowly for me. He also said he was sorry for making me cry."

I felt like I'd been punched in the stomach. She knew exactly what I had been through; she'd been there. I took her hand and held it, not caring for a second about the odd looks the other workers gave me. Sophia, the beautiful soul that she was, curled her fingers around mine and took a break from harvesting.

"When Rietveld walked away, Emiel walked me down the gangplank. I don't recall if there were others there, but at some point, we hurried away from the pier. I had trouble walking as fast as he wanted me to. We went around a corner somewhere and he put his cloak over me. The thing dragged the ground as he guided me through a bunch of alleys. The inn appeared like magic at the end of one narrow byway. It felt magical anyway, because he told me to go back to my parents and to forget this whole night. But that I should leave

Masdam and the Kingdom of Deigs forever if I wanted to stay safe.

"I don't remember going inside the inn, but I do know my parents cried when they saw me. Mother threw what I'd later be told was a ransom note into the small hearth. After we left for home, they sent word to your family, Lina, but my father blamed yours for the whole event. He was always saying how your father's bragging would get them all killed."

I tried to absorb all of this new information, these happenings that were in such contrast to what I had thought was true all these years.

"Your mind is far sharper than mine," I said. "It's amazing you have all these details in your head still. Do you know what happened to me? How I got home? I don't remember much."

"Oh, I saw you. When I was hiding behind a barrel waiting for Emiel to return. He had gone to check something. The other pirate was carrying you down the pier and then he disappeared into a building. I don't know where. You were both soaked to the bone. He was so handsome. I think you were bleeding and unconscious. Not sure if that part is a memory or one of the many dreams I've had about that day and night."

I released Sophia's hand and began peeling the flowers apart again, needing to do something with my hands, with this jittery feeling growing inside me. Zavi had rescued me? No, that wasn't true. Couldn't be.

Star dumped a full bowl of crimson stamens into the larger bowl in the center of the linen sheet. "Maybe Zavi crawled through the captain's quarters window. It's big enough on the larger ships."

I dropped the flower I was working on. "And what? Jumped into the bay with me unconscious?"

Phoenix shrugged. "Maybe? He is half-Fae. He could have held you with one arm and swam you both to the pier. You were smaller then, so I would think it's possible."

My teeth ground together. I felt like I was coming apart at the seams. "Do you remember anything else about Zavi?"

"No, just that he had nice eyes."

"I remember screaming." I felt my hand at my throat, surprised by the touch, like my fingers were not my own.

Sophia's kind gaze darted to my face. "Rietveld probably hit you to shut you up," she said, her tone gentle despite the harsh information she was delivering. "Darling," she said, now looking at Bram, "please don't crush the stem. We use them in baking and in some medicines."

"Sorry." Bram gave her an apologetic grin and set down the split flower he'd been rolling between his fingers.

Sophia smiled at him and then at Phoenix, who rolled her eyes and smiled back.

"No problem, love," Sophia said.

I recalled a bump on my temple during that time. Was it from Rietveld striking me? I couldn't bring any memory of that moment forward. Was this how Zavi had felt? That his past was just out of reach? I wondered if his memories had all returned by now or if the strain on him had forever blackened a few like what had happened to me.

"I don't hold any anger toward them," Sophia said. She took a quick drink from her cup of hot tea, then set it back on the ground. "Rietveld is a very powerful person. Even here, though I don't believe he comes here himself. I imagine those men, well, that man and that half-Fae male, were doing their best in a terrible situation."

"Really? I think you're too generous with your forgiveness. Why didn't my parents tell me you were alive? Why did they let me believe you were dead?"

"I don't know," Sophia said.

"They didn't talk about the event even once to me."

Phoenix ran an absent hand over Sanne's tangled hair. The girl sniffed and rubbed her nose with her arm.

"They acted like Rietveld was a great contact," I said, anger sharpening my words. "They never even aimed a frown at him."

"Did they know it was him?" Sophia asked. "They might not have. My parents only found out later on through one of their contacts in Masdam."

"Maybe not. And if they were tossing letters from you without reading them, maybe they were also throwing out letters from your parents to them without seeing what information was inside. It kept us all in the dark." It was a possibility, sure. But I doubted it.

Sophia nodded.

Star put another stamen in the bowl. "Speaking of letters, we could pen one to Zavi and see if Emerald can find him back in Ashrahl."

She hadn't looked up, but the suggestion was aimed at me. I glared, shutting that thought down.

"Why?" Sophia separated the stem from her flower. "And why is he in Ashrahl?"

I pushed my plate away. "I have a story to tell you."

. . .

After filling her in on all the details and answering her questions, we feasted with just her family inside the main house. Over spiced eggplant stew, sweet rice, fragrant saffron bread, and pomegranate juice, I reunited with her parents, two people who I had absolutely adored as a child.

"You're the same mischievous girl you've always been," Sophia's mother, Iyana, said. "And don't worry. We won't tell a soul and our employees are good at keeping our business private."

Sophia's father, Mazun, poured steaming cups of tea for all of us. "I want to personally thank Emiel and Zavi for their change of heart and their courage in standing up to Rietveld. It's horrible to imagine losing all of one's memories. Did Zavi have a lead in finding his brother?"

Sophia had told her parents everything.

"Not really," I said, glad my voice was steadier than I felt inside. "Just that he was most likely in the city, working for Rietveld and completely ignorant of his past."

I kept to the facts. If I let myself feel too much, I'd go mad. What was I supposed to do? Forgive him? Truly? Sophia was alive, but Zavi had said himself that he had been a true pirate and had shed innocent blood.

Phoenix leaned over and whispered in my ear, "What is going through your head? Do you want to go somewhere and talk?"

Star's fork was halfway to her mouth, but she paused and gave me a look that said she could stop eating now and talk if I wanted. After so much time spent together, we almost read one another's minds. I was so grateful for them.

I waved their offers off and tried to eat. My stomach wasn't having it.

Had I made a huge mistake in letting Zavi go? Could a person truly change?

Sophia's parents had their heads together. Her father was squeezing his eyes shut and her mother was whispering quickly. I felt terrible for bringing this all up again. It had to be traumatic for them as well as us.

Mazun glanced my way. "Know that you are in our kingdom now."

"You make us sound like royalty," Iyana said, chuckling and taking another sip of her tea.

"We aren't that, but we're damn close. The king and queen hold us in high favor."

Sophia nodded, grinning. "We orchestrated their wedding feast. Did you know that?"

"I didn't. That's wonderful."

The rest of the day was perfection. Perfection with a hole in the middle of it. A hole the size of a Fae pirate turned bard whom I was having a lot of trouble hating.

37

ZAVI

How had Rietveld made it to Ashrahl so quickly?

With a burlap bag over his face, Zavi saw nothing as he was dragged through the streets. Bloodied from falling to his knees with his hands tied behind his back and searing with pain from his stitches where the ibisgon had pierced him, he was more than ready to be done with this day.

Great idea, Zavi. Go looking for a man who doesn't even know you and who works for a man who loathes you. Just let him know you're in town creating trouble. Lovely idea. Yes. Very clever.

Old Ones save him, he was the biggest fool. He'd honestly hoped that somehow Emiel would know it was him, his brother, the one Emiel had trusted above all, loved above all through their entire lives.

A rough hand tugged the bag from Zavi's head. A strip of sunlight nearly blinded him and he winced. He had been dumped in the center of a circular sand pit surrounded by close-knit buildings. Arches, windows, and arrow slits blackened the light brown expanse of structures that hugged the circle of sand.

"What is this place?" He hadn't meant to speak the question aloud, but his head was hazy for one of a million reasons.

He was answered with the low growl of a dragon. Swinging around, he looked up to see a mountain dragon— one of the fire-breathing ones from the Shrouded Mountains in the Fae Realm of Lights—with a white-haired man sitting on its back. No, a Fae. A full-blooded Fae if Zavi was to guess. Because only the Mist Knights of the Fae realm rode mountain dragons. The rider didn't dismount but simply stared down at Zavi and the others inside the sand pit with him.

Rietveld, Emiel, Drukker, and Lord Casparji stood beside one another, talking quietly.

"If you're plotting an elaborate death for me, can I get some details? If I'm about to die, I might as well know what the show will be like."

"Shut it, tavern rat." Rietveld's voice boomed across the arena.

Because that was what this place had to be. Although there were only three levels of steps leading from the sand to the buildings that surrounded it, they were set up to seat a small crowd. Zavi was relieved that no crowd was currently gathered. Perhaps that was a good thing. Maybe. Maybe not.

"May I ask how you managed to get here so quickly?" Zavi said to Rietveld, Casparji, and Drukker.

He gave them a grin because he was just that amount of crazy at the moment. Why hadn't he killed Rietveld when he'd had the chance? He'd worried about the aftermath, but this was exactly as bad.

Zavi looked up at the dragon and rider. "Did you haul

them here? What did they offer you for that? I thought Mist Knights only worked for King Lysanael and Queen Revna."

The dragon leapt and spread its wings, making everyone startle, even Rietveld. Rider and dragon gracefully landed beside Zavi. Rietveld glared at the rider, who ignored the crime lord and slid from the massive scarlet beast.

"I am only here as a special favor to my commander," the rider said quietly enough that only Zavi could hear. "My commander seems to have dealings with this man." The way the rider said man told Zavi exactly what he thought of Rietveld. "I have fulfilled my duty and will go." His eyes found Zavi's. "I can see you are of my blood."

"Only partly."

"It doesn't matter. At my nod, run to the dragon. I will haul you onto his back and we will leave this pit."

"I can't. They have my brother." Zavi jerked his chin in Emiel's direction.

"The human?"

"Yes."

"You've adopted him as your own."

"I have."

A sad smile crossed the Fae dragon rider's face. "I have one lodged in my heart as well." He said it almost absent-mindedly, like he hadn't meant for Zavi to know. "Well, if you have a change of heart, I'll be around. Shout for Marius and I will hear you."

Without another word, he jumped back onto his dragon. The creature shrieked, and everyone bent in fear. The dragon and his rider lifted into the sky and flew from view.

There went Zavi's only chance out of this mess. Not that riding a dragon was any safer than dealing with a crime lord.

❦ 38 ❧

LINA

That night, behind the Ofandrus family's house, under a ridiculous sky of brilliant stars, I stood beside Phoenix and Star, our arms linked and our faces stretched into smiles.

"Where's Emerald?" I looked around. I hadn't seen the dragon in several hours.

Star and Phoenix exchanged a look and I frowned.

"Spill it, friends. What is going on?" They were definitely up to something.

"I never told you about my first year in the military, did I?" Star broke away from us and began walking down the gentle slope to the path that led through the saffron fields.

I followed her and Phoenix was on my heels.

Star looked up. She couldn't keep her gaze off the night sky when it was like this. I remembered finding her on the rooftop time and time again when we first started staying at the hideout.

"I wasn't a good person, Moth. I really wasn't."

"You? I doubt that." I nudged her shoulder with a finger and chuckled.

But she didn't grin and she ignored my teasing push. "I murdered someone. In cold blood. For no good reason at all."

I stopped and Phoenix bumped into me. She set a hand on my arm, but her gaze was on Star. I could tell she knew this story already.

"Star, why didn't you tell me?"

"To protect you, really. Because the man in question knew your father. I worried that, someday, he might ask and you might have to answer."

"Who was he? Why did you have to kill him?" There was no way she hadn't had a very good reason.

"It was a mistake. He was in the wrong place at the wrong time. Another man had attacked a woman in my unit. I set a trap for him and planned to end his life before he could hurt anyone else. It was a moonless night. I couldn't see well. I went for his throat and found out too late that it was the wrong man. I could have spared him, but he would have told my captain about the setup and my attack. It was his life or mine, and I chose mine. I am no innocent."

"Why are you telling me now? You know I wouldn't hold that against you, but why now?"

"Because I planned to kill someone. Someone bad, yes, but still. And then I murdered a man who hadn't done anything wrong that I knew of. I ended his life to protect my own, to hide my crime."

"But you wish you hadn't. You have never done anything like that since."

"I learned from it, yes." Her big dark eyes flicked to my

face and her look said she wanted me to infer more from this sad tale.

"I am lucky to be your friend. You aren't that person anymore."

Phoenix lifted a fallen saffron flower petal and released it into the night breeze. "Neither is Zavi."

I shook my head. "We don't know that."

"Don't we?" Star asked. "You can read people. Even when Zavi was at his worst, was he willingly hurting you?"

I tugged at my sleeves. "No. But he stole from us. He lied. He is the monster I had nightmares about for years."

"He *used* to be a pirate," Star said. "He's a bard now. And I call him a friend."

Phoenix picked up another petal and rolled it between her fingers. "People can change."

"But he robbed us after the whole bard thing. He hasn't changed."

"Wouldn't you rob someone to save one of us?" Star said, her eyes crinkling at the corners.

I huffed out a laugh because of course I would. We'd all done exactly that. We'd stolen and stolen and stolen until we'd had the funds to help one another escape our horrible kingdom. Pressing the heels of my hands against my eyelids, I let my laughter rise up again. "I'm a hypocrite. That's what you're telling me?"

"Yep," Star said.

Phoenix snorted a wry laugh. "If the shoe fits..."

I opened my eyes to see them gazing at me, amused looks on their lovely faces.

"Since Zavi's trauma with this memory stone," Star said, "he has been different. At least, from what he's told us and what we have seen. That's all anyone can go on. We witnessed his kindness toward the children and little Emerald. The way he helped us sail here even when we were all hating him. How he begged forgiveness. These are not the ways of a bad person."

"We all have dark and light," Phoenix said.

She was right. They both were. "And that dog loves him."

"Yes," Star said at the same time that Phoenix said, "Totally devoted."

Could I do it? Could I forgive Zavi and let my heart love him? I swallowed, unable to say any of that out loud yet. "You never told me where Emerald is."

"She should be"—turning, Star squinted at the sky above the house—"ah, yes. Right there."

I spun to see a small shape flying across the starlit heavens, heading toward us. I held out my arm and the dragon landed lightly near my wrist.

"Why is she red?"

Star reached over and took a slip of parchment from a tie on her leg. "To protect her from the ibisgon, we painted her with berry dye."

Of course. "Smart. What is that?"

Phoenix leaned over Star's shoulder to examine the parchment. "It's the note we sent to Zavi."

Oh, I remembered Star bringing up that idea earlier. "I can't believe you did that behind my back."

Phoenix tilted her head. "Yes, you can. It's for your own good anyway."

Star lifted the note. "There's no reply."

Emerald pecked at my hand and stared into my face.

"What is it?" I asked.

Her snout rapped my hand again, then she rose into the air. She circled above us, then hovered low over our heads.

"She wants us to follow her, doesn't she?" Phoenix said. "I bet something is wrong with Zavi."

"How do we even know that Emerald found him?"

Emerald dove at me and landed on my shoulder. I held still, wondering if I was about to experience a dragon bite for the first time. She closed her talons on the shoulder of my tunic, bunching it as she lifted off. She dragged me forward a step.

"I guess we are following her. Now."

39

ZAVI

Rietveld looked at Zavi like he was a pile of dung that he'd stepped in with new boots. "It's unfortunate that you've chosen to rebel against me once more. I informed your crew that your body was found in Masdam. They are currently on their way to join me here to do my bidding. I've offered them sums they can't refuse. The only issue I see is you being alive; it's a problem easily remedied. I'm finished with games regarding your punishment."

Zavi swallowed, memories streaming through his head.

His crew. Lagsny. Brodie. Thompson. Faraine. Tahiren. He had taken most of them off the streets of various port cities where they'd been eking out a living through begging or stealing, all orphans like him. Most of them were good people. Maybe not Brodie, but the rest had hearts of gold. All of them were brave to a fault. He couldn't help but smile, recalling music nights on deck, blisteringly hot days exploring lost islands, and the way they'd come together when they'd lost a crew member to their dangerous profession. They had been an extension of his and Emiel's family.

And they thought he was dead.

He could argue that they wouldn't stoop so low as to work for Rietveld, but he didn't want to give Rietveld any fuel to burn them. Rietveld could simply dredge up a crowd of his men and kill the whole crew when they showed up. No, maybe they would wiggle out of Rietveld's clutches without Zavi making it harder. It would be better for them to pretend to be all in. Of course, that was the plan that had gotten him cursed in the first place.

"You won't find a better crew in the world," he said as he tried to slip a hand out of the knot behind his back.

Emiel frowned at him. What was he thinking? Had Zavi broken through to him at all? He had to be curious about the scar. He was just afraid of the pain. Zavi definitely understood that. It was a very specific agony and he'd never forget it even if he lived for many more decades.

Rietveld jerked his chin at Emiel. "Run him through, Emiel."

Zavi tugged harder on the knot holding his wrists tight. Emiel walked toward him, unsheathing the short sword at his belt. He wore a curious expression, studying Zavi's face as he went. Suddenly, Emiel's features twisted and he paled, halting.

Rietveld took a step closer. "What is it? Do the job or you'll join him."

"Aye," Emiel said, his voice rough.

The curse was biting at him. He must have recognized Zavi in some very small way. Emiel stood in front of Zavi and set the sword's point against his chest, under the sternum. He would angle the thrust upward and into the heart. A quick death.

"The missing piece of the memory stone hidden inside you is in my pocket," Zavi whispered. "I would never blame you for killing me if you follow his order. Please remember that always. You are my brother even if you don't know it, and I love you dearly. I hope you find peace and joy somehow in this difficult world."

Emiel took a slow, shuddering breath, his gaze darting from Zavi's eyes to the place where Zavi's old scar was. He bent and spoke close to Zavi's face. "I don't know what you're talking about, madman."

So this was it. Emiel would be the one to end Zavi's life.

"If you meet a woman named Lina, please tell her I loved her like I've never loved anyone."

"No," Emiel whispered.

He drew back, spun, and threw the sword at Rietveld. The blade spun tip over hilt, then lodged itself in Rietveld's chest. Rietveld fell backward and Lord Casparji tried to catch him.

Rietveld was dead.

Zavi couldn't stop staring at the lifeless body of the man who had ruined his old life and given him a new one. The life that Emiel had saved.

Zavi's eyes were hot with unshed tears. Emiel might not remember him, but he was still loyal. It was part of his makeup, a trait woven into his flesh. And Zavi loved him for it.

Casparji swore as well as any pirate, his hands fisted and spittle flying from his lips.

Drukker, his blond hair mussed and falling over his

flashing eyes, shouted, "Take the man!" to Rietveld's two guards.

They ran for Emiel, who pulled a dagger from his boot, slipped behind Zavi, and cut Zavi's ties.

Zavi stood and tugged a pair of daggers from his own boots. "Thanks for that, brother."

"No problem, madman."

They lunged at the guards. The larger guard swung a mace at Zavi and Zavi ducked. He came up fast and rammed his blade into the guard's throat. The man dropped, blood spilling down his front. Emiel had been disarmed by the second guard, and they circled one another. Drukker and Casparji crept closer, their swords drawn now too and sweat showing on their faces. These weren't fighters, and they knew that as well as Zavi did. Once he and Emiel took down the second guard, it would all be over.

Zavi moved behind the second guard. The guard shuffled his feet, trying, as he had been trained, to keep his attackers stacked, but Zavi and Emiel were experienced. Emiel might have believed Zavi was insane, but he was fighting with him in the way they always had. Zavi's heart constricted. They adjusted as the guard did.

Drukker shouted. Zavi turned to see whom he was calling out to.

Twenty pirates wearing black sashes tied to their belts streamed into the arena.

❧ 40 ☙

LINA

Star, Phoenix, and I rode into the city on horseback, following Emerald's lead. Sophia had come alongside her father and five of his burlier-looking workers.

Zavi's words echoed through my mind. *You're the most beautiful thing I've ever seen, firefly. You absolutely glow.* I could have dismissed his pretty phrases as a way to get under my skirts, but it hadn't felt like that in his arms. That fire between us... A spark in the dark world... It had felt like a beginning and an end all wrapped into one. *Lina. My mate.* His voice had been low and soft, sincere. Reverent. That night on the ship had had the quality of an exchanging of vows. Some may have called me naive in thinking my first go round with a male would mean something so dear, but they weren't there. I had been there. I had felt the truth in his touch, his gaze, his tone.

Emerald's behavior had set my teeth on edge. Things had gone wrong with Zavi; I just knew it.

Zavi, I am coming for you.

Most of the streets were quiet, the inhabitants sleeping

except for the occasional child's cry or dog's bark. But along the main street, one establishment was raucous still at this late hour. The sign swinging over the door said *The Fiery Cauldron*. Women in embroidered tunics and scarlet trousers sang and lifted pints alongside men in less stylized tunics and darker red trousers.

Mazun lifted a hand to halt us near the tavern.

Star lifted herself from her saddle, standing in her stirrups and tugging the end of her cloak from beneath her. "The merchant class parties just like the lower class here."

Phoenix nodded. "Women and men side by side."

I smiled at Phoenix and Star. "We're going to have a lot of fun in this city."

"If we don't die tonight," Star said, raising an eyebrow.

Mazun dismounted, ran a hand through his tangled black hair, and headed into the tavern.

"Why are we stopping here?" I asked Sophia, who had been discussing something quietly with one of their employees.

"Father needs to let the local Watch know what's going on. He has a contact here."

"Must be nice having the Watch on your side."

Phoenix undid her braid and reworked it. "Or even on the side of justice."

I couldn't even imagine how enraged Father, Drukker, and Rietveld were.

"I love that kind of grin from you, Moth," Star said, easing her mare back a step.

Mazun returned and soon we were clomping down the city streets again, following the muted hue of Emerald's wings against the backdrop of stars. We left the area of nicer shops and newer construction, and the horses brought us into a section of Ashrahl crowded with old manor houses. Most of the roofs had fallen in and the old-style windows—windows never meant to hold glass—gaped like empty eye sockets. In some of the aged buildings, people in rags huddled around small fires that smelled of manure. Their gazes snagged on us as we passed.

A waterwheel churned steadily, splashing and clunking and covering the sound of our horses.

Emerald wheeled low and squawked quietly, seeming to suggest we stop.

Structures partially in ruins from age stood in what appeared to be a circle, a block or so around, if I had to make a guess. Through a dark archway, a bare stretch of sandy ground glittered under the stars. It was hard to see. The light from a torch and the stars slanted together and created odd shadows. Voices rose from inside the arena. I leaned forward and tried to see who was inside. I closed my eyes to focus and listen, but the voices were muffled and they echoed unevenly through the archway.

Mazun turned his horse. "We need reinforcements," he whispered. He waved, indicating that we should follow.

"That's the old arena," Sophia whispered as we made our way back toward the city's center. "Rumors are that Rietveld hosts competitions there between men and beasts. He and his associates bet on how fast the man will die."

Stones, that would be rough. How could anyone think of that as entertainment? "Disgusting."

We trailed Sophia and Mazun toward a three-story house along the main thoroughfare.

Mazun slid from his stallion. "I saw at least ten men

through the double-arched window at the arena. I don't like it. Hopefully, the mayor will give us a hand."

He rapped on the thick oaken door and waited. A squat fellow who looked surprisingly like a toad answered the door.

"What is it, Mazun?" The man blinked and scratched his scruffy chin. "I've been in bed for two hours!"

"Apologies, Lord Mayor, but this is an emergency. We finally have a chance to take down Rietveld and his operations. If we move now."

The mayor's scowl fled and left a wide grin in its place. He rubbed his hands together. "Oh, I love the sound of that. Tell me everything."

"If you're willing, ask Mistress Hamma if she's game, get mounted up, and rouse any soldiers you have in the area. Meet us at the old arena. If you're up for it, I'll fill you in as we ride."

"My wife will definitely be up for this. She hates that man more than I do."

I raised my eyebrows at Star, Sophia, and Phoenix. "I am absolutely in love with the way Laqqaran relationships work."

"The difference between Deigs society and ours is rather striking," Sophia said.

The respect in the mayor's eyes somehow reminded me of Zavi. But of course, everything was bringing him to mind the last few hours. I took a breath and sent up a prayer that he was still alive and kicking.

❧ 41 ❧

ZAVI

Emiel had frozen in place.

"It's me!" Zavi shouted at his crew. Old Ones, bless them. They were all here. Would they fight for him? "It's our crew, Emiel," Zavi said as he lunged at the guard to keep him busy. "Do you remember any of them?"

Casparji laughed. "Your former captain is as good as dead," he said, addressing the pirate crew. "He murdered Master Rietveld. Kill them both or your life is forfeit."

The crew stared at Zavi and Emiel, their eyes wide.

Brodie flipped one of the two daggers he held and sneered. "Rietveld said he was dead already."

Faraine's light blue hands flexed on her broadsword. She had as much Fae blood as Zavi, and sometimes Fae skin held colors that human flesh never did.

"Well, Rietveld is now a corpse," she said, eyeing the body. "How is he supposed to pay us if he's the one who is dead?"

Another group of what had to be Rietveld's men stalked

into the arena behind the crew. "Do it now," Drukker barked, "or you'll be hanging by sunrise."

The new men held swords to the crew's backs, and they started toward Zavi and Emiel.

Casparji smirked, his face flushed with rage or excitement. Maybe both. "Please, do keep fighting, Captain Zavi." Sarcasm slicked his voice. "I haven't had entertainment this interesting in a while."

Drukker chuckled and slapped Casparji's shoulder. "I wish your daughter were here to witness this."

Everyone had paused, as if no one knew quite what to do or who was on whose side.

Casparji nodded. "She'll come around. Don't worry. I know exactly where she is hiding and no one can keep her from me. A father has rights, even away from his kingdom."

If only Lina could hear that. She'd be enraged and destroy everyone in here. Zavi couldn't help but smile at the thought of his fierce mate. Even though he'd lost her, he would always love her.

A figure moved between two of Rietveld's men...

42

LINA

My blood boiled as I walked out of the archway and glared at my father. "Well, you're going to have a hard time exerting your supposed rights, Father. Not when I'm holding one of these." I lifted my dagger and wiggled it. My heart was racing. "In fact, why don't you try saying that one more time."

All heads turned toward us. There seemed to be a sort of standoff happening. But where was Zavi?

"Lina?" Zavi's voice filtered up from the arena's center and through the crowd.

I gripped my dagger and stepped forward, trying to see around a bunch of very scary-looking fellows. I wasn't too worried though because the mayor, his soldiers, and a load of other heavily armed folks flowed into the arena behind me.

"Take her. Take them all!" Drukker called out.

The men around us turned to fight the mayor's soldiers. Swords clashed, shouts went up all around, and suddenly I was fighting a man three times my size. Phoenix, Star, and

Sophia fought beside me. Star threw knives and thrusted blades, picking up new ones that those downed had dropped. Phoenix had a short sword and was spinning and striking, a look of rage in her lovely features. Sophia scrambled up a half-crumbled wall support and began picking off fighters with her bow and arrow. There was so much going on, but I couldn't turn to see if Zavi was all right. I had enough to deal with. I kicked upward, sending my shin into the big man's stones. I missed hitting him straight on and he drove toward me, knife extended. I dodged the strike and jumped beside him, cutting him deep along his side as I moved.

"Lina!" Zavi's voice was a lighthouse in this storm.

"I'm here!" I stabbed the big man in the side and he dropped to a knee.

One of the soldiers finished him off with a slice of his sword.

I shoved my way through the pirates and Rietveld's men, driving toward Drukker, who had hidden behind a column.

"You're pathetic." I snaked my hand around the column and snatched his arm. I dragged him out.

"Lina! Stop. We can work this out."

"You're about to have a lot of trouble on your hands. I don't think you'll have time for a wife." I turned and shouted, "This one has heavy pockets!" into the fray of miscreants, who were more like me than I wanted to admit.

Three men ran at Drukker as I slipped away to find Father.

He had his sword in his nondominant hand and was parrying off strikes from a pirate whose shirt had been ripped down one side. A Masdam Watchman came up behind the pirate and knocked him down with one blow of his club.

I faced my father. "The days of you running my life are over. Your life is over if you don't surrender right now."

The end of his sword wobbled not five inches from my nose. "I only ever wanted to raise you the way I had been taught. I love you, daughter."

"Bull shite. You educated me, then took away any need I had for a brain. You tried to force me into a cowardly, abusive man's bed. You hit me. That isn't love. Love is what I have found with my friends. And maybe with a certain pirate here. Last chance, Father. Lay down your weapon and give up, or I'll call Mazun over here. He won't be nearly as merciful as me."

His gaze flicked over my shoulder and I saw Mazun there, glaring and flanked by Ashrahl Watchmen and two members who I assumed were part of Zavi's crew, what with the black sashes and all.

Father set his sword down.

"Tell me you're sorry." My voice cracked, but I cleared my throat and said it louder. "Tell me you're sorry." He wouldn't mean it, but I wanted to hear him say it.

"I only—"

I set the tip of my dagger under his chin. "No. That isn't an apology."

"I...I'm sorry." His eyes flashed with rage.

"Beg me not to end you for all the horrible things you've done."

"I will not," he said through gritted teeth.

"Moth." Phoenix's voice wove through my anger and grief. It was a reminder that I wasn't a monster.

Did I want to kill my own father? I cleared my throat. Tears threatened to roll down my cheeks, but I forced them to dry right on up. Lifting my hand, I flipped my knife and hit him across the temple with the hilt. He went down like a stone.

"Someone come clean up this rubbish."

I spun to rejoin the fighting, but rough hands grabbed me around the middle. I rammed my elbow into my attacker's nose. He shouted and released me. My legs buckled. I was suddenly on the bloodied ground. I tried to leap back up, but my legs weren't working. What was...

A dark spot showed on my tunic. I pressed a hand to my side. With fighting going on all around me, I'd been stabbed and hadn't even noticed.

"Lina!" Zavi broke through the chaos and knelt beside me.

His eyes widened at the sight of my wound. His green, green eyes. But I didn't see my kidnapper in his gaze. I only saw the one who treated me like I was the best treasure in the world. He touched my face, then my wound, and he hissed.

"Who are these other men?" I asked.

"My crew. They're fighting for me."

"I thought so."

Two of the fighters wearing black sashes took down three of Rietveld's men.

A whip-thin man burst through two men wrestling over a knife behind Zavi.

I pointed, the motion making my vision waver. "Look out!"

Zavi lifted me with what seemed to be no effort at all, then launched a front kick into the assailant. The man grunted and dropped back, but he kept his feet. He came at us again. The others were too close now. There was no room for Zavi to move or to lift his foot.

The world grew hazy at the edges. "Just drop me!"

Ignoring me, Zavi held tight, turned, and took the stab of the thin brute's knife. Wincing and growling, he lurched backward. Still holding me, he shoved himself into the attacker. The man's knife, covered in blood, clattered to the arena's stone steps, and the wielder fell under another of Rietveld's men. A boot hit his head and he was knocked out.

I was floating. All sounds faded to a low murmur.

"I've got you, firefly." Zavi's chest vibrated as he spoke against my head. "Don't let that glow fade. I will be lost in the dark."

❧ 43 ❧

LINA

Nightmares flooded the darkness.

Drukker stood over me, ten feet tall and bristling with anger. *"You will be mine. I will find a way."* He raised a hand and closed it slowly like he could trap me inside.

Father and Mother shimmered into the nightmare. *"We will punish those who have aided you in defying us."* Their words mingled together and echoed off unseen walls.

A gentle hand took mine, but the darkness would not fade.

Inside the dark, Drukker, Rietveld, and my parents grew fangs like the Fae and ran at me. Their fingers extended to become talons like the Unseelie Fae were known to have. I shuddered and wrapped my fingers more tightly around the gentle hand. They tore at my hair and clothes.

Whispers rode over the chaos and my screams. "Do not give in, firefly. Lina, please, show the world that ferocity I adore. Please."

The speaker was invisible, but I knew it belonged to the hand that held mine. If I could only open my eyes and stop these horrible dreams, maybe then, death wouldn't come for me. If I could just see him...

Sounds filtered through my nightmares.

"...part Unseelie..." It was a familiar voice, but whose?

"We can't risk it." Another voice I knew but couldn't place.

"We must risk it."

Their words grew muffled and I faced Drukker and my parents in my nightmare. I gripped the gentle hand ferociously. Strength flowed from the hand and joined with my own righteous anger. I grew taller than Drukker and my parents, and my blood boiled.

"You have been beaten at your sick game. I am no longer under your control. I. Am. Free."

A whirling light burst from my chest and split the dream specters into a thousand pieces.

A breeze cooled my blood and my flushed face. The darkness softened to a dim light, then I opened my eyes fully to see Zavi holding my hand. I let out a long, stuttering breath. My lungs felt like they had been crushed, but the nightmares were gone. I was alive. Here, with Zavi. Relief shone in his gaze. His fangs showed as he smiled, and dark circles hung beneath his eyes.

"I will forever owe the gods a favor," Zavi said, resting his forehead on my hand.

I started to reach for his head with my free hand, but someone stopped me. A slightly gray-skinned half-Fae held my other arm fast, a paintbrush poised over me.

"Unseelie?" I croaked.

The magical healer smiled down at me. "Yes. I'm using Unseelie rune magic on you." She touched my temple. "I hope it works. I only have a smidge of Unseelie blood from way back in my family tree. And don't fret about this magic. Your bard there has threatened me within an inch of my life. I have been duly warned to be very careful with you."

His lips lifting in a lazy grin, Zavi focused his green eyes on me, and I ached to curl into his arms. Did I trust him finally? I couldn't deny the comfort and strength he'd given me. In my nightmares, there hadn't been room for any anger toward him. It had been nothing compared to the rage I felt toward my parents and Drukker.

Zavi moved a lock of my hair away from my forehead. The touch felt even better than the healing runes.

"You're lucky you were seriously injured in Laqqara, not in Deigs, because there are a few here with Unseelie blood."

"And none at home," I said. "Yes."

Magic coursed through my temple and down my body in cool waves.

"You had a terrible fever. How do you feel now?" Zavi asked.

"So much better."

Zavi looked over me to the healer, who nodded.

A heavy feeling blanketed me. "I didn't ask for that magic…" I said, slurring.

Sleep whisked me away.

A DAY—OR MAYBE TWO—LATER, I WAS UP AND ABOUT THE plantation. I took daily walks with Phoenix, Sophia, and Star. Sometimes Zavi would join us, but he wasn't pushing. Once I had proved I was going to live, he had given me space. It was a distance that I tried to appreciate, but in reality, I loathed.

Phoenix, Star, and Sophia strolled through the fields with me, telling me everything that had happened after I'd gone down in the fight at the arena ruins.

"And your ex is now in a Laqqaran prison," Sophia said, "which I find particularly delightful."

Drukker in prison. I laughed hard and winced at the pain of my healing injury.

As we walked, dust rose from the path through the fields and Sophia detailed the end of the fight, how Zavi had carried me away as his crew finished routing our enemies, and how the mayor had ordered Drukker and Father to a long sentence here in Ashrahl.

Around us, the saffron blooms were ghosts—scattered, wilted petals that hadn't made it into the baskets. But the plantation was still beautiful. Tall trees with thick trunks lined the back of the property and birds dipped in and out of the fields to catch bugs. The waterwheel at the far western border of the plantation sparkled in the sun. I was so unmoored, but the sensation was fantastic. I had no one to please. No set future. I could go any which way I chose from here. I could stay or go, as Sophia had put it yesterday.

"What happened with Zavi's crew?" I asked.

"They had a very wild party with their captain," Star said, "then they sailed away."

"They left Zavi?" I scanned the area. Was he out here somewhere?

Phoenix shrugged. "He wanted them to. Said he hasn't been a pirate in a while and he doesn't plan on returning to the job. Mazun and Iyana have offered Zavi and Emiel employment."

"What is Zavi doing now?"

Star grinned and watched our feet as we strolled on. "He is making sure everyone cares for you properly."

"I don't need that."

"We know," Phoenix said, "but it is really sweet."

Sophia steered us to the left, heading for the river that ran alongside her family's land. "We asked him to stay on as a farmhand. He hasn't said yes or no yet."

Phoenix took my low ponytail and twirled it around her finger. "Because he is waiting to see if you'll have him or reject him."

They were blessedly quiet. I needed more time to think. I wanted to forgive him and to believe he was a new person, but when I felt that way, I could just imagine myself on the day of the kidnapping and... I pursed my lips and tried to calm my thundering heart.

"Do you want help deciding?" Phoenix asked.

Well, I spoke too soon about the whole quiet thing. "What do you mean, exactly?"

Clasping her hands at her chest, Phoenix grinned like a madwoman. "Imagine if we told you he had left on his ship. For good."

My stomach dropped.

"See?" Phoenix pointed at my face.

"She's right, you know," Star said.

Sophia took my arm and we stopped at the edge of the river. "Oh, looky there. I had no idea you were taking a swim, Zavi. Sorry to bother you."

"Sophia, you are a liar," I said.

Emerging from the shadow of a massive oak, Zavi swam to the far side of the river, his bare shoulders glistening with water. He hadn't noticed us yet, or he was acting as if he hadn't. With his back to us, Zavi stood in the shallows near the short drop-off, and the water lapped the smooth lines of his lower back. Raising his hands, he slicked his hair back and water cascaded down his body. The scars from the ibisgon attack gleamed white. He had healed incredibly fast. Lucky Fae, with all that magical blood.

"So many muscles," Phoenix whispered in my ear.

I rolled my eyes, but I couldn't actually look away. I didn't think he was wearing trousers either.

"Gee, I think a foot soak would do you some good." Star bent and began untying my boots. Sophia and Phoenix joined her.

"Get off me." I nudged them away with my knee and they dissolved into laughter before hurrying away and leaving me on the bank. The meddling jerks.

Zavi turned and gave me a fantastic smile, teeth white in his tan face. "I agree with them actually," he said over the shushing of the current.

Words filled my mouth, but I held them in. I was in two pieces. One wanted him. No holding back. The other kept staring into his green eyes and searching for my enemy. But that defensive side, that part of me that was still ready to do what I needed to do to protect myself and to protect Sophia, couldn't find the kidnapper in Zavi's steady gaze. He just... wasn't him anymore.

Zavi swam slowly to my side of the river. He definitely wasn't wearing a stitch of clothing. My swallow was probably audible even over the river's noise. With careful movement, he approached me.

"May I?" he asked, gesturing to my feet, which were tucked under me.

I shucked off my boots and let my toes submerge in the cold water. A sigh left me. It was wonderful. Zavi stood in front of me, partially obscured by the river from the waist down. He cupped his hands and poured water over my ankles, then higher over my shins and knees. I leaned back on my elbows and watched him, the side of me who wasn't yet convinced about Zavi making me study every shift of his features.

Zavi was eyeing me too. "Hold on."

He walked over to a knot of grass a couple of feet away and brought back a dagger. The dagger that had been on his belt ever since I'd met him. Holding the weapon out to me, he smiled sadly.

"There," he said. "You have the upper ground and the only weapon. You are in control of this moment. Not me."

"I'm not afraid of you."

"Really? Because you look like you're trying to decide where exactly to stab me."

A chuckle bubbled up and I let it out. "I'm not going to stab you, but I appreciate the gesture you're making here."

I set the dagger beside me, and some of the grief in Zavi's eyes lightened.

"Progress," he said.

"What happened with Emiel?"

"Not much. He won't talk about the memory stone. It definitely affected him more severely than it did me. Iyana and Mazun asked him to stay and work."

"They asked you too, right?"

"They did."

He scooped more water over my legs, then ran his fingers from my knees down to the arches of my feet. It felt divine.

"Is Emiel here now?" I asked. "What is your plan?"

"He's in the courtyard, working with a new colt and his mother. He has always been very good with animals. I told him so and he looked ready to punch the grin right off my face."

The autumn breeze blew around us and made the fallen oak leaves dance.

"Why is he angry with you?"

Zavi pursed his lips. "I think he's confused and his head is fogged. He isn't thinking clearly about me. The curse is so much worse for him. I wonder...never mind. Talk to me about how you're feeling. Please."

"No, tell me. What do you wonder?"

"If I manage to talk him into the surgery and uncurse him, will he ever be the Emiel I knew and loved or will he be changed forever?"

I took his fingers and turned one hand over, spilling the water he had cupped. I pulled him closer. His unclothed hip, still submerged, brushed my leg, and my cheeks flushed. He leaned against the bank and held my hand, his thumb skating across my knuckles and giving me more delicious shivers than simple handholding should ever accomplish.

"Well, you're a tricky Fae. Why don't you just knock him out with some goblinbloom?" The mild relaxant, hallucinogenic plant was very popular in the Fae realm, or so I'd heard.

His eyebrows lifted and he sniffed a laugh. "That could work."

"I think you should do it. If I were in his shoes, I would want to know my past. I'd definitely want to remember my brother, if I had one. I always want to know the truth about everything in my life."

"Makes sense."

"What do you mean?"

"You were lied to and controlled, well, somewhat, by your parents. Then I lied to you multiple times."

"Some of those lies weren't your fault."

"Some were." He met my gaze, his eyes unblinking.

His admission wasn't the first one he'd made to me, but this one sank into my heart and warmed me. If I closed the distance between us, we would be together. He would be my mate, ready to support me, love me, to live this amazing life with me. I felt a pull between our bodies, like some rare magic wanted us together in every way.

"I'm glad you aren't trying to excuse the robbery or your past crimes."

"No excuse is good enough. Not even saving Emiel. He wouldn't have wanted me to rob you and lie in order to find him and uncurse him."

"So the kidnapping from his side happened...why, exactly?"

"He thought he was working for someone else. Not Rietveld. By the time he figured it out and had royally screwed up, he was trapped. Do as ordered or end up in pieces fed to the sharks outside Kruid Bay."

I nodded.

Zavi turned away from me and began walking back to where he'd stashed his clothes. He left the dagger with me.

"I'll leave today," he said, "and I'll take Emiel with me if he'll come. You won't have to look at us after today. Never again."

I was in the water, striding toward him before I knew I was moving. A rush of longing more powerful than any river's current washed over me, and I wrapped my arms around him and set my head on his bare back. The pull between us sizzled with his skin against me. He smelled intoxicatingly wild—like the river and forest—such a Fae sort of scent. He twisted in my grip, his eyes wide.

"Are you stabbing me?" He looked down and around, a grin tilting his lips.

"Not today. But you aren't going anywhere."

He cocked his head to one side and his gaze swept over my eyes, cheeks, and neck like a soft touch. "I'm not?"

I shook my head. I didn't trust myself to speak right this second. Too many emotions were tumbling around in my heart.

He narrowed his eyes. "So you can have your chance to murder me tomorrow?"

Water droplets hung from his thick eyelashes and sunlight beamed through the trees to slant across his high, sharp cheekbones and his strong jaw. His eyes were the color of pine trees at dusk.

Old Ones, save me. I was so far gone for this male.

He smoothed the fallen wisps of my bright red hair behind my ears and kissed my forehead. The cold of the river and the heat of his skin felt amazing.

"Firefly, I will follow your light as long as you allow it. To the ends of the realms and back again."

The two sides of me crashed together and the invisible link between us grew more powerful. I felt as though no matter where he went or what I decided, I would always know him and love him.

"Lina," he said, his voice so very quiet and low like a drum's beat, "You are my home. I will always love you even if you can't find a way to see the person I am now."

I drew back a little and looked at him straight on. My heart sang with my decision. "I love you, Zavi. Will you stay here and live with me? Will you marry me?"

A smile burst across his face and it stole my breath. He lifted me and I wrapped my legs around him.

"Yes, Lina." He kissed me, his tongue drawing across the side of my mouth. Heat poured through me. "Yes," he whispered, kissing my neck, "yes, yes, yes."

I kissed him back and I didn't keep it soft and sweet. I wanted more. So much more.

44
ZAVI

"I'm not sure if I'm excited Lina will be dressed to match me or if I'm worried I'll pluck the eyes from anyone who looks at her too long." Zavi smoothed the open front of his long dark red vest. They were dressing for the wedding in one of the Ofandrus family's guest chambers.

Sophia's brother, Burzin, snorted a laugh. "Her attire only matches in hue. I doubt you two would make it through the ceremony if she was equally exposed."

Burzin had returned that morning from a trading trip to Saxonion, the kingdom directly north of Laqqara. He'd agreed to be one of Zavi's blessings at the wedding today. Three people were required to walk in front of the groom and three others in front of the bride.

Zavi eyed himself in the mirror and saw Burzin behind him, trying to tie his shoulder-length hair back at the base of his neck. "You look much better in red than I do."

Burzin bowed and chuckled. "Thank you, brother."

"I still haven't quite absorbed the fact that your family is giving me their surname. I can't tell you what that means to me."

Damn, he was not going to cry. No. But to have a family, and not only a family, but one as amazing as this one? It was something he'd never even tried to wish for.

Burzin handed over a mug of mead. "Let's share a drink together."

They sat at the small round table near the chamber's window. Outside, everyone was gathering to walk to the crossroads stone where the wedding would take place.

"Will your crew be here soon?" Burzin took a swallow of his drink.

"I'm not sure."

They had left two weeks ago. Zavi rapped his fingers on his mug as yet another image of Lina flashed through his mind. Her fiery hair against the blue of the sky. The feel of her hand in his was pure magic...

"They had a lot of loose ends to tie up concerning Rietveld's death and their future," he said.

Burzin was grinning when Zavi looked at him again. "You are solidly in love with her, aren't you?"

"Why do you say that?"

"Because you have a certain look on your face, and you are definitely not thinking about right now and this conversation."

Zavi had to laugh at himself. "I am in love with her. Have been for a while now."

"I'm glad you'll have one another. Plus, you'll make living here more exciting, I'm sure. We needed some new blood. So this crew of yours, they're going to work for the mayor now, right? Or was that just my father's wild idea?"

"They are, and it was Mazun's idea, yes. A brilliant one."

Standing, Burzin glanced out the window. "Well, it's time."

Zavi couldn't leave that chamber fast enough to suit his hammering heart.

I'm coming, my mate. Today will be ours.

❦ 45 ❦

LINA

Zavi was to meet me at the crossroads stone, an ancient rock adorned with rune carvings. I wore a short dark red shirt with a dangerous slit down the front. My Laqqaran trousers were embroidered with luminous purple saffron flowers and my feet were tied into a pair of very complicated sandals. The gold beaded band that Sophia had woven through my crown of braids and across my forehead was my favorite part of the wedding attire.

I walked behind my three blessings, Sophia, Phoenix, and Star. They parted, found a place to stand in the small crowd, and there, in the shadow of the crossroads stone, stood Zavi.

He gave me a grin that said he was more than ready to be alone. My cheeks heated fiercely and my pulse raced. A little unsteady from the two mugs of mead I'd had before leaving the house, I approached him and he took my hand.

"My firefly. You are stunning."

The joy on his face reflected my own. I couldn't wait to make him laugh, to curl into his arms, and to build a life together. The long dark red sleeveless vest that he wore hung open and loose to show his chest and narrow waist. His trousers were the same color as his vest and he also wore a pair of complicated sandals, but they were somehow more masculine. We were doing this in full Laqqaran tradition to demonstrate our commitment to making a life here.

The suntalker—a Laqqaran religious leader—joined us, her dark hair braided into a headpiece that mimicked rays of sunshine.

"We come here to witness the joining of two people from distant lands," she said, her voice melodious and strong.

The gathered crowd was full of familiar faces and strangers. I didn't see Emiel anywhere, but surely he had come since everyone else had.

With her arms around her children, Phoenix blew me a kiss. Star winked and rubbed Emerald's chin; the dragon had perched on her shoulder. Wolfling had shown up again. It was horrible that Rietveld had driven him off the night we were at the arena. The dog sat beside Sophia now, his shaggy tail flapping up and down.

"We have welcomed them to our kingdom and our traditions, and they have embraced our ways." She focused on Zavi and me. "Place your hands on the stone."

The stone was cool to the touch and the runes under my palm almost seemed to spark, but that could have just been my imagination. I looked at Zavi, who raised an eyebrow at the stone.

His gaze dusted across my face and yearning for him pulsed through me. He could satisfy every bit of that yearning with that mouth, those hands, and that mind. When he looked at me like that, the world disappeared and it was only him and me. Alone and on fire in all the best ways.

I gave him a chastising look. After all, this was meant to be a holy gathering and his eyes were full of naughty imaginings, but I couldn't quite stop smiling. He grinned and stepped closer, his body nearly touching mine. The pulse of love and desire beat between us, like a drum that ordered me to step even closer.

Zavi's crew had arrived. They stood near my friends and Sophia's family and staff.

The suntalker raised her gold-painted hands to hush the crowd. "I dedicate the bond between Zavi and Lina to the sun, to the heat, to the light that feeds us in body and soul."

She had us face one another and join hands. Zavi's fingers were so warm and when he moved or readjusted his grip, the place where our skin met almost seemed to sizzle. With a long ribbon the specific purple of saffron flowers, the suntalker bound our wrists.

"In the presence of their blessings and their families," the suntalker continued, "both chosen and born, and under the divine sunlight, I declare these two bound by marriage."

A cheer rippled through the crowd, hands clapping and some ringing small bronze bells that seemed to be Laqqaran tradition as well. The suntalker untied our wrists, lifted a bell from the ground near her feet, and rang it soundly.

Zavi grabbed me and kissed me hard on the mouth. "My mate. I adore you and will do absolutely anything to prove myself to you over and over again."

I held the back of his neck, and his hair fell over my fingers. I pulled him closer, inhaling the salt and bergamot scent he always had. I smiled, realizing I would find out why he had that scent, what soaps he preferred and what oils he wore in his hair. I would know him better than anyone I had ever met. A lightness filled me as we walked through a corridor of our loved ones. Phoenix and Star stepped forward and hugged me tightly.

"You saved us, Moth," Phoenix said. "And I am so grateful." Tears shone in her eyes.

Star gripped my shoulder and stared into my eyes. "It's true. We wouldn't have had the stones to see this through without you leading the way. Thank you, friend."

I kissed them each on the cheek. "You are the most blessed of blessings in history. I am lucky to have found you."

We hugged again, then I turned to see Zavi smiling widely. Warmth surged through me. He wasn't hurrying me. He respected my friendships and delighted in them as I did. I hoped Emiel would come around soon and be the brother Zavi needed.

With Emerald flying above and Wolfling bumping Zavi and wagging his tail, we continued our quick trip down the corridor of happy faces. Bells rang, people cheered, and Zavi only had eyes for me.

In the bedchamber Sophia had ordered prepared for us, a large and sumptuous room on the second floor of the manor house, Zavi lifted me and tossed me onto the bed. Black silk curtains blocked the light from one half of the overly cushioned, completely indulgent sleeping surface. He tugged at them, pulling them back so the sunlight spilled from the window onto my body.

"Much better."

I laughed. "Getting old, Fae bard? Need more light to see your lover?"

He growled, ripped his long vest off, and crawled on top of me. In between the kisses he set on the skin exposed by the deep slit in my shirt, he whispered, "You are not my lover. You are my mate. It is so much more."

I sighed as his lips found a sensitive spot on my neck above my collarbone. "Aside from the obvious, what does it mean to you?"

"I feel the need to show everyone that you are mine. Obnoxious, I know. I desire you more than I have ever wanted anyone. My attraction to you feels like a matter of life and death. There could be more to it as we grow closer. My Fae blood might surprise us now and then."

"Our love will be a grand adventure," I said.

He nibbled my ear and I shivered, loving every moment of it. "The best adventure."

"I want you to teach me all you know about the arts of the bedchamber."

A chuckle shook his shoulders as he leaned into me, shifting his weight onto an elbow. "The arts."

I slapped him on the arm playfully. "Call it what you like, but you know what I mean. Don't hold back."

Kneeling on the bed, he drew me up until I was on my knees too. "I wouldn't dream of it, firefly."

He unlaced my shirt and threw it on the floor. Bending his head, he drew his lips over my breast, and my breath caught, my heart hammering in my chest. His hand smoothed down my body from my shoulder, over my chest, and down my stomach.

"Shh, love. Calm that heart of yours. This is a long journey. We won't be sprinting tonight."

Heat pulsed in my belly and lower. His fingers drifted between my legs and he strummed my body through my clothing. My thighs clenched, my whole body tingling.

"What if I want to sprint?" I panted out. I wanted him now. In every way.

His grin was decadent. "This will be worth the wait."

"You're incredibly arrogant, you know that?"

"You're not exactly humble," he said, his laugh dusting over my flushed skin.

He eased me onto my back and eyed my trousers.

"Yes, please," I said. "Let's be done with all of this."

"On that, we can agree."

He slid my clothing off and leaned back, his eyes sparkling with admiration. I felt like a goddess.

"I'm trying to summon up words to describe what you do to me, but..." He shook his head.

"Your turn." I unbuckled his belt, untied his trousers, and wrapped my arms around his neck. The feel of him against me sent a shock of desire through me so powerful that I felt unsteady.

He held me tightly and nipped his way from my ear, along my neck, and then between my breasts. I inhaled and let my head fall back, goosebumps dancing down my body. His tongue found my nipples and he teased and bit lightly, bringing a gasp from my throat.

"Too much?"

"No. Good." I took his head in my hands and eased him back in place.

He smiled against my ribs and lowered me onto my back.

His kisses were as light as a feather's touch as he dipped below my waist, then lower. I dug my fingers into his hair and tugged. Pleasure rippled up from my core and soon I was drawing him to eye level. I took hold of his hips, marveling in the feel of the bone beneath his smooth skin. I wanted to explore every inch of him. The sensation of his abdomen muscles contracting under my palm was magical, the scent of him all around me, the heat of his length against me…

Gazing at me with those beautiful eyes, he whispered, "Whatever you wish from me, I will do my best to give. Just say the word. I am yours through and through and through."

I pulled him down and kissed him, tasting his tongue and the corner of his mouth, and biting teasingly as he thrust into me. Pleasure drove up my body and the world was bliss.

He went to his elbows, and his arms cocooned my head.

"My firefly, my mate," he whispered against my temple.

His hips shifted forward and back, every move powerful and unflinching, and I took it all, savoring the exquisite joy of being joined with the only male I had ever loved, the only person I had ever loved like this. We were one. We were light. We were the most shining moment.

I wrapped my legs around him and held him to me. I was on the edge of breaking into glittering pieces of sensation and it was the most marvelous feeling. Nothing could hurt me here. I was free here. Alive. Fully myself and fully in love.

"Lina, my Lina…" His breath coursed through my hair and his body shuddered.

Pleasure crashed over me, unmaking and remaking me, and I whispered his name, my voice a wish and a promise. "My Zavi, my bard, my mate."

EPILOGUE

Zavi

Fighting a chuckle, Zavi drew the covers over Lina's shoulder. She was snoring like a sailor who'd had a barrel of grog, and gods, how he loved it. He loved everything about her. She could do no wrong. They had been in bed for nearly two days, with the staff bringing them various meals on trays. They had eaten by the fire, telling one another tales about their wild nights in Masdam. She had stolen so many rings. He chuckled then, unable to keep his joy contained.

Sniffing and mumbling, Lina rolled over.

He dropped a kiss on her temple. "I'll be back in an hour."

He dressed quickly and slipped on a pair of boots Mazun had ordered for him the day after the wedding. They'd been showered in gifts that arrived in tidy, wrapped packages of silk and linen. It was too much generosity. Truly, far too much.

With one last glance at Lina, Zavi slipped out of the bedchamber and headed down the corridor to the stairs. He had to help Emiel. Lina would understand him leaving the wonder that was their bedchamber for that very good reason.

Downstairs, he bid good morning to the man who brought them luncheon, then he hurried out the kitchen door to the small cookery garden behind the house. Emiel was already there, settling a flat stone into the path that snaked through the raised beds of cabbage, root vegetables, and some herbs he wasn't sure he had seen before now. Emiel's tunic was soaked through despite the early hour. His brother was a hard worker and started his jobs before the sun was up.

"You've always risen early to finish before the sun drops toward evening."

Emiel halted in his work, then turned slowly, eyeing Zavi over one large shoulder. He looked terrible. He'd gone paler than ever and was hollow-eyed.

"Don't shut me out, Emiel." Zavi knelt beside him and lifted the next stone. He worked the flat dark gray rock into the void Emiel had dug while Zavi was still in bed. "You're dying and you know it."

With a grunt, Emiel sat back and bowed his head. "You're right. I don't know what is happening to me, but...but I don't feel right at all."

"Please. Let us check out what gave you that scar. The one that matches mine. I swear on my bride that I am telling you the truth about this. You are my brother."

Emiel looked up and met Zavi's gaze. "Fine. Cut me open. I'm about to die anyway, so what is there to lose?"

Zavi clapped once and jumped up. "That's the spirit!" He took Emiel's hands and pulled him to standing. "Come, let's find someone who is ready to slice and dice you."

"You have the absolute worst bedside manner. Has anyone ever told you that?"

"We were pirates, brother. And though we have left the life of crime and ocean shenanigans, some things are tougher to shed."

Emiel grumbled something unintelligible and followed Zavi back into the house.

IN LESS THAN AN HOUR, THEY HAD THE CURSE UNDONE, AND Emiel was blinking and staring up at Zavi from the healer's table. The memory stones—his and his brother's—lay side by side on the healer's desk in the corner.

He leaned on the table and tried not to lose patience. If he could have his brother back, his life would be complete. Without him... Well, he didn't want to imagine that this wasn't going to work or that Emiel's mind was too far gone to heal.

The one window's light painted a stripe across the small room that had been built onto the western side of the house.

"Emiel? Please say something."

Emiel touched the bloody stitches. "Zavi?" He sounded like himself again, saying Zavi's name in that quick way he had when they were young.

Zavi crumpled onto Emiel's chest. "Yes, brother. Yes, it's me." He fought tears and laughed into Emiel's tunic. "Gods, I'm so glad to have you back."

"Welcome to our home, Emiel," Lina said, grinning wildly

as she said the word *home*. That was what the plantation was for her now. Her true home.

Lina's hair was pulled back into a quick knot, her lips were swollen from kissing, and she had never been more beautiful. She stood by the table, one elegant hand on the edge.

"Glad you're back," she said to Emiel. "I've been waiting to meet you."

Emiel smiled and shook his head like he was attempting to clear it.

Zavi exhaled. Stones, he was relieved. "Do you remember much?"

"I remember you, the orphanage...I also remember..." His gaze cut to Lina. "Days that I would rather forget."

Zavi set a hand on his brother's shoulder. His face was going to split in two from smiling. "Don't worry about that. We are all about new beginnings here. If you want them."

Emiel nodded, then shut his eyes. Zavi snatched a pillow from a stash of bedding items on the shelves under the hanging dry herbs.

"I am very dizzy," Emiel said.

But his speech was clear.

The part-Unseelie healer dipped her gray hands in the basin on the side table. "He should sleep and heal. You can return this evening."

Zavi kissed Emiel's forehead. "I love you, brother. Take your time. I had the same curse. Not sure if you recall my tale. It's a nasty bugger."

Emiel's chest moved up and down evenly.

"Don't worry. He's just asleep," Lina said. "Right?" she asked the healer, who nodded.

"I have only seen a curse similar to his once," the healer

said, "but I can tell when someone is on their way toward death. He is not. Most assuredly. I will take the memory stones to the mayor. Perhaps they can send them back to the Unseelie realm for destruction."

Lina eased forward and spoke into Emiel's ear. "Emiel, if you can hear me in your dreams, you make sure you live because I need someone to tell me who is and isn't crooked in the world of jewelry around here. I assume you know more than Zavi since you've been working in Ashrahl."

A laugh spilled from Zavi. Lina would never stop surprising him with her cleverness.

Zavi set a hand on Emiel's chest and took a deep breath. His brother was alive and his memory wasn't completely gone. It was an absolute miracle. *Thank you, Old Ones. Thank you so very much.*

The healer shooed them away from Emiel.

Zavi escorted Lina out of the healer's room and into the garden. "What's going through that gorgeous head of yours?"

"I have decided I'm going to open a jewelry shop at the market. Then I'll be surrounded by shiny things all day."

"You're glowing again." He put her hand on his arm and kissed her knuckles.

"I have a feeling I'll be doing that pretty often from now on."

"If I have anything to do with it, you will."

She spun into him. He wrapped her in his arms, and he began to sing.

"A beauty with light fingers,
She'll steal your heart away,
And then on New Year's morning,
She'll dance the day away..."

Lina kissed him on the mouth, then on the tip of his nose. "Oh, my handsome bard, how I adore that voice of yours."

Zavi didn't deserve this happy life, but he would hold it tight for as long as fate permitted. "I will sing to you until the end of our days, and I will happily provide as many naughty romance books as I am able."

Laughing, she kissed him until he was dizzy.

READERS,

Thank you so much for diving into this story! I hope you enjoyed reading it as much as I loved writing it for you. If you are new to the Realm of Dragons and Fae world, try The Fae King's Assassin (an enemies to lovers story), The Unseelie King's Rebel (a touch her and die story), and Bound by Dragons (novella prequel to upcoming series about dragon riders featuring Marius and Ragewing, who met Zavi in the arena).

If you'd like to see bonus art first, character interviews, behind the scenes stuff, and extra material from The Pirate King's Thief, be sure to join my newsletter. https://www.alishaklapheke.com/free-prequel-1

Thank you again for reading!
Alisha

AFTERWORD

Amsterdam inspired much of Masdam, the capital city in the kingdom of Deigs. This story takes place in a fantastical version of the late medieval period, but has multiple allowances for my own fun interpretation. I am by no means tied to real history or places that are actually found on our real world maps. I do enjoy traveling and studying history though so I often use my experience to flavor my worlds.

As for *The Princess Bride* influences, well, you can see how Zavi had a bit of Wesley and the Dread Pirate Roberts in his personality, yes? I have adored that movie ever since I watched it as a child. So good! The quirky humor and ensemble cast is exactly my type of thing.

I hope you enjoyed the story! If you did, you might go on to read the others in this world—*The Fae King's Assassin*, *The Unseelie King's Rebel*, and *Bound by Dragons* (which is a prequel to a 2024 series which will begin in full with *Kingdom of Spirits*).

Thanks for reading!

ACKNOWLEDGMENTS

Thank you to Laura Josephson for the amazing editing (Why do I talk like Yoda when I get tired? 😄), to my Dragon Divas for reading the ugliest, earliest forms of my stories, to Tessonja Odette and Hanna Sandvig for the critique work, to my Uncommon Crew for the support, to my Typo Hunters for your eagle eyes, to my Denners (Alisha's Dragon Den FB group) for the love and motivation as I write and market my work, to my Moontree gals for the rum and pirates on demand, to my Turtles for keeping me sane in the wild world of publishing. And last but certainly not least, thank you to my family and friends for humoring this daydreamer and being the best of the best. I love you all forever.

ABOUT THE AUTHOR

USA Today bestselling author Alisha Klapheke wants to infuse readers' lives with unique magic, far-flung fantasy settings, and romance. Her inspiration springs from an obsession with history, years of world travel, and the fantasy she grew up reading when she was supposed to be doing her math homework.

When she's not writing, Alisha teaches Muay Thai kickboxing, Brazilian Jiu Jitsu, and Krav Maga to kids, adults, and the occasional country music star at her school just south of Nashville. That may be why writing fight scenes is her favorite.

9 798988 835806